"There's no reason you can't become my mistress."

"You've been alone with me long enough that whatever respectability you might have had is gone. Your reputation, should you have had one, is in tatters."

A look of alarm crossed Eliza's face. But all she said was, "I can't imagine I should make much of a mistress for you. It is years since I put on a spinster's cap, and besides, I am covered with freckles."

Lord Hartwood roughened his voice. "Freckles or not, I need a mistress." Taking a breath, he let his tone soften as he prepared for the final insult. "Do not fear, Miss Farrell. Though I will ruin you, I will pay well for your services. I am heartless, but my purse is deep."

As his words sank in, her freckles stood out more sharply against the growing pallor of her face. He reached out and slowly let his fingers drift along her shoulder, languidly drawing a line down the front of her dress, along the muffled curve of her breast.

"So tell me, Miss Farrell," he murmured, bending to whisper into her flaming, pink-tinged ear. "Will you become my mistress?"

Romances by **Jenny Brown**

LORD LIGHTNING

Lord Lightning

JENNY BROWN

AVON

An Imprint of HarperCollinsPublishers

AVON BOOKS
An Imprint of HarperCollins*Publishers*
10 East 53rd Street
New York, New York 10022-5299

Copyright © 2010 by Janet Ruhl
ISBN 978-0-06-197605-6
www.avonromance.com

First Avon Books paperback printing: October 2010

Avon Trademark Reg. U.S. Pat. Off. and in Other Countries, Marca Registrada, Hecho en U.S.A.
HarperCollins® is a registered trademark of HarperCollins Publishers.

Printed in the U.S.A.

10 9 8 7 6 5 4 3 2 1

For Alicia and Lisa.
With thanks also to Val-Rae,
Alison, Edith, and Linda.

Lord Lightning

Chapter 1

London 1818

The ability to predict the future for others was
a blessing for which Eliza Farrell hoped she
was sufficiently grateful. But her gratitude would
have been far greater had her own future not depended so heavily on the accurate employment of
that skill. As the Theatre Royal's doorway atten-
dant guided her down the dim passageway that
led from the street to a small room located to one
side of the stage, Eliza struggled to recover the
confidence which had, until now, enabled her to
withstand so much adversity. She had left nothing undone when preparing for this meeting with
the actress who would be her first paying client.
She had studied the horoscopes diligently and
consulted the works of the authorities when she

found herself in doubt. But still, if she were to fail!

A clamor in the passageway outside the dressing room announced her client's arrival. Eliza clutched the handle of the bulging flowered satchel that held her almanacs and prayed for strength. Then Violet LeDuc swept into the room. The actress paused at the doorway only long enough for Eliza to take in her stately height, the perfection of her rounded figure, and the peevish way her eyes narrowed as she caught sight of Eliza. An older woman fluttered a few steps behind her: the neighbor who, upon learning of Eliza's predicament, had so kindly offered to put in a few words for her with her mistress—the very words that had resulted in the present interview.

But who would have imagined the quiet, faded older woman would have led Eliza to such an Aladdin's cave as this? The late afternoon sun filtering through the sooty skylight high above sent reflections glittering off the jeweled buttons and golden braid of the costumes piled on every available surface. The air was thick with an indefinable odor—the actress's scent, perhaps? Eliza had no experience with such things, but whatever it was, it mingled with a hint of sweat and a whiff of the pork pie some actor had left uneaten on a table in the corner.

Eliza suppressed the pang of hunger that rose as she caught sight of the food. It had been a long time since she had eaten. Still, if all went well and she satisfied her new client, she and her father would again have money for food.

But only if all went well.

After a measured pause, Violet acknowledged Eliza's presence with a nod so faint it ran no risk of disarranging her artfully arranged golden curls. She seated herself on the bench facing the dressing table set against one wall and gave a quick glance at the mirror above it, favoring it with a smile much warmer than the one with which she'd greeted Eliza. Only then did she swivel around and demand of Eliza, "What do the stars command? Should I travel with His Lordship to Brighton?"

As the actress's voice, so well adapted to the stage, reverberated through the cramped dressing room, it threatened what little confidence Eliza had left. Still, she schooled herself to show nothing but calm as she opened her satchel and extracted from its depths the two horoscopes she had so carefully prepared the night before. The feel of the rich, velvety paper against her fingertips was reassuring. She had spent her last carefully hoarded shillings on that paper, hoping its quality would convince her client of her professionalism. Cautiously she pushed aside the pots of paint and powder that covered the tiring table and laid out her charts. Only then did she trust herself to reply. "The stars command nothing," she said. "They merely describe your character. It's the choices you make that determine your fate."

The actress snorted. "Spare me your sermons! You sound like a governess, not an astrologer, and you look like one, too. Where is your turban? Where are your veils?"

Eliza fought down her dismay as she glanced at her second-best gray merino gown. Surely this woman didn't expect her to dress like a Gypsy.

"Well—" The actress's voice softened. "Perhaps I am being too harsh. With Madame Esmerelda gadding off to take the waters I have no choice but to rely on you. His Lordship will be here any moment. So tell me quickly, what must I do? Madame Esmerelda would have already given me my answer, not these mealymouthed excuses."

"And have charged you three times the fee," her dresser muttered behind her. "Give Miss Eliza a chance. She may not look the part, but she told my Henry such things about his past as no one could have known. And she predicted to the very day when he would be hired on at the counting house."

Violet sighed. "You do have such a way with hair, Harriet. I suppose it's worth humoring you." She turned back to Eliza. "Perhaps I spoke too quickly. But the matter is pressing. So answer me this: Should I go to Brighton with His Lordship or stay in London to play the leading role in *A Rake and His Conquests*?"

As Eliza took one last look at the nativities of the actress and her lord, she was glad she had taken such pains with them. No blots disfigured the circular maps of the heavens she had drawn so carefully the night before. The costly black ink she had used made the spindly planetary symbols stand out clearly against the creamy tint of the paper. And despite the actress's harsh glare, the ancient symbols still spoke to her. Her confidence restored, she bit her lower lip as her Aunt Celestina had so often admonished her not to do and said, "You are very close to achieving success in your profession. Jupiter, the greater benefic, is poised to enter your House of Public Fame. But it is a poor time for matters of the heart. The Lord of the House of Love is conjunct with Saturn, the greater malefic, which spoils whatever it touches. So you shouldn't leave the theater for any man."

Violet's eyebrow lifted quizzically. "You say I will achieve success in my profession, but from what you've just told me I wonder if you understand what exactly my profession *is*."

Eliza directed her gaze toward the gaily-colored costumes that filled the dressing room. "Do you not earn your bread by acting in this theater?"

Violet laughed. "If I had to live on what I earn here, I'd have starved to death by now. You *are* an original, and a country miss, too, I would wager. How long have you been in London?"

"Why, these two months."

Violet leaned back against the tiring table. "Two months in the city has not been enough time to rub off all your country notions. Would your advice to me differ if you understood that I earn my bread by keeping His Lordship happy? Would that change your prediction of my success?"

Eliza blushed as the full import of the actress's words struck home. Had she made a complete fool of herself?

"What do the stars tell you if that's the case?" the actress pressed on. "If I give in and go with him and help him carry out this wild scheme of his, will he make me his wife?"

So *that* was what she wished to know. As usual, the question asked was not the question the client wanted answered. But Eliza's heart sank. Violet would not like what she had to say. "I can't see him marrying you," she said softly. "The connection between the two of you is a Third House matter. It is one of business, not of love. Besides, the aspect is separating. Whatever the relationship was, it is coming to an end.

"And there is more." Eliza hurried on, wishing to get past the unpleasant facts as quickly as possible. "You have Saturn in the House of Children and Venus in the House of Illness. You could not give this lord of yours an heir, and a lord must have an heir. Any marriage between the two of you would end unhappily."

Violet turned pale. "Who's been telling you my secrets? How did you learn of my misfortune?"

"No one told me anything. I can read it from the chart."

Violet wheeled around to face her dresser. "You told her, you little snake. You gave away my secrets so she could pretend to tell my fortune."

"I told her nothing!" Harriet protested, shrinking back from her mistress's upraised hand. "I just passed on the information she asked me for, just the birthdays you gave me and the times and places of your births."

"A likely story." Violet sniffed, then she turned back to face Eliza. "You'll have to do more to prove to me you aren't just a clever fake."

Eliza picked up the actress's chart and held it up to her face to hide her consternation. It had never occurred to her to pump a servant for information before reading a nativity. There was no need. The information was all there on the chart—in the numbers and symbols so full of meaning to anyone who, like herself, had spent years learning how to interpret them. It was intolerable to be accused of trickery precisely because she had been so accurate.

But she would have to tolerate it if she were to earn the guineas she needed so badly to save her father from debtor's prison. This was the first client she had found after months of searching. If only she had realized that a paying client would be so different from the villagers of Bishops Ridley who had always consulted her Aunt Celestina when they were worried their husbands might be straying or their children might die of the summer's bloody flux. They had known her aunt from childhood, so there was no need to convince them that her prophesies could be trusted. But as proficient as she had been at predicting their futures, her aunt had been a respectable woman. She would have known no more than Eliza about the life of a woman like this.

The actress glared at Eliza with calculating eyes. She was so golden, so blonde, so beautiful, and so sensuous. How could Eliza not have

realized she was this nameless lord's mistress—
a woman paid to supply him with sexual pleasure? Still, she ought to have guessed it. Had she
not been told that in London women of dubious
virtue were the *only* ones willing to pay to learn
what their horoscopes might tell them?

But even so, there must be something in these
horoscopes she could use to win back her client's
trust, something more promising than her blasted
hopes of marriage. Catching sight of the heavy
gold bracelet that sparkled on one of Violet's elegant wrists, Eliza remembered one of her aunt's
adages: "If love is lacking, look for money," and of
course, there was money in abundance on Violet's
chart. She brightened.

"I can see you have already risen from great
poverty to riches," she said. "And your fortune
will continue to grow if you invest your money
carefully. The strength in your chart lies in your
self-reliance. Not on the help of others."

"Without the help of others, I'd still be selling
flowers in the Haymarket," Violet retorted. "How
could I possibly get by without the help of men
like His Lordship?"

At least this was a question Eliza could answer
with ease. Pointing to the pie-shaped segment of
the chart that described such matters, she said,
"The Lord of your House of Wealth is Mercury.
It stands in the Third House, where it is naturally strong. That suggests you could earn more
wealth by investing in something of the nature

of Mercury—some method of improving local travel, perhaps. A scheme of building roads—"

"There's that canal Sir Thomas has been going on about," the actress interrupted. "He's told me he could make me rich if I let him put some small part of my savings in it, but I thought that was only flummery."

"Is Sir Thomas rich?"

"As rich as Croesus—and all self-made they say."

"Then perhaps you can trust his advice. A self-made man would understand investment. Is he a good man?"

"What would I know of goodness in men?" snapped the actress. "But he's handsome, anyway, and very attentive—and far less temperamental than His Lordship. He already has children—his wife died giving him his sixth, and he respects me as an *artiste*. Perhaps *he* would make me his wife—"

Violet stood up. As she took a step toward Eliza, her eyes darted from one horoscope to the other where they lay on the tiring table amid the spilled powder and rouge. "Perhaps you do know something," she said. "But can you tell me about His Lordship? Can you ferret out *his* secrets with your charts?"

Eliza nodded, relieved to have moved on to an easier topic. "Oh yes, his character is very clear."

"To you, perhaps, who've never met him," Violet said with a wry grin. "But not to those of us who've had to deal with him."

Eliza could not help but smile. Then she said,

"His Lordship is a fiery man. He has great pride and courage. He shows strong loyalty to those who serve him faithfully. He has an excellent wit and wishes others to admire it. He is also a fine actor and loves to play a part. Because the moment of his birth was ruled by Venus there is much pleasure in his life and much affection. Indeed, he has a much greater need than the ordinary man to give and receive affection because he is a Leo. It is the sign of those who are born to love."

"How very interesting," said Violet, with a guarded look. "But what about his constancy?"

Warned by the actress's tone, Eliza paused before replying, anxious not to make another misstep. "I think His Lordship could be very constant in his affections, were they fully engaged. Though it's true that his Sun is opposed by Saturn, which could mean his ability to love might develop only as he got older. Still, once it was awakened, he would be a very faithful lover."

She glanced down at the chart again to allow herself another look at His Lordship's Saturn, before adding, "If he has difficulty expressing his true nature, it's because there's some hidden sorrow in his life—something to do with his early life. Did his mother die when he was young?"

It seemed likely. The nameless lord's nativity bore the same conjunction of the Moon and Mars that appeared on her own chart, and her own mother had died in a carriage wreck when Eliza was only eight.

But Violet disposed of that possibility, saying, "No, his mother is most definitely alive—far too alive according to him. There was some great broil between them in his youth and any mention of her will send him into one of his rages."

"Well, that would fit, too. The Moon in a chart describes the mother and Mars may often be expressed as anger," Eliza said. "Still, I would expect he experienced something painful in his childhood. Saturn is the Lord of his House of Early Life and it stands in that house, too, making it more powerful. His childhood must have been one of suffering."

"Suffering is not a word I should think of in relation to His Lordship." Violet laughed. "His home is like a palace. He has more riches than he can spend. And if that weren't enough, he's so handsome it's hard to understand why he bothers to keep a mistress as there are plenty of women of the ton who would gladly take on the role *gratis*. No, the only suffering in his life is the suffering he causes others. He's notorious for the pranks he plays on people." Violet paused and the expression of scorn that had previously filled her face was replaced by one that held a hint of curiosity. "Does his chart tell you why he's such a rake?"

Eliza examined the chart again then answered, "I see nothing here that would explain it." But even as she spoke she wondered. She knew so little about such matters and doubted her Aunt Celestina had known much more. The only rake they'd encountered in Bishops Ridley had been found in the pages of Mr. Richardson's novel *Clarissa* and they hadn't had his chart.

More to reassure herself than for the benefit of the actress she went on, "His Moon is in Taurus, Venus's sign, and it stands in the Eighth House, which would be read by some to mean he was very passionate. But even so, Jupiter, the planet of good fortune, is in his Seventh House of Marriage. So, I do not see a rake here." She tapped one finger on the powder-spattered top of the dressing table. "I see a man who needs love and who is capable of intense devotion. The woman he loved would be very fortunate."

Several other actresses had drifted into the room, attracted by the sound of conversation.

"Who's she talking about?" one asked.

"I'll let you guess," Violet said. "A fiery man, prideful and courageous, with a strong need of affection. Oh yes, don't let me forget—he's loyal and constant in love."

The other girl looked mystified. "And who, pray tell, is this paragon?"

"That's the joke of it, Sally." Violet laughed. "This loving, constant man she's sketched out for us is none other than Edward Neville, Lord Hartwood."

"Lord Hartwood? That is a good joke, indeed." The girl giggled. "Lord Lightning, a loving, constant man? Why he's monstrous proud of his profligacy. I've heard him stand right here and brag that he'd never give his heart to a woman for even a single moment."

"Indeed," Violet said.

Eliza put out a hand to steady herself against her chair. It was almost too much to take in. Violet's nameless lord was Lord Hartwood? Even living in obscurity in the tiny hamlet of Bishops Ridley she had heard dreadful stories about the notorious rake the world had nicknamed Lord Lightning thanks to his shocking behavior.

Violet turned back to face her, her rosy lips curled in disdain. "What a fraud you are. For a moment you had me thinking you could tell the future. But you must have learned what you knew about me from someone you bribed. Too bad you forgot to question them about my protector." Rage had turned her even features ugly. "I am glad I hid Lord Hartwood's identity from you. Had I not done so, scandal alone would have told you all you needed to sketch out his character."

"But what I described to you must *be* his character," Eliza protested. "At least it must be if the time and place of birth you gave me were correct. But if they *were* correct, I don't care what scandal says about him. Lord Hartwood must be exactly the man I described to you."

"Then you are a charlatan. All the world knows Hartwood's character. And all the world knows of his heartlessness, too."

"Then perhaps all the world is wrong," Eliza snapped. But even as she heard herself speak those words, she wondered how she could have been so mistaken. She picked up Lord Hartwood's horoscope again and peered at it, muttering under her breath as she scanned the symbols she had so carefully drawn the previous evening. What had she missed?

It was true the new planet, Uranus, stood at the top of his chart. Any planet in that position described the reputation the native would earn in the world. But with Uranus, who could say what it meant? It was so unfair to have new planets to deal with—planets about which the ancients knew nothing. Sir William had done the world no favor by discovering this one.

But she'd ignored Uranus in making her interpretation. Perhaps that was her mistake, as any planet placed at the top of a chart must be important. She recalled now how her aunt, who had maintained a correspondence with many of England's most distinguished astrologers, had speculated toward the end of her life that the new planet might indicate explosions, eccentricities, and sudden, unexpected events. If that was true it might explain the personality Lord Lightning showed to the world. Then she remembered something else: she had assumed the conjunction of His Lordship's Mars and Moon described an accident like her mother's. But her own Mars-Moon conjunction stood in the House of Travel where it might well describe a coaching accident. Lord Hartwood's afflicted planets were set in a different house: the troublesome Eighth House which governed Sexual Relations. Placed there it might indeed describe a man who directed his anger at women or even a sexual pervert. Eager to confirm that this had been her mistake, she looked up at the glowering actress and demanded, "Has Lord Hartwood hurt you?"

Violet shook her head no.

"Are his tastes in love abnormal?"

"Far from it."

"Why then do you disparage him?"

Violet looked uncomfortable. "He's a very cold man, not a warm one as you described him. He says cruel things. And from the start of our connection, he has shown so little interest in pursuing the delights of love that I've wondered if he keeps another woman."

"He doesn't force himself on you against your will?"

"Far from it. Indeed, I wish he would force himself upon me more. I would feel more confident of retaining his affections if he would give in to the normal passions of a male. But he doesn't. He shows no passion at all, but just toys with me. It's quite unsettling."

"Then it is just as I thought," Eliza announced triumphantly. "You have listened to too much idle gossip. The lustful libertine your friends describe is not Lord Hartwood. He is more complex. His need for love is there. Perhaps you cannot see it, but it is most definite and strong, though I do wish someone who knew him better could shed more light on his true character."

"Perhaps I can," drawled a deep male voice.

"I wager I know Lord Hartwood's character far better than any of you, having known him intimately these past thirty-two years."

The women packing the small dressing room sprang back to open a path for the pale-haired man garbed in elegant evening dress who stood at the doorway, so tall the crown of his lofty beaver top hat almost brushed the lintel. He balanced a large jeweled dagger lightly in his right hand and flourished it before making a stabbing motion in the air. Then he took a single step forward and, with a powerful flick of his hand, sent the knife sailing into the corner, where a harsh squeak revealed it had glanced off its target, a large gray rat. The women shrieked as the animal scampered away. Eliza managed to maintain the outward appearance of composure—glad that her aunt had taught her to suppress all sign of feminine weakness—but she was no less perturbed. Even Uranus at Lord Hartwood's midheaven had not prepared her for this!

"I don't like vermin," he said coldly. He strode to the corner and picked up the knife, running a finger along the side of the blade as if cleaning it. Then he stalked back toward Violet. The jewels on the dagger's hilt sparkled more brightly with his advance. As the actress cowered back against the wall, Lord Hartwood closed in and brought the dagger up slowly toward her chest until it touched the top of one rounded breast projecting from her low-cut bodice, just above her heart. Then, before she had time to react, he grasped the blade with a swift motion of his other hand, twisted the blade, and snapped it in half.

"You were so frightened, my darling Violet," he said in a soft mocking tone. "But there's no need for fear. It was only a papier-mâché knife that I found in the prop room. I took a fancy to it, imagining myself for a moment in the role of Hamlet. But you needn't fear me. The knife was as harmless as I am. It couldn't have hurt you any more than your insults could have hurt me."

Violet rounded on Eliza, her face flaming. "Now see where your foolishness has led us! Here's Lord Hartwood himself, and now, I wager, you shall have a taste of that bad temper you were so sure he didn't have."

Eliza bit her lower lip, determined to show no hint of the dismay she felt. The golden guineas she had been so close to earning had been swept away in the storm that had blown up between the actress and her protector—the golden guineas that were all that stood between Eliza and ruin.

Violet, meanwhile, had recovered herself as best she could. Turning back to her protector, who still loomed over her, she said, "This is only some foolish girl who's come to read the players' fortunes, Your Lordship. She's an imposter and knows nothing about the stars. Please don't take offense at her foolish ramblings."

"On the contrary," Lord Hartwood protested with a cold smile that did not reach his dark brown eyes. "Your seeress is a deep well of wisdom. I have been standing outside your doorway these past five minutes and am much diverted by the character she's given me. 'Loyal and loving. A man who must have love to live.' How refreshingly different." He paused, and his eyes hardened. "But you made it clear you don't share her good opinion of me."

Violet blanched, and Eliza wondered what else Lord Hartwood had heard, his mistress's words disparaging his sexual performance? Clearly Violet thought so. After shooting a furious look at Eliza, she took a deep breath, faced Hartwood, and said, "I shall not mislead you, Your Lordship. My regard for you has changed. Though I appreciate all you have done for me, I cannot accompany you to Brighton. If I did, I would have to give up the leading role in the theater's new play. I don't believe that your feelings for me are strong enough to justify such a sacrifice."

Hartwood gestured toward Eliza. "Was it for help in deciding this matter that you took counsel with the little fortune-teller?"

"Yes."

"And you've taken her advice, though you've just assured me she's a deluded fool?"

"It had nothing to do with her."

"Then what does it have to do with?" He paused, his dark eyes glittering. "Were the jewels I bought you not to your taste? Was the house I purchased too small? Or was it my lack of interest in your skills between the sheets that disgusted you? Come, tell me. I would like to know." As he spoke the last phrase, he began to walk toward Violet, pushing her back with each step.

He was a much better actor than Violet. The chart had not lied there. He was the classic Leo, part actor, part spoiled child. He used his whole body when he spoke, his long, strong hands expressing the tension he kept out of his voice. Everything about him demanded he be noticed, even the things he had no control over like the startling contrast between his pale blond hair and gleaming mahogany eyes.

He drew even closer to Violet. "Is my only reward for the kindness I have shown you to be that you abandon me? And that you do so *now,* when I depend on you to help me claim my inheritance?"

Backed almost to the wall, Violet stood her ground, shaking her head decisively. "I've chosen to act the lead role in Saturday's performance. I was only offered the part because Helena took ill so suddenly. It could make me the first actress in London. It would be the making of me—"

Hartwood cut her off coldly. "*I* have been the making of you, Violet. Did you really think the director selected you to fill that role because of your talent? You read your lines tolerably, but so do many other girls. No, it was the hope he might draw on my deep purse to pay off the theater's debts that motivated him to choose you." Lord Hartwood rubbed his forefinger over a large glass jewel embedded in the broken hilt of the stage dagger. "How quickly you've forgot where you came from and what I've done for you. But it is only as I expected; I've never found women to be capable of loyalty."

He tilted his strong chin upward, clearly aware of the many female eyes following his every move. "What you choose to do is of no importance to me," he said, shrugging his exquisitely tailored shoulders. "As you've guessed, I have grown weary of you. You'll be most easy to replace."

With that, he bowed ever so slightly, still staring at the mortified Violet. Then he slowly removed an enameled golden snuffbox from his pocket, withdrew a pinch of snuff, sniffed and savored it, and with a dry ironic laugh said, "And they say that *I* am fickle."

Chapter 2

Edward Neville stood outside in the alley where he'd retreated after making his perfect exit. Though he had carried it off well, considering the circumstances, he needed a moment to collect himself and master the rage welling up within him. He breathed deeply and smashed one fist into his gloved palm, feeling the heavy signet dig into the flesh. He'd made a fool of himself. Again. He'd treated Violet as if she were something more than a trollop with little to recommend her beyond a well-formed pair of legs and a willingness to display them. And even more foolishly, he had hoped to get something in return for his many kindnesses—to be exact, two weeks' worth of loyalty. It was so little, but she had refused him even that much.

The old familiar pain rose within him, and

again he slammed his fist into his hand. Women were incapable of loyalty. He might just as well have expected some mare he'd bought at Tattersalls to recite Hamlet's soliloquy.

But even so, Violet would have come with him had it not been for the interference of the self-appointed seeress. It was she who'd talked Violet into walking out on him just when he needed her most. It infuriated him. He'd so looked forward to bringing the superbly vulgar Violet with him when he went to Brighton to fulfill the terms of his brother's will. Though he would still find pleasure in having his mother totally at his mercy after all these years, without Violet at his side it wouldn't be the same. To pull the thing off properly he must find a replacement for her. But he could think of no one.

The Season was in full swing, and though none of the ladies who would acknowledge his acquaintance were part of the ton, the demimonde, too, had its balls and routs, its visits to the theater and its nights in the gambling hells. Even if he'd known someone suitable, it was unlikely he would be able to pry such a ladybird from the delights of London without offering her carte blanche. And *that*, his adventure with Violet had just brought home to him, was too high a price to pay.

Just then he heard footsteps behind him and the swish of a woman's gown against the pavement. He felt a surge of relief. Violet must have tallied up all she had got from him and decided not to throw it away. He unclenched his fist, grateful that after her absurd display of independence Violet had finally seen reason.

But the woman who stood huddled in the alley was not Violet. It was the little fortune-teller, clutching a lumpy satchel and dabbing at her eyes.

How like a woman to willfully destroy his plans and then act as if *she* were the one to be pitied! But her display should not surprise him. Women were always in tears, those damnable tears that let them get away with everything.

A sudden thought occurred to him: Why should she get away with anything? He needed a woman for his scheme. Why not abduct the little seeress and force her to play his whore? His closed carriage stood only a few feet away, the coachman at the ready; it would be only a matter of a few moments to overpower the chit. Once in the carriage, her ruin could be completed, and then what choice would she have but to come along with him?

But as quickly as he imagined the scheme, he saw that it was flawed. Whatever the world might think of him, he had no taste for rape. And, besides, he needed a willing helper.

Still, the woman deserved to pay for her damnable interference. There had been something so consoling about the idea of her abduction. He rather hated to give it up. It wasn't right that the little fortune-teller should get off scot-free. Could he not indulge in just a tiny bit of abduction? Just enough to frighten her out of her wits and ensure she would never again pull a trick like one she'd just played on him?

Lord Lightning chuckled. A plan was beginning to form in his mind, and there was nothing he liked better than a plan. His black mood began to lift. There were times when it was a definite advantage to have no morals.

After dawdling indecisively for some time in an inconspicuous alcove near the theater doorway, Eliza, who still had her morals but very little else, reminded herself that there was no point in blubbering. Aunt Celestina would have been disgusted with her. It was time to buck up and go on, to prove herself worthy of her forebears. But bracing thoughts like these, so comforting only days before, now fell flat. How could she go on, when she had no place left to go?

She pulled open her tiny netted reticule. As she had expected, all she found within it was four pence ha'penny. By now the bailiff must have taken her father off to debtor's prison, after seizing the few possessions her beloved aunt had left her that her father had not already gambled away. What a fool she'd been to welcome her father's unexpected reappearance after her aunt's death and to let him take her with him to London. He'd not been attracted by love for his long abandoned daughter, but by the small hoard Aunt Celestina had so carefully saved for Eliza's future. At nine-and-twenty she should have known better than to greet him like the small girl who had so missed her vanished papa. Her aunt had warned her about trusting him, just as she had warned her against so much else that might cause her to repeat her mother's errors. But it was too late for regrets. She dabbed at her face to get rid of her shameful tears and squared her shoulders.

But just as she stepped out onto the pavement, she felt a strong, gloved hand come from behind her and grasp her by the arm. It pulled her toward the large closed carriage emblazoned with a crest that waited some dozen yards down the alley. She struggled to free herself and was about to cry out for assistance when a cultivated voice growled into her ear, "Do not attempt to resist me, my pretty one. If you do as I bid, I will not harm you."

She recognized the voice—and she recognized the sense of drama. It was Lord Hartwood.

As he drew her toward the carriage, a liveried postillion opened the door smoothly, allowing her captor to shove her inside. Then the elegant lord clambered in, taking a seat at the far end of the deeply upholstered bench as the coach door shut with a well-oiled click. He signaled to the coach-man with a single rap on the compartment's roof and the carriage began to move.

She was being abducted! She knew she should be alarmed. But as she breathed in the aroma of well-oiled leather and the subtler scent of the var-nished burled maple paneling that surrounded her, it was not alarm she felt, but relief. For a few moments longer she could postpone facing the fact that she had nowhere to live, no one to turn to, and four pence ha'penny with which to plan her future. It was even possible that despite his cynical pose, Lord Hartwood had been so impressed by her earlier reading of his character that he wished to know more. Had she found a patron after all—one capable of showering her with the golden guineas needed to stave off disaster?

But one look at her abductor dispelled that notion. A sneer darkened his eyes and narrowed the sensuous lips that in other circumstances might have been described as inviting. His eyes drilled into hers, and suddenly she knew why they called him Lord Lightning. His eyes raked up and down her slender figure, lingering on the bodice of her dress as if with his gaze alone he could divest her of that garment. Eliza shrank away from him, sliding toward the other end of the bench, and raised one hand protectively in front of her chest.

"Lord Hartwood—" she began, but he cut her words short.

"Did your fortune-telling tricks not warn you to beware of a man with fair hair? Were you not cautioned to make no short journeys? Or do you read the stars only for those you attempt to bilk?"

"What do you mean?"

"You will address me as 'Your Lordship,'" he admonished her. "And you will remember at all times the respect owed to my rank. What's your name, young woman?"

"Miss Farrell, Your Lordship."

"Well then, Miss Farrell, you've greatly displeased me with your damnable interference in my life. Now that you are completely in my

power, I'll make sure you don't play such tricks
again. Would you like to consult the stars to find
out what I have planned for you? Will your almanac teach you how to escape me?"

His vehemence caused his snuffbox to slip from
his pocket and roll onto the floor, but he did not
stop to pick it up. "But of course, you wouldn't consult the stars to learn your own fate," he taunted.
"You're a fraud, some scullery maid looking for
easy money—no, you speak too well to be a scullery maid—a lady's maid perhaps. But whoever
you are, I've had enough of your meddling."

At these words, something in Eliza snapped.
The nerve of the man. Calling her a jumped up
lady's maid? She who was a direct descendent of
England's finest astrologer!

"I am no fraud," she retorted. "I was trained
in the practice of astrology by my Aunt Celestina
who studied with her father, who was William
Lilly's great-grandson. Your insults can mean
nothing to me."

"Surely," Lord Hartwood responded in an unpleasant tone, "though my insults may mean nothing, you must fear for your safety at my hands."
And with that, he reached out one languid hand
and caressed her thigh. A shock ran through her
body. No man had ever touched her in such a
brazen way. She twisted her neck sharply, pulling
away from him. The man was impossible. It was
time to put an end to his nonsense.

"Your Lordship," she snapped, "I, too, have
read the novels of Mr. Richardson, which you

have apparently confused with real life. Had you not caused me so much distress just now in the theater, I might find your posturing amusing. But though you may have the reputation of a Lovelace, I am no Clarissa. I am a woman of some nine-and-twenty years, quite past my prime, with my living to be earned, no thanks to you. And you have caused me quite enough trouble for one day."

"Surely," Lord Hartwood said, his hard look now replaced by something very akin to amusement, "though not Clarissa, you must owe me a little bit of terror. After all, I do have you in my power."

"Oh don't be silly," Eliza countered. "We read Miss Austen now, not Mr. Richardson, and the ladies in our modern novels only run off with bounders when they fall prey to their devastating charm—not because some man drags them off in a closed carriage."

"I am abashed, madam," replied Lord Hartwood, "to find you do not consider my charm to be devastating."

"I have no idea if your charm is devastating or not, for you have favored me only with your bad temper. Though, on reflection, I'd imagine you have charm enough when you choose to use it—at least, you would if you really have the Libra ascendant that's on the chart I drew up for you."

Lord Hartwood lifted one pale eyebrow. "So you truly believe that drivel you spouted to Violet?

You actually think you can divine my character with your mystical documents?"

"There is no need for you to insult my art," Eliza said firmly. As she spoke, a part of her watched in astonishment as she administered a set down to a man who was, after all, a powerful nobleman. He, too, appeared to be astonished. His deep brown eyes had widened and he was clearly having trouble maintaining the harsh expression the role he had taken on required. He removed his beaver hat with a flourish, revealing a startling mass of pale, tousled curls, and said in an ironic tone, "Accept my apologies, madam. In the future I shall refer to your art only with the greatest respect."

"Thank you, Your Lordship. I am glad to hear it. But I am annoyed with you, too. I so badly needed the money Violet had promised me for my help. And I would have earned it, too, were it not for you. It was what I told her about *your* character that ruined everything."

"But what you said was all so complimentary." The expression of amusement still flickered across Lord Hartwood's sensual lips. "I found it refreshing to hear myself described in such unfamiliar terms. *A kind and thoughtful lover. A man who lives for love.* I'm more accustomed to being compared to Byron—though my crimes are mild compared to what he's accused of."

"Of course they are," Eliza said brusquely. "Lord Byron's chart is far more afflicted than yours. I've studied it."

But then she remembered with a pang that the

birth time she had for the incestuous poet was accurate, coming as it did from Lord Byron's mother who had consulted Aunt Celestina for help in governing her unruly son. She had no such certainty about the accuracy of the horoscope she had erected for Lord Hartwood. In fact, it was probably wrong.

She sighed. "In truth, I have my doubts about the information I was given about your birth. My interpretation would not have seemed so wrong to those who know you if the information you'd given Violet was correct. But if you had deceived her, it would explain why they laughed at the character I gave you."

Lord Lightning's eyebrows rose. "Do you have the effrontery to accuse *me* of dishonesty?"

As anger flooded over her captor's handsome features once again, Eliza remembered he'd also earned a reputation for being a fearsome duelist. Had she not been a woman she was sure he would have slapped a glove against her face and demanded she meet him at noon in some remote spot where he could put a bullet through her.

"I accuse you of nothing," she protested hastily. "But it was dreadful to be held up to ridicule like that when I so badly needed patrons. And I can't believe I would have so misread your character if the birth information Harriet gave me had been accurate."

His lips tight, Lord Hartwood said, "I was born on the twenty-ninth of July in the year '85. Exactly as I told Violet. There would be no point in lying.

I'm the son of a nobleman. The circumstances of my birth are a matter of public record."

"And the time of your birth?"

"At half past ten in the morning."

"How do you know that?"

He stretched out one long and elegant hand, drawing her attention to the lace peeping out at his cuff and the heavy signet ring he wore on his third finger. "I was born the son of a baron, a possible heir, so these things were noted carefully. And besides, my mother always used to complain that I had interrupted her plans for the morning with my inconvenient appearance in her life."

"If that is so, then the date and time I used to construct your horoscope were correct, and my interpretation of your character must be accurate, too, no matter what Violet might have said." After giving this a moment's consideration, she continued, "But it is strange that Violet, a woman who has been so intimate with you, should have preferred to hear something to your disadvantage."

"Yes, very strange indeed," Lord Hartwood said, his lips tight.

"She said you were cold and heartless. But that cannot possibly be true. You were born while Libra was rising in the sky—the sign ruled by Venus, planet of love, and besides, at your birth the Sun was in the sign of Leo which alone would give you a need for love far stronger than that of most other men."

"Perhaps Violet could not see those aspects of my nature because she has not your gift of proph-

ecy." Lord Hartwood said quietly, "Though, of
course, there's another explanation. One you may
have overlooked. Perhaps she learned something
about my character in the six months she spent
living under my protection. Perhaps they taught
her that I am, in fact, a cold and heartless man.
You would have been well-advised to have paid
some slight attention to the unsavory reputation I
acquired over the past fifteen years."

Then, as if to punctuate his words, Lord Hartwood rapped on the front wall of the carriage, and
the coachman whipped the horses into a gallop.

It would not do to have her treat her abduction
as a joke. As bad as his reputation might be, it was
such that nobody dared to laugh at him. Yet twice
in a single afternoon this insignificant woman
had done just that. Clearly, it was time to move on
with his plan and put some fear into her. He'd had
enough of her sitting here, full of complacency,
her green eyes gleaming with pride at the thought
of how well she'd sounded out his character. He
twisted his lip into what he hoped was a frightening sneer and asked, "Do you know why I took
you up into my carriage?"

She shook her head no.

"Your meddling, based though it might have
been on your knowledge of the stars, has denied
me the services of my mistress. But I must take a
mistress with me when I go to claim my inheritance. The terms of my brother's will require it."
That wasn't entirely a lie, though it wasn't the

truth, either. "So," he said, reaching toward her
and cupping her chin in his hand as he fixed her
with an appraising gaze. "Since you convinced
my mistress to leave me, you will have to take her
place."

That caught her attention. Her sea green eyes
stared at him, wide with disbelief.

"Surely you're joking."

"I have never been farther from joking," he
said, hoping he could keep his sardonic expression from cracking. It would be hard work to
keep up the pose of unbridled lust for long. With
her schoolmistress's air and her carroty hair tied
up in a tight knot beneath her cheap lace cap,
she was ludicrously unlike any mistress he had
ever seen. Still, the threat would give her a well-
deserved fright before he left her off at the side
of the road, much shaken by her narrow escape
and with a far better understanding of the high
price to be paid for interfering in the affairs of
her betters.

He favored her with what he hoped was a lascivious leer. "There's no reason you can't become
my mistress. You've been alone with me long
enough that whatever respectability you might
have had before you entered my carriage is gone.
Your reputation, should you have had one, is in
tatters."

A look of alarm crossed her face. Good. She
was responding exactly the way he had planned.

But all she said was, "I can't imagine I should
make much of a mistress for you. It is years since

I put on a spinster's cap, and besides, I am covered with freckles."

He roughened his voice. "Freckles or not, I need a mistress. You drove away Violet, now you must take her place." Taking a breath, he let his tone soften as he prepared for the final insult. "Do not fear, Miss Farrell. Though I will ruin you, I will pay well for your services. I am heartless, but my purse is deep."

As his words sank in, her freckles stood out more sharply against the growing pallor of her face. Her consternation was clear, which was pleasing. She would not laugh at him again any time soon. Now on to the grand finale. He reached out and slowly let his fingers drift along her shoulder, languidly drawing a line down the front of her dress, along the muffled curve of her breast. He lingered just above where he thought her nipple might be hidden under the thick wool and inscribed a spiral there. Her eyes widened with shock.

"So tell me, Miss Farrell," he murmured, bending to whisper into her flaming, pink-tinged ear. "Will you become my mistress and yield your body to my lust?"

He expected her to shriek, or perhaps to faint. He drew on his military training to be ready if she were to strike at him. But there was only one reaction he had not expected: that she would raise her gold-flecked eyes and look deeply into his and then, speaking so softly that he had to strain to hear her, murmur, "Yes, Your Lordship, I'll be your mistress. Yes."

"Yes?"

Lord Hartwood repeated her assent in an odd croaking tone, and Eliza saw the haughty lord's pale lashes flutter open in surprise. She, too, was quivering with shock at what she had just said. Had she really assented to his scandalous proposal? Had she gone mad?

There was still time to pretend she had been joking—to laugh off her assent and slap his hand away. The look of astonishment—or was it dismay—that filled his face as she gave her assent told her he hadn't expected it. But she couldn't bring herself to unsay the fatal word.

How could she? The bailiffs must be already at the house. Her few belongings would be set out on the street, to be hauled off later and sold for her father's debts. And her father would be back in debtor's prison. It had been only this morning he'd told her, "Be patient, sweetheart, my luck will change and I'll pay your inheritance back to you, doubled in value. You wait, someday I'll buy you a coach and four and you'll ride around town like the lady that you are." But his luck never changed. It never would. And now, faced with this monstrous offer, what else could she do but agree? Lord Hartwood's coach and four were not imaginary.

But still, she must make sure Lord Hartwood

really meant what he'd said. So after lifting his hand from her bosom and depositing it back in his lap, she said, "There *is* a condition on my acceptance, Your Lordship. You must immediately send twenty pounds to the warden of the Marshalsea and instruct him to pay off all my father's debts."

"So twenty pounds is the price you set upon your virtue?" Lord Hartwood inquired coolly.

"Is that too much?"

"Not at all," he said quietly. "One of Violet's earbobs would've cost that much, and I've given her far more than one. You shall have your twenty pounds."

"And there's something else," she added hesitantly, her hand twining around the handle of her flowered bag. "I must save my books. They are all I have left and without them I cannot practice my art. They were my aunt's, passed down to her from our ancestor, the great astrologer Lilly. If my father runs up new debts—and he will, for he cannot keep from gambling—the bailiffs will come and take them. I shall consider the sacrifice of my virtue well rewarded, if only my books can be saved."

Well, that was a corker! He had heard many a hard luck tale from the women he'd taken under his protection: They said they sold themselves to help their sick children or aging parents, but never before had a woman sold herself to him to save her books. He looked away, unwilling to let her see how hard he was struggling to keep a straight face. When he turned back toward her, her face held such a look of strained anxiety that he knew she feared he would not agree to so extravagant a demand.

Gently he reassured her. "It is no great matter to preserve your books. I could send a letter for your father to sign, stating that, in view of the twenty pounds I've paid him, he signs over the ownership of all books in the possession of his daughter, which I will hold in trust for her. That way he can't take them back even if he runs up further debts."

"So my books would truly be saved?"

"Indeed," he said dryly. "Though not your virtue."

"My virtue can be of little interest to anyone but myself," she replied coolly, reassuming for the moment that fusty schoolmistress's air of hers. "Certainly its value must be far below that of my codex of Maternus—or the Ptolemy's *Tetrabiblos* of 1635. Besides, at nine-and-twenty I am well beyond the age where I could expect to marry. I can face the loss of my virtue with equanimity if I can save my books."

She paused for a moment, clearly wondering if she could press for anything else. Finally she spoke. "There is one thing more. You must find someone to feed my poor Pup. Leaving him with my father would be like condemning the poor creature to death. But don't give the money to my father. He would wager it away at cards."

He nodded, but said nothing. She stopped for

a moment, cocking her head like a small sparrow waiting to take flight. Then watching his face carefully, she added, "I do not wish to appear greedy, but I am afraid I must ask you for yet one other thing. But I promise you this will truly be the last."

"You drive a hard bargain," he said severely, folding his arms across his chest. What would she ask for this time? A peck of birdseed? A length of twine? Never before had he heard such odd requests from a woman he had taken into keeping.

She took a deep breath, clutching her hands together, and then hesitantly explained, "I must ask that you grant me twenty-five pounds more when our connection is over. I would not ask for it, except that I see no other way. When you grow tired of me, I must have some funds with which to reestablish myself and find a place to live."

"Forty-five pounds, then, and some dog food," he said in his most quelling tones.

"Yes, and that letter you promised, to save my books. I find these terms most satisfactory."

The time was long past when he should have brought down the curtain on this ridiculous scene and left the little fortune-teller by the side of the road. But the glow suffusing her otherwise plain face made it difficult to pursue such a course now. The lesson he had hoped to teach her had backfired completely. Far from filling her with fear, his threat to ruin her had filled her with hope. So it was a puzzlement to know how to proceed. Though he knew for a certainty that his sins ensured his final resting place must be hell, he could not find it in himself to snuff out the hope he had aroused in such a forlorn creature.

And besides, he really did need a mistress. A mistress was vital for the proper claiming of his inheritance.

But could he make a mistress out of such unpromising material? Even for someone as fond as he was of unlikely pranks and eccentric behavior, it was hard to imagine how such a scheme could succeed. Her freckled face bore no hint of the sensuality a mistress must possess. And who would believe her to be a strumpet when her manners were those of a country schoolmistress?

Yet he hesitated to dismiss her. While her looks were unpromising, the hope he had inadvertently kindled in her now lent a certain brightness to her features. She appeared to still have all her teeth, and her face, though thin, looked well nourished enough to suggest there might be some pleasing curves hidden beneath the shapeless bodice. Her neck was long and graceful, and her skin was flawless, like unglazed porcelain. He suddenly found himself wondering what she'd look like stripped of the figure-obscuring drab gray dress.

But what if she turned out to be a virgin? Deflowering maidens could be iffy and his tastes had never run in that direction. Plus, he needed a willing helper for the weeks ahead, not a miserable ex-virgin bewailing her ruin. Still, there had been a striking lack of wailing from the little seeress so far. She was a bold puss for all of her

Quaker manners. And she was better than nothing, which was his alternative at such short notice.

So why not accept her ludicrous terms? Should it work out, as unlikely as it seemed, he'd have a brand-new mistress to bring with him to his mother's home in Brighton, one who had the advantage of being easily disposed of at the end of the fortnight. Should it not, he could simply send her back to town with her forty-five pounds and the letter about her books.

In any case, the evening would be diverting. The chit offered him novelty. And he'd been known to spend far more than forty-five pounds for an evening with a woman whose favors had promised him far less entertainment.

Chapter 3

That the evening before her might hold the prospect of entertainment was the very last thought in Eliza Farrell's mind. She had sat in stunned silence as Lord Hartwood had informed her that he found her last offer acceptable and would take her on as his mistress for the term of the next fortnight. He had explained that he would send the money to free her father this very night and make the necessary arrangements to feed Pup. Then he had drawn forth from under the carriage seat an exquisite folding gentleman's desk upon which he began at once composing the letter to his man of business in London.

It was only as she sank back against the luxuriant velvet squabs, with her heart pounding louder than the hooves of the carriage's horses, that Eliza realized that—exactly as Aunt Celestina had predicted—her impetuosity had led her into disaster. It would be only a matter of hours until she learned what it meant to be a fallen woman ruined by a notorious libertine famed for his hot temper and cold heart.

She was glad that the falling dusk obscured her features so Lord Hartwood could not see her dismay. But she had given him her word, and as soon as she had done so, he had begun to fulfill his side of their bargain with such immediate dispatch that she could not see how to extricate herself from the situation.

At least her beloved books would be forever out of the bailiffs' reach, though she quailed when she recalled what it was the libertine lord had demanded in exchange for their safety. She glanced furtively at her new protector, his handsome face lost in thought as one elegant finger absently stroked the side of his aristocratic nose. What could he be expecting? Aunt Celestina had never discussed such matters with her, and though the whispering of her neighbors in Bishops Ridley had given her some hints about what could happen between an unchaperoned woman and a man, she had not been brave enough to ask her aunt for the details.

Well, she would find out soon. She'd made sure of that, so there was no point now in lamenting her fate. She must set herself to bucking up and getting on with it in a way that would have made her aunt proud—had her aunt been willing to ignore what exactly it was she was about to get on *with*.

Her consolation must be this: If she could get through whatever it was that Lord Lightning would demand of her—and if it was not so dreadful that when it was over she must fall into a hectic and fatal decline like Mr. Richardson's Clarissa—in a fortnight she would return to the world equipped with the books she needed to practice her craft and a fortune of twenty-five pounds. But as she stole one last glance at the intimidating nobleman beside her, she prayed that whatever Lord Hartwood would make her do would not be too unbearable.

As dusk engulfed the carriage, Edward, too, found himself praying the upcoming hour would not be too unbearable. He had long prided himself on his talent for pleasing women, but he had rarely exercised that talent over the past few years, bored with the company of the sort of women who were drawn to a man whose reputation was as fatally damaged as his own. He'd had enough of the women of the demimonde with their coarseness and their continual demands on his purse and of the society women who watched him undress with feverish anticipation, as if the removal of his shining top boots would reveal a cloven hoof and the doffing of his buckskins, the lashing of a forked tail.

He shifted uneasily in his seat as the carriage rumbled through the falling darkness toward his town house. How irksome it would be after the fleeting moments of pleasure were over: yet another woman to be beguiled and placated, another woman whose fickle affections, once his, must somehow be tolerated.

He sighed and drummed his fingers against the rich wood that paneled the carriage door. He was already beginning to regret having made one of those impulsive gestures for which he was so famous. But having made it, he would go through with it. However distasteful it might be, he would use the passion he'd arouse in the mousy fortune-teller during their initial sexual encounter to seal her to him. He could not afford to have her disengaged were he to take her to his mother's house. He would need to command her loyalty for the brief fortnight that would follow, though he did not look forward to the hour it would take to accomplish this. A bit of brandy would help.

As he glanced at his mistress-to-be through lowered lids and saw how the blood had drained out of her face, making her freckles stand out starkly against her pale white skin, he realized it might serve them both were she to become foxed, too, so they could get through the necessary unpleasantness quickly. When all that was over he could leave her and get on with the real pleasure he had been looking forward to all day. Only this afternoon he had purchased a copy of Mr. Keats's controversial new long poem, *Endymion*. It awaited him now in his valise. Yes, he thought wryly, his new mistress was not the only one who loved her books.

* * *

It was dark when they arrived at Lord Lightning's town house, so Eliza was able to form no idea of the exterior, save that it appeared to have a great number of windows and a decided air of elegance. Her new protector guided her wordlessly from the carriage, his fingers barely brushing her shoulder. Even so, his touch set her nerves to jangling.

Unseen hands opened the tall oak doors as they approached, revealing a grand foyer dark with aged paneling, but Eliza had no time to marvel at the magnificence revealed to her. Lord Hartwood motioned her toward a wide staircase lined with portraits where an obsequious housekeeper awaited her. Showing no hint of surprise at the way her master had materialized out of the darkness with a strange woman in tow, the housekeeper simply curtsied to him politely and led Eliza to a luxurious bedchamber where she left her alone.

The light from the three-branched candelabra the housekeeper had brought with her flickered fitfully. But even in the near darkness it reflected off the highly polished surface of the marquetry table standing beside a large, richly cushioned bed. It brought out the subtle sheen of the silken fabric that covered the walls and glinted off the golden highlights of the plasterwork adorning the painted ceiling far above her head.

But there was no time to be lost in gazing about at the magnificence of her surroundings. At any moment Lord Lightning would return and she would learn, for better or worse, exactly what it was he would require of her. Her empty stomach, which had been growling with hunger only a moment before, lurched. Thoughts flooded into her mind, unbidden, and ungovernable.

To what unimaginable act might he subject her? To what humiliations might she be exposed? Surely her aunt would not have warned her so frequently of the danger of giving way to her passion had those dangers not been considerable.

What had possessed her to agree to Lord Lightning's offer? Her aunt had taught her to control her fiery Aries Ascendant. Eliza knew better than to give in to the impulses of the moment—or at least, she had thought she did. But she need only look now at the huge bed that dominated the center of the room, its dark paneled headboard piled high with the thick pillows whose richly embroidered satin covers gleamed dully in the dim candlelight, to know how completely she had acted without thinking and wonder how high the price would be that she would pay.

If only Aunt Celestina had not died. Her aunt had so often helped her rein in her unruly nature. But her aunt was dead. And all Eliza had left to hold on to after all her years of loving care were the very books whose rescue had put her into Lord Lightning's power—those and the secrets of the astrologer's art her aunt had passed on to her.

Eliza reached into her satchel and pulled out a handful of almanacs. Perhaps even now her aunt's teachings might give some insight that could help her survive the oncoming ordeal. She *had* seen good in Lord Hartwood's chart. She must not lose sight of that, no matter how intimidating he might seem when she found herself alone with him here in the dark.

Her fingers searched through the bag's contents until she felt the velvety smooth surface of the paper on which she had drawn His Lordship's natal chart. She drew it out and laid it on the side table, but it was too dark for her to read it there. Since the little light present in the chamber fell almost entirely on the bed, she seated herself gingerly on its edge where it was just possible for her to make out the tiny print of her almanacs.

Though she knew she did not have enough time to calculate the exact positions of the planets at this hour, there was one technique that might provide some reassurance. Her aunt had learned it from one of her German correspondents. It had the advantage of requiring almost no calculation, so it would take her only a few moments to extract the information she needed. But as she heard the sound of a door opening behind her and swung around to face it, she realized she would not have even those few moments.

Lord Hartwood strode into the room. A footman followed behind him carrying a tray on which rested a decanter, glasses, and a plate of dainties. Silently the footman set the tray on a side table and then bowed and removed himself from the room.

She was alone with Lord Lightning.

He had removed his exquisitely wrapped neck cloth and now was garbed only in a loose silken shirt, its top buttons open, and in pale superfine breeches that fit his long legs like a second skin, displaying his muscular calves to advantage. His shining Hessian boots were gone, replaced by soft kid dress shoes which muffled his steps as he moved soundlessly across the room toward the bed.

The dim light gilded his pale curls. How could she have not noticed before how very large he was—and how magnetic? She felt herself drawn into his orbit, like a small planet caught in the grip of a fiery sun. She knew she should resist, yet that sun was so magnificent. She should be appalled to find herself here—scandalously alone in the bedroom of a libertine—and a half-clothed libertine at that. Yet she could not help but admire him.

But there was little time for that. Lord Hartwood was observing her, too. His dark eyes glinted in the candlelight, their expression hard to interpret. As they rested for a moment on the books and papers spread out upon the bed, a half smile flickered across his lips. "So you even take your books to bed with you, do you?"

At the sound of his deep and resonant voice, Eliza bit her lower lip and reached for the paper that bore his horoscope. But anxiety made her clumsy, and her hand knocked it off the richly embroidered counterpane. It fluttered to the floor, but before Eliza could rescue it, Lord Hartwood reached down to pick it up. He peered at it for a moment in the dim light, then handed it back to her.

"So what do your stars tell you now, little seeress? Will you survive your visit to Bluebeard's Castle?" His long form lounged against the bedpost. One languid arm snaked around it, making the strong muscles of his broad shoulder stand out as they strained against the thin fabric of his shirt.

Instinctively, Eliza drew back. Then, with as much sangfroid as she could muster, she replied, "I cannot say. You interrupted me before I had finished with my calculations."

"What was there for you to calculate? You've already told me my character is an open book to you."

Eliza ignored his sarcasm. "Your character is complex, my lord. There are warring strains within your nature. But as I have just such a disposition myself, I feel certain I shall be able to furnish the proper interpretation, if you would be kind enough to grant me a few more minutes."

Despite his desire to get things over with quickly, the woman's refusal to be cowed caught his attention. At her first sight of him, clothed as he was for the evening's sport, her face had quivered with an emotion he believed was fear, and yet she had responded to him so steadfastly— with something in her brave green eyes he had never seen in those of a woman he'd brought to his rooms. With a qualm he realized it might be innocence.

"Continue with your labors," he heard himself saying, much to his own surprise, as he strode over to the large comfortable armchair that furnished one corner of the room.

A vivid blush colored her cheeks as, her fingers shaking, the woman picked up one of her almanacs and quickly flipped through the pages until she found the entry she was looking for. Then she peered intently at the horoscope—he wondered if it was his or her own—her eyebrows furrowed in deep concentration.

Her lack of self-consciousness, so unusual in the women with whom he was acquainted, gave her face an elusive charm, and he rather enjoyed watching her as she worked. Though as her head remained bent over her work, he remembered the ultimate purpose of this interview, and some of the pleasure he had been feeling abated. Alone with her now, he felt, as he had not felt in his carriage, the enormity of what he was about to do to her. Such innocence should have been saved for some honest, earnest man, who could have shared the delusion of love with her—at least for the first few times. Not to Black Neville's son, cursed with Black Neville's cold unloving nature.

But it was too late for regret. She'd made her bargain. He'd paid to free her father. Her books were safe. So shaking off his doubts, he strode to the side table and decanted the brandy into a glass. He held it up to the light and lost himself in contemplation of its warm amber glow, while she went on serenely consulting her charts.

Only a few moments later did she look up. A wide smile filled her open features. "It will be all right," she said. "Uranus sextiles your Venus by solar arc, while Jupiter conjoins your Moon and Mars. Your anger will be tamed by love, and good fortune will come from—" Here she blushed again, more prettily this time. "Well, from the things associated with Mars."

"The god of war?"

"War, yes. But in astrology he is also lord of iron, fire, anger, and, well—" she hesitated again "—of manly passion." The little fortune-teller's blush had spread beyond her face and now flowed into the portion of her freckled chest that was visible at her throat.

Manly passion, indeed. She must really be a virgin.

He swirled his brandy in the glass, inhaling deeply as the vapors released, then drained it down. It was a shame to abuse a good brandy by guzzling it so quickly, but he felt himself in need of the instant resolve the brandy would furnish. Then he stretched back in his chair and gazed at his quarry, enjoying the artless way in which she displayed her rounded and surprisingly graceful arms as she grabbed at her books and stuffed them clumsily into her bulging valise. But his appreciation of this display was cut short as he noticed the quivering of her hand. The woman was trembling.

Had he been a kinder man, her anxiety might have caused him to take pity on her and let her go. She was so completely out of her depth. But he was not a kinder man. He was Lord Lightning, and the woman should have taken more care than to get herself into this situation. Why should he give in to sentiment just because she was an innocent?

But even so, her hope-filled words had cooled his enthusiasm for what must come next. She would not find love with him, no matter what she saw written in the stars. He was not capable of it, and only a very foolish virgin would have been so naïve as to admit to a libertine like himself that love was what she hoped to find in their upcoming tryst.

It reminded him forcibly of why he avoided virgins.

But things had gone too far now for him to stop without looking like a fool himself. So it was time to get it over with.

He stood up and walked over to the sideboard. In a moment he had filled a second glass with brandy and brought it to where she sat so stiffly on the edge of the bed.

She took it willingly, though as her small fingers brushed his when she reached for the glass, he realized they were ice cold. He was about to warn her to drink the brandy slowly and to savor the delicate aroma, but before he could say a word, she slugged it down as quickly as he had drunk down his.

Her swallow terminated in a choking sound, followed by a violent fit of coughing. He reached his arm around her shoulders and pounded on her back until the coughing stopped.

"You're supposed to sip it, not suck it down like a sailor guzzling grog."

"But that was what you did. I only followed your example."

"Well that should teach you not to. Don't you know I'm famous for setting a very bad example?"

The girl smiled, rather charmingly. Then she sank back against the pile of thick pillows that furnished the bed.

She looked so odd lying there amid the pillows on which he had entertained some of the most beautiful—and wanton—women in the kingdom. But it was not just her modesty that made her different from them. He struggled to define what it was. Then it struck him. It must be that ridiculous spinster's cap of hers—the first object of that kind to ever have made its appearance in his bed.

As if she had read his thoughts she raised a hand to her cap, though after she touched it she stopped. "Would you prefer I remove my cap?" she said, uncertainly. "Is that customary?"

"Quite." As was much else she would soon discover. "It does look rather uncomfortable with all those pins."

"It is. The pins dig into my head. But such caps are meant to be uncomfortable. They are the very soul of propriety."

"Then you must remove it directly. Too much propriety is likely to send me into a fit of sneezing. I am quite allergic to it."

He was relieved to see her smile, and even more relieved when she tilted her head toward him and let him pull out the pins that affixed the cap to her hair. When he had removed it, he placed it gingerly on the table beside the bed. If only it turned out to be as easy to divest her of the rest of her garments.

Without the cap her hair was surprisingly thick and lustrous. He leaned toward the candelabra and pinched out all but one flickering flame. Then, gazing at her with his most smoldering look, he murmured, "Your eyes are beautiful in the candlelight."

It was meant to be mere moonshine, but as the words left his mouth, he realized, with some surprise, that they were true. Her eyes were striking—large, green, and luminous—though disturbingly intelligent. He could see in them, too, the effort she was making to control her fear.

"There's no need to be frightened," he assured her. "You will experience only pleasure at my hands. And if there should be some unexpected consequence of our connection, you may rest assured I will open my purse generously to deal with it."

He felt a burst of self-satisfaction. That was far more than his brother had done for any of the women he had impregnated. But he quickly suppressed that thought. It would not put him into the mood he needed to establish.

Next he reached out and gently pulled the remaining pins from the girl's hair. It broke free from the tight knot in which she had confined it and tumbled across the linen pillowcase. The river of thick curls, no longer carroty, glowed auburn in the dull light of the single candle.

He stroked one curling lock on the pillow where it had fallen, delighting in the springy feel of it. It was so clean, so silken. Then he let his fingers walk up the long tress, following it upward to her nape, which he stroked with a slow, soothing motion, until he saw her relax and nestle deeper against the pillow. Her skin was warm and velvety. He let his fingers brush across the softness of her lips. Then he raised her hand to his own mouth and slowly, teasingly, kissed the tip of each finger. As he did, he noted with surprise the eagerness with which she reached out to feel the texture of his lips. Carefully he let his tongue come out to greet her fingertip. Then, imprisoning her finger with his lips, he sucked it into a kiss. The sensation that filled him as her delicate skin met his searching tongue was far more stimulating than something so innocent should have been.

A wave of desire swept over him. By Gad, he wanted her! But even as he felt himself respond, her finger hesitated and withdrew, warning him to slow down. There were new delights to savor here.

Yes, a voice murmured in his mind, *the delights of despoiling innocence.*

He ignored it. She knew what she was in for when she agreed to come here with him. There was no need for conscience to interfere. Innocent or not, she was just another woman, fickle and greedy like the rest, babbling of love as they all did before they got their claws into a man. So what if she was a virgin? They all started out that way, but they got over it. Why should he care if she imagined their coupling might lead to love? He'd teach her something about love—about the hot piercing pleasure to be found in merging bodies, and when she learned it she'd become like the rest of the cold, hard women who sought him out and then abandoned him.

Yet he was unnerved by the gentleness of her hand, which now stroked his stubbled cheek. Her probing fingertips brushed over his lips, stroked the indented place in the center, then brushed the side of his nose before moving upward to the smooth place on his cheek where no beard grew, touching, learning, and making it clear she had never before, ever, touched a man.

He suppressed another qualm. Why make all this fuss about her innocence? There was nothing shy now about the way her caressing hand was making its exquisite way down his neck, to his shoulder and the opening of his collar, sending shivers of pleasure down his spine. Her fingers rested briefly on the tuft of pale blond hair that rose beneath his throat, and combed through it gently, before she reached down to the first fastened button of his shirt and stopped.

His own hand shaking now, he reached up and gently undid that button and the next, allowing his shirt to fall away and leave his chest naked.

Her hand dropped and she let him take control again, but her huge green eyes kept drinking him in. There was a haziness to them now. Their clarity had been replaced by something more dreamy. The brandy must be taking effect.

Taking direction from the way she'd just touched him, he let his hand glide gently down her cheek and along her neck to her shoulders and arm. He felt the tiny hairs on her biceps rise in response to his feather-light touch.

There were buttons on her bodice, too. When he undid them one by one, she made no protest. He slid one hand under the loose shift that was revealed and pushed the thin fabric of the shift aside. To his surprise, she wore no stays. He made the most of that discovery, cradling the rounded breast he found beneath. It barely filled his hand, but though it was so much smaller than Violet's luxuriant orbs, it was firmer and delightfully resilient; her rosy nipple was surprisingly beautiful, too, domed and swollen.

She gave a little sigh. He reached further inside her shift, brushing along her torso, his fingers dancing toward her soft mound of nether curls. As he felt them spring against his fingertips, he wondered if they were as fiery as her hair, but his attention was wrenched away from such speculation as he felt her hips rise to meet his exploring hand. Emboldened, he pulled her closer with his other arm and pressed the length of his body against hers, letting her feel for the first time what he had in store for her. But as his swollen manhood rubbed against her abdomen, she tensed and jerked away from him, and he saw what must be fear flash in her eyes. It was replaced a moment later by the most disturbing look of trust.

He stilled, then drew back, aware again of what he was taking from her.

But it was too late for regret. She'd gotten what she wanted and she'd pledged him this in exchange. This breast was his to caress as long as he wanted. Her thighs were his to kiss, to suck, to crush beneath him.

More roughly than he had intended, he pushed her shift aside again and seized her rosy nipple in his mouth, flicking his tongue against the swollen flesh. A ripple swept through her body. He hoped it was passion. He feared it was shock.

As he hesitated, she stirred beneath him and moaned.

"Lord Hartwood—" she began, reminding him she didn't know his Christian name. No matter. Whatever she had to say, he didn't want to hear it. He touched his mouth to hers, silencing her with a kiss. Then he reached his hand back inside her shift and let his fingertips trace designs on her abdomen, gentling her. He heard her breathing quicken.

Louder this time she said, "Lord Hartwood, I need—"

His lips closed on hers again. He would give her what she needed. As if by accident he let his fingertips brush against her womanly nub, pleased when she writhed against him. He was surprised to find her already swollen and surprisingly wet. He longed to bury his face there and fill himself with her scent, but he held himself back, not wishing to scare her. Carefully he extended one finger into the opening of her secret passage. But the little gasp she gave as his searching fingers prodded more deeply was not a gasp of pleasure.

He stopped. He lifted his head, his eyes locked into hers, and he saw the shock that registered there.

Her eyes betrayed her. She had learned, at last, what manner of man he really was. Though she would go through with it and live up to her side of their bargain, he knew, as clearly as if her voice had whispered the words, she regretted making that bargain.

She gave a tiny gasp and her mouth started working. It would all come out now, her loathing and her disgust. He could not bear to hear it. He must silence her the only way that was left to him. He must fill her with himself and forcibly make her his. He must corrupt her, give the beast within himself what it demanded, and be once again what he knew himself to be: selfish, irresistible, and damned.

But something held him back, something he'd thought had died in him long ago. Something that whispered he had sinned enough.

Filled with dread, he pulled away from her and let her speak.

"I'm sorry to be such a ninny," she began softly. "But this is all so unfamiliar. I . . . I never expected

to be a mistress so I haven't studied the subject.
And even if I had wished to study it, my aunt
would never have let me read the sort of book that
could have furnished me with instruction. The
books I *have* read always stopped short of telling
me exactly what it is that happens next."

A wave of laughter swept through his body,
replacing the dismay that had filled him only a
moment before.

"So that's it?" he choked out. "You would like to
study up on the subject before we proceed?"

"Well, of course. One likes to know what one is
about. And this is so much stranger than what I
had imagined."

"It is, indeed," he said. "It is, in fact, far stranger
than anything *I* ever imagined."

But as true as that was, with an odd sense
of relief, he realized it was over and that it had
ended far better than he would ever have imagined it could. To be sure, there was still an ache in
his manhood, an echo of the lust that had over-
powered him only a few moments before. But
the blackness that had threatened to engulf him
was gone. She had dispelled it with her ability
to remain herself when he had been swept away.
And somehow, by remaining herself, she had
shone light into a place within him that had not
known light before.

When he had recovered his ability to speak, he
reached over and put his arm around her, shelter-
ing her. He inhaled the delicate scent of her hair

and said, "I think we have both had quite enough learning for one night."

Was it a look of disappointment he saw flit over her face? He could not credit it, yet that was what it looked like. But of course, she must fear he would hold back the payment he had promised her. He let his eyelids drift shut as he searched for words to reassure her she would not leave penniless when he sent her away the next morning, but his mind was moving slowly—the brandy perhaps, or perhaps the aftermath of his wrenching inner struggle. When he opened them again he realized no more words were needed. The brandy had had its effect on her, too, and his new mistress—the virgin—had dropped off, snoring quietly, into a faintly sodden sleep.

Chapter 4

At dawn, Eliza awoke with a painful pounding in her head and in some confusion as to where she was. She lay beneath the covers of a huge satin-draped bed, clad only in her shift. On the wall across from the bed was a painting of scantily clad nymphs disporting themselves with a satyr. She had a fuzzy memory that on the previous night she, too, had disported herself in a manner not all that different from the nymphs. Indeed, as she grew more awake, it struck her that during the course of the night she must have become a fallen woman. But try as she would, she could not remember the details.

She remembered drinking the fiery brandy that had burnt her throat and set up a strange buzzing in her head. She remembered Lord Hartwood coming into the bed with her and the gentle way he had taken her hand and allowed it to explore his body. She remembered, too, the surprising discoveries she'd made as he'd explored her body, before she'd become frightened and gasped out something—anything—to postpone whatever it was that was about to happen. But after that she remembered nothing. Nothing at all.

She shuddered. Perhaps what had followed had been so horrible she had had to blank it out to remain sane. She had heard of such things happening. But somehow, remembering how Lord Hartwood's soft lips had felt on her fingertips and how gently he had caressed her bosom and so much more in that shocking but surprisingly delicious way, it was hard to believe that something so terrible had followed.

Gingerly she explored her body. Except for the throbbing in her head, nothing hurt. And most oddly, her underdrawers were still in place. She knew from what little she had heard that ruin should involve the removal of her drawers.

There was a knock at the door and a maid came in, bringing with her a tray on which reposed a cup of tea and some toast. She set it down beside Eliza, curtsied, and just before making her exit, informed her that when she had finished with her breakfast Lord Hartwood would be pleased to see her in his study.

She sipped her tea; her stomach was not yet up to dealing with toast and at the thought of having to see Lord Hartwood, it heaved. Eliza could not imagine how she would face him again. But she must, if for no other reason than that there was no other way to determine what had happened. It was a good thing her Aries Ascendant gave her courage. She would need it to get through the upcoming interview.

Unlike Eliza, Edward awoke with a surprising feeling of lightness in his heart and a sharp appetite. The light that filtered through his curtains seemed crisper than usual, the air, more bracing. His valet, who always tiptoed as quietly as possible in the morning, having suffered in the past from the uncertainty of his master's temper at that early hour, was greeted with a hearty "Good morning" and an unexpected smile. Edward was surprised at his own good humor—good humor that was all the more surprising considering the abortive nature of the previous evening's encounter.

But it was exactly that which was the source of his unusual lightness of spirit. Somehow, last night, he'd done the honorable thing, though to do so had gone much against his natural inclination. The warm, happy feeling he felt welling up within him now must be that emotion with which he had almost no experience—the satisfaction of a virtuous deed well done. He savored it. Such a feeling was not likely to come his way again. He had no intention of making a habit of virtue.

He finished his breakfast, dressed with his valet's help, and then made his way down to his study. Of course, after what had happened, he'd have to dismiss the little fortune-teller. There was no possibility now of making her his mistress. That was vexing, to be sure, as he would have to face his mother without a mistress in tow. But he'd pay off the girl generously despite what had happened. No doubt she'd be thrilled by her narrow escape.

He basked for a moment more in the glow cast by his unaccustomed act of charity, then he turned back to business. There were a few more letters to write before he headed out to Brighton, in particular, a delicate one addressed to his father's ex-mistress, Mrs. Atwater. She would serve his purpose almost as well as a mistress of his own, and it would be a simple matter to enlist her in his scheme as she was so very fond of money.

But no sooner had he trimmed his pen than there was a rap on the door and a footman announced, "Your Lordship, Miss Eliza requests a moment of your time."

Miss Eliza? He searched his mind, wondering to which lady of his acquaintance the footman might be referring. Then he realized. It must be the little fortune-teller. He hadn't even asked her Christian name.

He barked out his permission for her to enter, and she came into the room, closing the door gently behind her. She made her way over to his desk and stopped awkwardly before him with a look on her face much like that of a pupil who had been sent to the headmaster's office. She was clad once again in her heavy gray wool Quaker's dress with her auburn hair bound up in a tight knot at the back of her head. She had even more freckles scattered across her flaming cheeks than he had remembered.

In the clear light of morning, it was inconceivable to him that such an ordinary creature could have inspired him with the passion he remembered sweeping over him the previous night. But swept over him it had—until he had been stopped in his tracks by that unaccountable need not to hurt her. The memory brought with it the disquieting vision of her auburn hair let loose and spread around her, and as their eyes met, he realized with some surprise that, despite his good intentions, the oddity of the situation left him with no idea of what to say to her. Eliza stood silent for a moment, too, twisting her fingers together, clearly finding it difficult to speak.

Finally she blurted, "Your Lordship, though it is embarrassing to admit it, I am not at all sure of what took place between us in the course of last night. So I must beg Your Lordship to answer me frankly. Am I ruined?"

Her predicament was far from humorous, but, even so, he was tempted to laugh. Though he was not used to thinking of himself as a man much given to laughter, something about being with Miss Farrell made laughing easier. He collected himself. "Your reputation is gone as you have spent the night unchaperoned in my house. But beyond that, nothing happened."

"You are very certain of this, Your Lordship? There can be no mistake?"

Her face bore such an earnest look as she waited to learn her fate that he experienced once again a most unexpected burst of happiness at the thought that he had not, after all, made her his victim.

"I am completely certain," he said gently. "You may go to your wedding bed secure in the knowledge that you are a maiden still. The brandy was too much for both of us. You dropped off into a sound sleep early on. I did so shortly after. No harm was done."

The relief that flooded her features was followed almost immediately by anxiety. "Then you did not make me your mistress?"

"No. I thought better of it. It was a foolish idea and I've given it up entirely."

Her face fell. "Then I shall have to pay back the money you sent to my father."

"There is no need to do so. Consider it a gift. And here—" He opened a drawer in his desk and took out some banknotes, which he placed at the edge of his desk so she could reach them. "Here are fifty pounds. Our arrangement is over. The money will help you get settled again somewhere new."

She made no move toward the notes, but simply said in an uncertain voice, "So you wish me to leave?"

"Surely that must be what you yourself would wish for."

Surely it should be, Eliza thought. But oddly, it was not.

Though she should be feeling only relief that she had escaped the consequences of her rash and headstrong decision the previous day, and escaped them, moreover, in possession of fifty pounds she could never have earned on her own, Lord Hartwood's words had filled her with a sense of loss. She struggled to account for this wholly unexpected emotion, but could come up only with the explanation that though she had read the horoscopes of many distinguished and powerful men, this was the first time she had been given the opportunity to observe such a man in person and see the planets on his chart come to life. It was hard to taste such delight so briefly and then be forced to leave it behind.

And there was something more: Despite all the terrors of the previous night, there had been something exhilarating in the upheaval that had taken place in her situation. It had been frightening, to be sure, but the glimpse of his world that Lord Hartwood had given her made it hard to resign herself to returning to the dull life of a bookish middle-aged spinster.

She sighed. Aunt Celestina would have called her ungrateful and she knew she should be glad she was not a fallen woman. But as she watched His Lordship's long elegant fingers toy with his pen—those very same fingers that had awakened such inexplicable feelings in her body the previous night—she knew that even though he had not ruined her, Lord Hartwood's subtle touch had awakened something in her that would not easily go back to sleep. The morning light, which poured through the window, illuminated the tuft of silvery curls at the base of his neck, reminding her how her exploring fingers had discovered its silken texture and the warmth and richness of his golden skin. A sensible woman would have delighted in her narrow escape, but the effort it took to force her mind away from that memory told Eliza how far she was from being sensible.

Besides, Aunt Celestina was dead, and she had no one now to turn to for protection but the father who had abandoned her shortly after her birth, who had greeted her arrival in London with happiness, to be sure, but only because it meant he could gamble away the small inheritance her aunt had bequeathed her. So she stood before Lord Hartwood and chewed her lower lip like a schoolgirl as she pondered her next step. At last she spoke. "If I should wish to stay, my lord? What then?"

What then indeed? Edward sighed. He should have known after the events of the previous night that nothing involving the little fortune-teller would be easy.

"Yesterday you spoke repeatedly of the importance you placed on finding a mistress to accompany you to Brighton to claim your inheritance," she reminded him.

"I did."

"Might I not be that woman still?"

Not likely! He would not go through another

night like the last one. If she put herself in his power again, he would take her. "I assure you," he said curtly, "I no longer have any desire to make you my mistress."

"Was it my freckles?" she asked sadly. "Did it appall you to discover I was so completely covered with them?"

Freckles? What had they to do with anything?

"Or was it because I didn't know what I was doing?"

Suddenly it struck him what she was asking. "Your freckles make you surprisingly attractive," he lied nobly. "And besides, virgins aren't supposed to know what they're doing."

"Then why do you no longer want me? You said it was important that you take a mistress with you to Brighton."

He frowned. He should have known he would not be left to savor his one good deed. Like all women, she would not leave without first making a scene.

Testily, he explained, "I do not want you, Miss Farrell, because, as much as I wished to take a mistress with me on this accursed visit, I realized, just before it was too late, that I couldn't afford to make *you* that mistress."

"But I asked so little! You said yourself, I asked less than the price of your last mistress's earbobs."

"Indeed. And that proves my point. Had you not been so utterly unsuited to the role of mistress, you'd have asked for a great deal more." He saw her flinch, embarrassed at his words. "Miss

Farrell, do you realize that I might have given you a baby had things gone to their natural conclusion last night?"

"But surely it takes much more than one such experience for that to happen," Eliza replied. "It must be quite difficult, or why would so many wives have come to Aunt Celestina for advice when they were unable to conceive?"

"It takes but a single moment to conceive a child."

The look of shock on Eliza's face made him thank whatever restless spirits still watched over him that he had not taken her last night.

"Eliza," he said gently. "I'm not used to the society of women like yourself. The women of my world are hard and calculating. I'd come to think all women were like that, so by being as you are, frank and open, you've taught me something new about women that I'm glad to know." Though she'd also taught him that in the future he must give women like herself a wide berth. Given another scene like last night's, he knew what the outcome would be. It was only one of his famous unpredictable quirks that had saved her.

Still, he felt a moment of regret at the thought of having to give up all contact with her. There was something so novel about being with a woman who had not sought him out because of his blackened reputation or the size of his purse. Nor could he deny that it had given him an odd sort of pleasure to hear the glowing terms with which she had described his character, even though she was, of course, completely wrong. But that reminded him how impossible it was that she should stay.

He cleared his throat. "You spoke last night, as you looked at your horoscopes, of love. Had I truly made you my mistress, it's likely you now would think yourself in love with me. If that had happened, I would have had no choice but to dismiss you immediately—to protect you from yourself." He saw her poised to make some reply but did not give her a chance to contradict him. "The touch of a woman's body, no matter how intimate, does not open my heart to love. I cannot love. Were you to love me, I could only damage you."

"But surely, my lord, you could *learn* to love?"

"It's unlikely." He glanced at the heavy signet ring on his third finger. "My father, Black Neville, was a notorious rake who nearly ruined our family to satisfy a mistress's demands. My brother was even worse. He seduced a gentlewoman, and when she fell pregnant, he abandoned her. Attempting to bear his child sent her to her grave." He pushed his chair away from the desk and stood up. "That is the nature I inherited. I am my father's son and my brother's brother. You would be wise to believe what I tell you, rather than become another of my victims. Believe me, I cannot love."

Eliza felt her heart go out to him. A Leo who couldn't love! And yet, the words he spoke so bleakly were so completely at odds with the life and warmth she sensed imprisoned behind his harsh façade. He must be wrong. But even if he was not, whatever had hitherto been his experience in life, the chart she had examined the previous evening told her he stood on the brink of a great change. If ever he was to be able to break free and open up his heart, it was now. But to make the most of it, he would need her help.

He had turned away from her, and all she could see of him was his tousled pale curls. There was something so vulnerable about the sight. She yearned to reach out and comfort him. But as she leaned toward him he snapped to attention and swiveled back, fixing her with a look that seemed to strip her clothing off her body and made her quiver to her very bones.

No, she could not be his mistress. He was right about that.

She hadn't understood the words he'd muttered last night about opening his purse in the case of unexpected consequences. Her heart contracted at the thought that she might have borne him a bastard child! She remembered, too, the feeling of wrongness that had swept over her even as her body had begun to respond so unexpectedly to his touch. Though his body had been in the grip of something irresistible, it had not been love, and even as she had responded to it, she had sensed that his passion had disturbed him as much as it frightened her.

But even so, her instincts told her that she must

stay with him, at least a little longer. He needed her help, this Leo who could not love. But how to get him to allow her to stay?

Lord Hartwood picked up the banknotes from his desk, rose, and began to walk slowly over to where she stood. He was back in character again, all Byronic hero. His brooding eyes expressed the agony of his own existence as they swept over her, filled with bleak regret. He sighed deeply, until it seemed his entire being must echo with the cry of his empty soul. She doubted anything she said could reach him now, he was so totally one with the role. But what a role it was, and how well he portrayed it! First Lovelace and now Lord Byron's haunted Corsair. That last sigh of his would have been heard clearly in the cheapest seats. But what a shame it was, in view of his own needs, that he kept choosing such unrewarding roles. Lovelace and *The Corsair* would not teach him how to love. But as that thought flickered through her mind she saw all at once how she might use his love of theater to reach out to him without exciting his fears.

"Would your purpose be accomplished," she asked, "if I were to *pretend* to be your mistress?"

"What do you mean?"

"I might go with you to Brighton and *act* the part of your mistress, though only when we were with others. You would not have to treat me like a mistress when we were in private."

* * *

The woman was mad. He could think of no other explanation. But at the same time, the boldness of her suggestion intrigued him. Others rarely matched him in his ability to come up with outrageous schemes, but Miss Farrell was making a habit of astonishing him.

"What would be the point of pretending?" he asked.

"Well, it depends, of course, on what you want a mistress for. If it were only to satisfy your lust, I can see that the arrangement wouldn't suit."

"Indeed it wouldn't."

"But I doubt lust was your reason for selecting me as a mistress. I am not a woman who inspires lust in men."

He could have argued the point with her, remembering the unexpected strength of the passion that had filled him when he had dallied with her the previous night, but he thought better of it. And besides, whatever had called out his surprising response to her, it was gone now. Perhaps it had just been the effect of the brandy.

"So," she continued in the same calm tone, "since your reason for wishing to bring along a mistress did not spring from carnal need, it is likely you had some theatrical purpose in mind. Leos are known for their love of theater." She paused in her discourse and gazed up at him through ginger lashes. "If it was indeed the theatrical aspect of having a mistress that motivates you, I believe I can fill the role to your satisfaction."

"Based on what?" he asked, fascinated.

"On the fact that I have always been accounted a very good actress."

He mentally compared the earnest little sooth-sayer with Violet and the other actresses of his acquaintance and again suppressed a smile. "I should hardly have thought that your life would've offered many opportunities for acting."

"But that is where you're wrong. My Aunt Ce-lestina was a great lover of the theater, so we spent many happy evenings acting out together the various parts in her favorite plays. At times, she would invite other gentlefolk from our neighbor-hood to take part in our performances. The vicar, who had attended the theater in London several times, told her I was quite the best Lady Teazle he'd ever seen."

"So you would act my mistress, with some help from Mr. Sheridan and the vicar?" he asked, unable to suppress his smile this time.

"With pleasure, my lord."

Really, he should make her take the money and get rid of her now, before some sentimental maggot in his head—some relative no doubt of the one that had bitten him the previous night—made him accept her crazy offer. But it was too late. It was a very speedy maggot and had already taken a good nip. As much as he wanted to, he could not bring himself to dismiss her.

Mad as it was, her suggestion had a kind of lu-natic appeal. It would be a relief to have a mistress with whom he did not have to pretend to feel passion. Nor could he deny that he would find her company entertaining. She was such an original; he would never know what she might say or do next. And the truth was he felt a certain regret at the thought of never seeing her again—though that would soon wear off, as he knew very well he was incapable of feeling anything for a woman. It was only the novelty of her belief that he might be loving and loveable that intrigued him.

Still if he were to send her away now, she might continue on in the belief that he had, tucked away somewhere, a loving heart. How better to dispel that fantasy than to take her with him. A few weeks with him would destroy any illusions she might have about his goodness, and without them she would lose her power to interest him.

And besides, if he agreed to go ahead with her ridiculous scheme, he *would* have a mistress to flaunt in his mother's face. It wouldn't matter whether he actually had sexual congress with her. Just to force his mother to dine with a woman she believed to be his mistress would be enough.

And if the scheme failed? He would dismiss her. There was little to lose in attempting it, and who knew? Perhaps the little fortune-teller could pull it off.

Chapter 5

"I am tempted to try your scheme," Lord Hartwood announced. He stood at the window, his pale curls shining like an aura in the shaft of light that illuminated him from behind. "I *do* need to bring a mistress with me to claim my inheritance, even if she be only a simulated mistress."

He was going to let her stay! Eliza felt an unexpected bolt of fear.

"But I am not at all convinced that you could play the part."

A second bolt: disappointment.

"How good an actress are you, really? Could you behave convincingly in such a role? Could you pretend to be a brazen woman? Could you carry on shamelessly in front of disapproving eyes? You will pardon me if I say I find it hard to believe you could carry off this particular role, no matter what success you may have had playing Lady Teazle with the vicar in your aunt's parlor."

Eliza's pride was wounded. She was a very good actress and surely she had given him as yet no reason to doubt it. She advanced on him, her newfound resolution making her bold. "Try me. I shall show you what I am capable of."

Lord Hartwood paced over to a sofa that stood by the wall. When he turned to face her, the corsair was gone; in his place was the theater director. "Very well. Pretend you are in my mother's parlor. Lord Mumblethorpe is sitting over there. He's very conservative in his views. Are you ready to put on a show for him?"

Eliza nodded. She strode over to the sofa and seized the lace antimacassar that lay on top of its cushions. She draped it around her like a shawl, letting the ends flutter down across her bosom, imagining it to be the fringe of the silken dressing gown Violet had worn. She spent a moment getting into the role, then with a delicate wiggle, she let her lashes drop seductively, took a deep breath, and turned to face him.

Lord Hartwood favored her with a moment of intense regard. It was hard to tell what he was thinking. But before she had time to react, he made his way over to her, swept her into his arms, pressed her against the hard length of his body, and planted a long and soulful kiss on her lips, while his other hand curved over her buttocks.

It took all Eliza's self-discipline to keep from tearing herself out of his embrace. Instead she focused on his kiss. His lips were as warm as they'd been the night before, and when he parted them slightly to suck gently on her upper lip, she tasted the faint flavor of coffee. She opened her lips as well. Immediately she felt his tongue touch hers as he deepened the kiss. Her knees felt weak and she thought she might swoon from the sensation. But she knew that if she gave him any sign that she was disturbed by his simulated lovemaking, he would dismiss her instantly. So she tried as hard as possible to display the same kind of cool disregard with which she imagined a woman of the world like Violet would have responded to such a caress. She moved her lips against his, following his lead, and pressed her hips harder against his body. She hoped he couldn't feel the frantic beating of her heart.

After what felt like a very long time, he let her go, and she stepped back, her heart still pounding.

"You did that surprisingly well," he said. His lips quirked in something akin to amusement, though his eyes blazed with the same fire as the night before. "You did not scream or faint but kissed me in a most mistress-like manner. That bodes well for the scheme."

Eliza nodded dumbly. Her heart was still racing, and she still felt the strange tingling somewhere deep in her belly, that his roving hands had awakened. It struck her that acting the role of his mistress might be as challenging as being a real one, and given the strength of her response to him, for a moment she questioned her own motives in continuing. But then she shook off her doubts. Her motive was only to help him get through a tricky period as his true character emerged. He would not really make her his mistress. She would not wish him to. This was only theater.

As if sensing her discomfort, Lord Hartwood announced mischievously, "I believe we must try that again, just to be sure," and he moved toward her again, his dark eyes sparkling.

This time he drew her into a delicate Sheraton side chair upholstered in stripes of pale green and pink and, when she was seated, dropped his pale head onto her lap. Arching his back luxuriantly like the lion from which his sign got its name, he raised his head, letting it rest against her breasts and nuzzling her gently with his cheek. She could feel her nipples harden as he did so.

It was infuriating! She appeared to have no control at all over her reactions. She prepared herself for the inevitable letdown she must feel when he became aware of her inability to carry off the role, but to her relief her body's involuntary response did not seem overly to disturb him.

"Ah," he said with a tone of contentment, letting his hand explore the underside of her breast. "I believe I could pursue this line of inquiry quite profitably for some time." He exhaled gently. "Should you like me to continue?"

"I should not," Eliza said as quellingly as possible. She struggled to compose herself. "I believe

I have shown you that I can handle whatever is required."

"Perhaps. Though I should hate to make such an important decision on so little information. If you were to go with me as my mistress, you would have to maintain the role for an entire fortnight. I must be sure you are up to the strain."

His dark eyes again twinkled as his hand gently brushed against her peaked nipple. As he did so, he scrutinized her face closely, until she felt she couldn't bear another second of this torment and must end it, if her failure meant leaving him. But just as she was about to leap up and free herself he removed his hand and said, "That is enough for now. I do not wish to put my own resolve to so fierce a test. I don't know where you got the idea you aren't attractive."

She went limp with relief, but forced herself to respond to his question, keeping her voice playful to match his tone. "How *could* I be attractive with such a multitude of freckles? The boys used to make fun of them when I was young. My aunt tried every nostrum anyone ever recommended but nothing would make them go away. And I have red hair, too. Can anything be uglier?"

"Young boys know nothing about it, Eliza. Nor do elderly aunts. As a man of worldly experience, I can assure you your freckles are rather fetching. And though it isn't the current fashion, many men are quite fond of red hair. If you gave it some attention yours could be truly beautiful. Don't underestimate yourself."

Eliza could feel herself blush. No man had ever spoken to her like this. But of course, theirs had been a very small village.

"On the other hand," Lord Hartwood continued, "your gown *is* a fright and fits all too well with your idea of yourself as a hopeless spinster. If you are to accompany me, we will have to do something about your clothing. I can imagine nothing less mistress-like than that gray sack you're wearing. But it is no great matter to correct that," he assured her. "I recently had the modiste prepare a new wardrobe for Violet, one created especially for this journey. It is still here. Her taste in clothing was that of a consummate strumpet." A nostalgic look flitted across his face. "Indeed, that was a great part of her charm for me. Perhaps some of her things might be made to fit you."

Eliza doubted it, remembering the actress's lush form, but she did not correct him. He had come so close to sending her away, and she knew he was still far from believing that her idea might work.

"I shall order her trunk to be brought to your room. Look through it and pick out something suitable," Lord Hartwood ordered. "I will meet you there in an hour. See what you can do with yourself in the meantime."

It was with mixed feelings that Eliza rummaged through the trunk filled with the clothing Lord Lightning had purchased for Violet. Piece by piece she pulled out the garments made for the woman who had really been his mistress, clothing as beautiful as Violet herself. As she examined them, she felt a burst of envy. If only she possessed a fraction of Violet's beauty! But even as the thought flickered through her mind, she reproached herself for it. Her mother had been given the gift of beauty, and that beauty had ruined her life. It was a mercy Eliza had inherited none of it. It was far better to have been given only the gift of good sense.

Yet, as she examined each of the gaudy garments, looking for those whose color would not clash with her red hair, she wondered if good sense alone would enable her to make a selection from the bounty that emerged from the trunk. She knew nothing about the construction of a fashionable ensemble. Her aunt had prided herself on ignoring the trivial details of dress that filled the minds of lesser women and had not thought it important to instruct Eliza about them. Until now, Eliza had not felt in any way deprived, especially since on her birthday each year her aunt had most generously provided her with a new costume made of sturdy material chosen for its ability to withstand wear and perfect for those occasions when they took tea with the other maiden ladies of the neighborhood and made their weekly visits to the poor.

She had been grateful to her aunt for the thoughtfulness had freed her from having to waste her own valuable mental energy on matters of dress. But now, as she fingered the rich silks and delicate muslins, Eliza had to admit she did not find the task distasteful. It was fascinating to study the kinds of garments a woman who *did* fill her mind with the trivial fripperies of dress might wear. She could not but feel excitement at the thought of selecting something to wear from the wealth of garments before her.

And the trunk held so much. Gowns of the richest hue, overdresses of the thinnest voile, petticoats made entirely of delicate, sheer lace. Never before had she imagined such clothing existed. And the undergarments! They were so brazen that when she pulled out the first one she was confused at first by its shape and odd construction. Then she realized what it was—a pair of lasciviously slit scarlet drawers—and dropped it as if it had been a burning brand.

She could not imagine herself wearing such garb. But she must do it if she was to accompany Lord Hartwood while playing the role of his mistress.

With hesitant fingers, Eliza undid the buttons on her old gray merino dress. Then, even more hesitantly, she took off her shift, until she stood naked. Only after sternly reminding herself that it was essential she do this to assist Lord Hartwood with his much needed transformation did she slip on the scarlet drawers with their scandalous lace-edged slit.

The waistband was generous on her smaller waist, but not too much so. She could not help but notice the pleasing sensation she felt as the silken fabric brushed against her most secret parts. Such a garment might well awaken improper thoughts in a woman less self-controlled than she was. How fortunate that she had the maturity needed to keep from being swept away. Next she donned a lacy petticoat, pulling the strings that secured it to her waist. One of her Aunt Celestina's eccentricities had been the belief that stays were unhealthy, so Eliza wore none. But the shapelessness of her usual garments and the thickness of their fabrics had given her no need for such an undergarment. This was not true of the pale rose mull gown she drew out of the trunk now. It was virtually transparent.

As she drew it on it occurred to her that another sort of woman might have thought twice about the consequences of dressing herself in a gown that revealed her figure so flagrantly to a man like Lord Hartwood. Again she was glad the nature of their agreement meant she need entertain no such worries. She was coming along with him to observe him, to assist. It was ridiculous to think he might find her body enticing. Though no sooner had she reassured herself that he could have no possible interest in her person, than she felt a stab of anxiety. What if Lord Hartwood was so disappointed when he saw her in Violet's finery that he sent her away and she lost the opportunity to aid him? She must do all she could to prevent that from happening.

It was not easy doing up the fastenings without the help of a maid, but she did the best she could, pulling the gown over her head and twisting it around to bring the hooks to where she could reach them. Her task was made easier as the dress, like the petticoat, was a bit too large. Violet had been far more voluptuous than Eliza. But still, with a few seams taken in, it would fit. There was a packet of pins in the trunk, and with them Eliza quickly adjusted the fit of the bodice.

She stood up, appreciating the unaccustomed softness of the fabric and hearing the quiet rustle the expensive muslin made as it adjusted itself to her naked body, its decadent, slippery softness whispering of unimagined delights. It was a pale and beautiful tint that couldn't have been worn for any length of time without immediately showing dirt. But clearly, a fallen woman like Violet did not have to worry about dirtying her clothes, not with all those other gowns to choose from. How astonishing to find herself clad in this masterpiece.

Though perhaps it was best to say "half-clad." For the dress plunged deeply in both front and back, revealing far more skin than Eliza would have ever dreamed of displaying. Nearly her whole bosom was exposed and though Violet had been taller than she was, the dress was alarmingly short, revealing her ankle and even a good bit of leg.

She looked around for stockings, but the only ones she found in the trunk were as improper as the rest of Violet's garments: black and lacy, with tiny pearls woven at intervals into the lace. She drew them on, securing them with a set of frivolous pink garters adorned with rosebuds.

She could barely summon up the courage to look at herself in the mirror. But in any event there was no time. A sharp knock on the door announced Lord Lightning's presence and he strode in.

"What have you done with the quiet little seeress?" he quipped with an amused gleam in his eye. "Brazen woman! Have you hidden her in the trunk?" He made a show of peering around the room. "Well, I see no traces of her, so you must be Miss Farrell after all. But I had no idea you hid such voluptuous curves beneath your demure Quaker's dress."

She brushed off his attempt at wit. It was ridiculous. Her, voluptuous?

Lord Hartwood walked around her, his eye carefully appraising the effect of the new clothing. "Walk across the floor," he commanded.

She took a few steps, still astonished at the feel of the luxurious fabric against her skin, but he stopped her.

"No, you walk like a Quakeress still. You must move with a more calculated air, as if your body were a magnet drawing to it the eyes of all who watch you. Here, let me demonstrate." And with that he strode across the room, head held high, chest thrust out, aping the sinuous movement of a self-aware beauty so perfectly that Eliza could barely resist collapsing into giggles.

"You truly do belong on the stage," she gasped out. "You are never so happy as when you are playacting."

"It is you who have decreed that we must play-act," he retorted. "Try it again. I wish to see you walk across the room as if you were the queen of the demireps."

Thus challenged, Eliza drew herself to her full height, pushed out her chest, and swept across the room.

"Better," Lord Hartwood said, "but you must try to imagine this time that your magnet is drawing all masculine eyes to your magnificent bosom." She felt her face redden, and her eyes darted down to her chest. It was hardly magnificent, at least not compared with the rounded orbs that Violet had so casually exhibited, but the scandalous dress most certainly did put what she had on display. As there was no choice but to throw herself into the spirit of the game, she reached one hand into her bodice, quite deliberately, and made a quick adjustment calculated to make the most of her endowment. Then, having assured herself that Lord Hartwood's eyes were fixated on that most interesting portion of her anatomy, she minced lasciviously across the floor.

"Never before have I had a mistress who has responded quickly to instruction," he told her. "But you make it clear I am not the only one of us with a penchant for playacting. Were you also born when the Sun was in Leo?"

She smiled, pleased he had shown interest in her art. "Not at all. My Sun is in Sagittarius. It is the influence of Jupiter in my Fifth House that gives me acting talent."

Lord Hartwood's lip quirked up in a wry smile.

"So you are the little fortune-teller, still, despite the fancy new plumage. Well, that just adds spice to your character."

Then his expression again became serious. "Despite the fact it *is* playacting, if we go on with this, you must take it deadly seriously. If you are to come with me to Brighton, you must remain in your role until I give you leave to stop. I cannot afford to have any more mistresses desert me, even pretend ones." His eyes had lost their gleam of amusement. "Do you fully understand me?"

She bent her head in assent.

"I am probably making a mistake by taking you along, but you amuse me and I do need to bring a mistress with me. So hear me out: I will take the risk of bringing you with me to Brighton—but only if several things are clearly understood between us. Are you listening?"

She nodded.

"First," Lord Hartwood said, holding up one finger, "you will do your best to behave in public at all times as if you truly were my mistress. You must be prepared to subject your person to whatever I do to convince others that is the case." To reinforce what he meant by this statement, he approached her and languidly drew one hand down her chest until it rested within her bodice, gently cupping her bosom before stretching his hand lower and stroking the base of her abdomen in a way that sent a delicious quiver through Eliza's entire body. She blushed, but did her best to maintain her composure as surely any real mistress would.

"Good," he said, after withdrawing his hand. "I see we understand each other.

"Next, you must be prepared to be the butt of considerable rudeness. My mother will not welcome you. For that matter, my mother will not welcome *me*. She tolerates my visit because my brother's will has given her no other choice, but she may very well take out the anger she feels toward me on you. So you must be prepared to accept her insults without any reply. Any response to her attacks is to come only from myself, as your protector. Can you manage that?"

Again Eliza nodded. This must be that conflict with his mother she had seen on his chart, the one that arose from the natal conjunction of his Moon with angry Mars. She was quite curious to see it play out in action.

"Finally, and most importantly," he said, fixing her with his steeliest gaze. "You are to understand that the role of mistress will remain only that—a role. I am famous for my lack of principles, but for all my depravity, I have long made it a rule to have nothing to do with virgins. I attempted to violate that principle last night, but came to my senses before it was too late.

"You have chosen to accompany me for some reason of your own. I imagine it has something to do with your poverty, or perhaps it is merely that, like most women, you find my outrageous behavior fascinating. But whatever your motivation, as long as you are with me you will be careful to do nothing—" he stabbed his finger in the air to underline the word "—absolutely nothing, in public or in private, to tempt me to violate that principle again."

He fixed her with a stern gaze. She could see no hint of the warmth she had detected there only a moment before.

"Do you understand me, Eliza? If you tempt me to misuse you, I will turn you out onto the street without a farthing, and you will have to fend for yourself. There must be no more carnal contact between us."

Eliza nodded again, relieved. He asked nothing of her she could not easily adhere to. She certainly had no desire to become his mistress in truth, no matter how strong the feelings might be his teasing touch called forth from her body. Yet she was somewhat mystified by the strength of the emotion that accompanied his demand. It sounded almost as if he was afraid that *she* would ravish *him*.

"There is one last thing, Miss Farrell," he continued. "Several times now, you have shared with me your astrological insights about my character and have gone on at some length about the foolish twaddle you call love. You will cease that nonsense. There is no place for any sentimentality in our relationship."

He assumed a pugnacious posture, as if he expected that his insistence on this last point would bring out the fight in her. But Eliza made no reply. There was no point in debating it with him. If the chart told the truth, what she saw there would unfold with or without his consent.

It seemed to take him a moment to realize that she was not going to give him an argument. Then, he let his voice drop and added, "If you play your role well, when the fortnight is completed I shall pay you generously. The fifty pounds I offered you this morning is already yours. If you are successful in playing the role of my mistress for the next fortnight, you will be rewarded with far more. But let it be clear: my money is all you will get from me. Don't delude yourself that you can redeem me. You will not convert me into some tame Romeo. Henceforth whatever you do with me, you do entirely as a matter of business. Do you understand?"

Eliza nodded once again.

"Very well," Lord Hartwood concluded. "I will draw up a contract formalizing the arrangement and spelling out the terms of your employment."

"You do not trust me without such a contract?"

"I trust no woman," Lord Hartwood said coldly. "No woman has ever given me the slightest reason to do so."

How quickly he swung from amusement to irritation. It must be another effect of that conjunction of his Moon with angry Mars. Afflicted moons often resulted in moodiness. But even though she was disappointed that he had drawn back from the camaraderie they had shared when they had rehearsed together, she had got what she had wanted. She would have the opportunity to observe his character as she helped him through a most interesting personal transformation. But even so, there was still one question she must have answered before she could give herself fully to his scheme.

"My lord," she asked, "why exactly is it that you must bring a mistress with you to Brighton? I know it has something to do with your receiving an inheritance, but the exact connection eludes me."

His glance shifted away from hers and she sensed he felt some reluctance to answer. He walked over to a table and picked up a small miniature in a silver frame, gazing at it earnestly for a moment before offering it to her for her inspection. The painting showed a thin young man with hair much darker than Lord Hartwood's own and eyes of a dull blue instead of his lively brown.

"This is my older brother, James," he explained. "My *late* brother, James, from whom I inherited the Hartwood title. Like myself, James showed himself to be the true son of our father, an unprincipled wastrel who'd inherited much of Black Neville's devilry. But during his final illness he appears to have undergone a deathbed conversion and repented of his sins. So before he died he drew up a very odd will. It obliges me to visit my mother for a fortnight before I can receive my full inheritance. In addition, he specified that the visit must take place within two years of his death. Until that period is complete, the portion of the estate over which he had control has been frozen. I have put the visit off as long as possible, but as the second anniversary of his death will

occur within the month, I can put it off no longer."
He paused, clearly searching for words. "Because
of the way James wrote his will, if I don't bring a
mistress with me when I fulfill the obligation he
imposed on me, I cannot enjoy all that he has left
me. Does that answer your question?"

She nodded, though it really didn't. Why
would a deathbed repentance have motivated his
brother to do something so shocking as to force
his own mother, a respectable noblewoman, to
consort with a fallen woman? It seemed a very
odd way to repent. But then, she reminded herself that having never been on a deathbed, she
was in no position to judge. Perhaps as he faced
eternity after ruining his own share of women,
Lord Hartwood's brother had hoped to reach out
from beyond the grave and set events in train
that would somehow rescue another poor fallen
creature. Though if that were the explanation, she
could see why it might satisfy Lord Lightning's
penchant for the absurd to bring along a faded
spinster instead.

But she felt a pang of disappointment as she realized that his eagerness to make her into his mistress the previous night had indeed sprung only
from his need to fulfill the terms of his brother's
will. Shameful as it was to admit it, she could no
longer deny she had been clinging to the hope
that, when he'd decided to make her his mistress
last night, Lord Hartwood had felt some attraction
to her. Clearly she *had* been deluded, and that real-

ization brought home again how heedlessly she'd acted in offering herself to him. It was fortunate she had escaped without harm, but now that she understood the true situation, she would heed his advice and put all thoughts of love from her mind. Clearly, if she didn't, she might be badly hurt.

But if a will was involved, that raised another question. "My lord, if it should come to light that I am not truly your mistress, but that it's only a role I am acting. What then? Would you lose your inheritance?"

"It is up to you to ensure that no one finds that out," he said grimly. "If you betray our scheme to anyone, you will be dismissed, immediately." Then in response to the worry that must have shown on her face he continued, "But I'm coming to think there's a good chance you will pull it off. Otherwise I wouldn't let you attempt it. You have spirit and intelligence and some acting talent besides, and—" his teasing smile returned "—you are also possessed of a more than tolerably fine bosom. I shall send for a seamstress to make the necessary alterations to your wardrobe and send out for shoes and bonnets. We will leave for Brighton in the morning."

Then, before she was aware of what he intended, Lord Hartwood reached over and, after taking her chin in his hand, gave her a most luxuriant kiss. It was a kiss of exactly the sort one would give one's real mistress, a rich warm kiss that lingered on her lips far longer than was necessary considering there was no one else in the room to observe them. But she took it in stride, figuring that, in view of what was at stake, Lord Lightning probably thought it best to take advantage of any practice he could give her here in private, before they went out into the world to play their roles in earnest.

Chapter 6

Though she enjoyed the journey, having never before traveled in the comfort provided by a private carriage, Eliza did not look forward to their journey's end. Her new protector's mood, which had been cordial when their journey had begun, cooled noticeably as they neared their destination. For most of their journey he'd ridden outside on the box with the coachman, leaving her inside alone with her thoughts. He had invited her to join him at his table when they stopped for luncheon, but his air of preoccupation had prevented any but the most superficial conversation, so she had been unable to find out anything further about what she should expect when they arrived at Brighton and his mother's home.

Right before their arrival, he ordered the coachman to bring the carriage to a stop and joined her in the compartment.

"Have you been having second thoughts about our arrangement?" he asked. "There is still time to change your mind." When she shook her head no, his upper lip quirked into a rueful grin, and he said, "Then you are fortunate in your composure. I've been quaking in my boots at the thought of the interview that lies before us. I have never been able to face my mother with equanimity."

"Your relationship with her is strained?"

"It is."

"And how long has this coolness between you persisted?"

"Only since my birth."

His tone made further discussion impossible, but in any case, there was no time for discussion. Lord Hartwood now held out a small, but exquisite, box toward her, saying, "It would please me if you would wear this now. It is most definitely not a gift, and I shall want it back later, but it's important you be wearing it when first you meet my mother."

He opened the box and lifted from it a heavy golden necklace studded with blue stones, each one the size of a robin's egg. Because of the size of the jewels, Eliza at first assumed they were paste, but after inspecting them briefly she had to conclude that if they were paste, they were paste of a very high quality indeed. They looked quite real.

"They are sapphires," he said tersely. "They were once the property of a rajah."

"They are very beautiful!"

"Perhaps. But so much misfortune has resulted from their purchase that I have often suspected they bear an ancient curse."

That surprised her. "I should not have believed you to be so superstitious."

"It isn't superstition that makes me say that, but scientific fact. Fifteen years ago, my father gave in to the demands of his mistress, Mrs. Atwater, and purchased this necklace for her. His extravagance brought the family close to ruin. To save the family, my brother was forced to wed a wealthy bride. But before he could do that he was obliged to abandon a young girl of gentle birth whom he had seduced with a promise of marriage and got with child. My mother insisted that I take credit for the girl's ruin so my brother's wedding could proceed without hindrance. That is what led to our rupture."

"Do you mean to tell me she forced you to take on the reputation of a cowardly seducer when it was your brother who should have borne the blame?"

"Exactly. The heiress's father would have called off the match in a moment had he learned the truth. But the girl died trying to give birth to my brother's dead babe, and since, with her dying breath, she only named a Mr. Neville as the author of her ruin, my mother insisted one Mr. Neville would do as well as another and that I owed it to the family to take the blame, no matter what the cost to myself."

"But that is monstrous! Had she no feeling for what was right? Why couldn't the match with the heiress have been made with you instead of your brother?"

"He was my older brother, my father's heir. No heiress would have wished to wed a younger son like me. But even if she had, my mother would not have tolerated it. James was her favorite. He always had been."

"But wasn't your mother grateful for your sacrifice?"

"Women aren't capable of gratitude," he said coldly. "James was my mother's darling, and she soon convinced herself that the girl's ruin truly was my fault, rather than accept that her favorite child could have behaved so dishonorably. She had always prided herself on the strength of her morals and flattered herself that her favorite son had taken after herself—instead of after our father."

"But if it was James who was guilty of causing the poor girl's death, not you, my reading of your character was correct—you are not guilty of the crimes that darken your reputation!"

Lord Lightning drew back, his face hardening. "I am guilty of far worse. Do not delude yourself. I was innocent of that young girl's ruin, but I was Black Neville's son and shared my brother's tainted blood. Once I had taken on the blame for my brother's crime, no decent woman was willing to be seen with me. It was only a matter of time until I had exceeded both James and my father in vice."

He fixed her with an angry look. "I've already warned you. If you indulge in sentimental fancies and persist in imagining that I'm something I am not, I will bring our connection to a speedy end. I am not a good man and you must never again forget it."

"I shall not, Your Lordship. You have my word on it."

He held up the necklace to catch the little bit of light that shone in through the carriage's window and smoldered deeply within the heavy azure stones. "Mrs. Atwater was extravagant, as women of her sort usually are, and fell upon hard times once my father was gone. Besides the necklace he'd left her nothing to support herself or the bastard he had given her. So after his death, I was able to purchase the necklace back from her, accursed or not. Allow me to help you on with it." He leaned over her and draped the necklace around her neck, fastening the ornate clasp.

The stones lay heavily on her chest. The pendent hung almost into her cleavage and emphasized how low her bodice was cut.

"It becomes you well," he announced. "The fire of your hair and the warmth of your eye contrasts with the icy coldness of the stones."

Eliza shivered. It felt as if the extravagant jewels were burning through her skin. Lord Lightning had paid for its purchase with his integrity.

Her face must have shown some of her distress. "I hope you are not about to give way to superstitious fear," he said. "The curse on these jewels has already been fully discharged—upon myself. I doubt they have any energy left to harm you."

Forcing herself to give the appearance of composure, she replied, "That was not what troubled me, Your Lordship. It is only that no matter how hard I try, I always end up losing bits of jewelry. My Aunt Celestina was constantly chiding me for it."

Lord Lightning's dark eyes brightened momentarily with that look he got that was so close to laughter but still kept something back. "You need have no fear that you will lose these," he assured her. "All eyes will be upon them. Besides, as soon as my mother has seen them on your neck, they will return to my custody. I will have made my point."

They soon reached the outskirts of Brighton. The thoroughfare became more crowded, and the carriage slowed. As Eliza gazed through its window, she could not but feel excitement at the thought of finding herself at a fashionable watering place at the height of the summer. They drove past a wide open area, planted in grass, which was bordered by a wide paved path on which ladies and gentlemen promenaded. Beyond it, in the distance she saw a rambling building that presented the oddest jumble of architectural forms, both classical and fantastical, squatting among a crowd of more ordinary buildings. It was topped by a rounded dome and flanked on each side by what looked like tall minarets.

"The Regent's pavilion," Lord Hartwood ex-

plained, curtly in a tone that suggested no desire
to play tour guide.

The air was moist and a stiff breeze blew
briskly, challenging the elegantly dressed ladies
for possession of their tiny parasols. Eventually
the carriage entered a narrower street and after
proceeding only a short distance, slowed and
then stopped.

It was with some trepidation that Eliza let her
new protector hand her out of the carriage and
lead her up to the elegant doorway of the house in
which she would spend the next two weeks. She
walked carefully, still getting used to the dainty
high-heeled slippers he had presented to her. She
did her best not to trip on the diaphanous skirt
that blew around her legs in the hot July breeze,
whipping up to reveal the lacy stockings beneath.

Though not conversant with the latest rules of
fashion, she knew the outfit she wore was not one
that by any stretch of imagination would be worn
by a lady. Her copper curls, which had been shorn
in front *à la Grecque* at Lord Hartwood's command, sprang forth from beneath the exaggerated
bonnet he'd chosen for her, topped with vulgar
artificial fruit. She wondered what his mother
would make of it.

She would find out soon.

His mother's house was narrow but elegant, its
façade covered with an unusual pattern of black-
and-white tile. There was a tang of salt in the air;
the sea could not be far away. The door swung

open at their approach, revealing a small vestibule paneled in some dark wood where a footman, bowing deeply, motioned them toward the door that led to a small reception room, explaining that Lady Hartwood would attend them shortly.

The room they entered was dark. Its single tall window faced the rear of the house and was draped with a heavy brocade swag. Lord Hartwood led her to a chair whose clawed feet and gilded scrollwork recalled the elegance of the past, though she noticed its upholstery was worn away in places and its cluttered ornamentation was far less elegant than the furnishings she had seen at his town house. Given the shabbiness that surrounded her, she should have felt herself less overawed than she had been by Lord Lightning's magnificent dwelling, but if anything she felt more uneasy. How would she cope with the coming interview with his mother? Back in London, where her new protector knew exactly what she really was, it had been easy to imagine herself playing her new role. But to actually be thought of as a fallen woman, to face another woman's scorn devoid of the propriety her aunt had considered so essential—she could not help but feel fear tap at her heart, though she sternly repressed it. There was no reason to give way to such shameful emotion. She was merely playing a role.

"You may as well sit down," Lord Hartwood told her in a low voice. "It will be half an hour or more until Her Ladyship can bring herself to greet us. After all, it has been only fifteen years since last she saw me."

"You have not visited her in all that time?"

"I was gone into the army for some years. Then, when I returned, she barred her door to me." He was unable to keep the bitterness out of his voice. "She had her reasons. Unlike my father and my brother, when *I* left the paths of righteousness, I did not keep my peccadilloes secret. Though my mother easily forgave them sins pursued out of public view, she could not forgive me my lack of hypocrisy. She sees me now only because she is compelled to by James's will."

"But if she hates you so, why is she willing now to welcome you and help you claim your inheritance?"

"It is to receive her own inheritance that she must tolerate my presence. James's will stipulated that if she did not let me attend her for a fortnight she would forfeit this, her permanent home. She has no other property of her own and no income save what I allow her. Because my father squandered her dowry on his mistress, she was left ill provided for at his death, and what James left her has been tied up by the lawyers pending this visit of mine. Indeed, since James's death, she has only been able to remain in her home through my sufferance. I've had my man of business pay her servants and allow her a comfortable allowance. It gives me a certain pleasure to know that it is only *my* efforts that stand between her and poverty."

"It does you credit. Given her hostility to you, it would have been understandable if you had allowed her to suffer the consequences of her neglect."

"I am not interested in earning credit," Lord Hartwood growled. "And did I not warn you against finding good in me where there is none?"

"Indeed you did, Your Lordship," she said, schooling her expression. "And I shall take care in the future to do my best to put the very worst interpretation possible on all your actions."

"Excellent! I wouldn't have it any other way."

Their discussion was interrupted by a loud scraping sound coming from the hallway. "My mother is coming," he whispered harshly. "Remain seated when she enters."

How unspeakably rude! But there was no time for Eliza to frame a reply, as the door to the parlor opened and a footman wheeled in a bath chair. As he pushed Lady Hartwood toward them, her son swung around from the side table against which he had been lounging and came over to rest his hand firmly on Eliza's shoulder. The gesture at once established his familiarity with her person and made it impossible for her to ignore his command that she remain seated. She attempted to remain calm and to behave as she imagined someone like Violet might do, who had been raised in poverty without the benefit of the kind of education in manners Eliza had received. But since she *had* been schooled in good behavior, her heart pounded with embarrassment as the older woman rolled toward them.

Lord Hartwood's mother was dressed entirely in black. Her only jewelry consisted of a jet mourning ring and necklace bearing a small miniature portrait outlined in hair. At first glance, it was hard to believe the woman before her was Lord Hartwood's mother. Where his figure was trim and muscular, hers had run to fat. Her coloring was dark where his was fair. But on further examination there was a certain similarity in the strong, Roman nose that was such a prominent feature of both of their faces. And certainly there was something similar in shape of the steely eyes with which they coolly regarded each other.

Head held high, Lady Hartwood let her eyes sweep over the face of her only remaining child, then rested them on Eliza, gazing for a long time upon the glittering necklace that hung between her breasts, before turning back to her son. Her face showed no trace of emotion. "So you have come, Edward," she said. "I trust you had a pleasant journey. We will dine at eight. I have invited some people of trifling importance to help celebrate your arrival. It's astonishing what people will do to be able to say they have dined with a title. Though, of course, no one of any consequence would wish it known that they had dined with you."

She motioned the footman she was ready to leave, but before she could go, her son spoke up. "How kind of you to welcome us so graciously, Mother. I don't believe I've had the pleasure of introducing you to my own particular friend, Miss

Farrell. She has kindly agreed to accompany me for this fortnight. Please see that she is given the room adjacent to mine."

Again his mother's gaze raked over Eliza, coming to rest on the sapphire necklace that dangled in her cleavage, but her features showed nothing but a steely determination to maintain her composure. "Unfortunately, the only room that is free to accommodate Miss Farrell is a small one in the attics where the other servants sleep." She favored Eliza with a look that would have curdled milk. "It is quite hot and uncomfortable at this time of year. But you may have her things sent up there."

A look of fury flashed over Lord Hartwood's face, but in a moment he recovered himself, and like his mother, arranged his pale features to show nothing but cold control, making the resemblance between the two of them more pronounced. "I trust you will still let me sleep in my own room."

"I cannot stop you."

He turned toward Eliza. "You need have no fear of suffering unduly from the heat. My room has always been a comfortable one. Please feel free to make it your own." He turned back to his mother. "Also, before I forget, I've invited a guest to join us at dinner. I hope you can accommodate her. It's been many years since I've seen Mrs. Atwater. I hope you will make her welcome, too."

"Invite all the whores in Brighton if you wish. It is just what my guests will expect of you. I doubt there is anyone in Brighton who does not know the intimate details of the situation into which your poor brother's will has forced me."

"I am relieved to hear it. Let's hope, madam, that you, too, understand the terms of his will and intend to abide by them. I have many other claims on my leisure and am otherwise not likely to linger here. Let there be no mistake about that."

"You haven't changed a bit," Lady Hartwood said bitterly. "You were an annoying child and you've grown into exactly the kind of vulgar, showy man I feared you would become. My only comfort lies in the thought that your father did not live to see you become his heir. He died believing it would be dear James who carried on the family name."

"I am so sorry that I wasn't able to oblige you by dying in James's place, Mama," Lord Hartwood said. "But you will be so good as to observe that I *have* shown up to fulfill the terms of James's will and that by doing so I may yet save your home for you. I should like some credit for that at least."

"You have got as much credit as you deserve already," his mother snapped. "I haven't thrown your trull out into the street. You shall have to settle for that." And with that she nodded her head and with the footman's assistance rolled slowly toward the door.

"Not exactly the return of the Prodigal Son," Eliza heard Lord Hartwood mutter when they could no longer detect the sound of Lady Hartwood's chair in the hallway.

"Indeed. I would hazard that your mother would far prefer to slaughter you than the fatted calf. But you are not blameless, either. Consider the provocation you offered her! Even if she had felt some tender feeling for you, she could hardly have expressed it in the face of such a calculated insult."

"She feels no tender feeling for me." His voice was harsh. "She never has. I never felt her hand on me as a child except in punishment." He wheeled around, fixing her with an unsettling stare, his dark eyes almost wild. "You aren't going to leave me now, are you?"

The hint of desperation in his voice was at odds with the pose of cool unconcern he affected. Reacting instinctively, she almost blurted out that he could depend on her, for it would be impossible for her to leave him now—but she caught herself and clamped her lips shut. The last thing she needed was to have him reproach her for a foolish partiality right now. But clearly he needed something, for in the silence that stretched out as she fought to regain her control, Lord Hartwood tugged savagely at his neck cloth as if it were strangling him. A flash of pain—real pain, not an actor's imitation—swept over his features as he demanded, "By Gad, Eliza. Answer me!"

She struggled to keep her voice level. "Of course I shan't leave you, sir. We made a bargain. I shall stay and help you do what you came here to do."

He peered at her intently as if weighing her words. Then his face gradually relaxed and he let his breath out slowly. After carefully readjusting the points of his collar, he said, "I believe you really *will* stay."

"Of course I will. What did you expect?"

He shrugged. "Expect? I would never attempt to predict a woman's behavior. I'll leave the predictions to you, my sage astrologer."

His lips had again assumed that smile that had so little humor in it. His face wore once more its usual look of detached disdain. Only as he prepared to follow the butler up the stairs did he turn back and allow his eyes to meet hers. To her surprise, she saw a hint of tenderness flash through them, one that recalled the pain she had observed in them just moments before.

"You did very well just now, Eliza," he said. There was almost no irony in his tone. "If I am not careful, I may find myself in your debt."

"I am glad you are pleased with my performance, Your Lordship," she replied briskly, curtsying to him. She would not again let herself forget the parts they were playing. His eyebrows rose at the exaggerated gesture. But he said nothing more, merely turning and ascending the main staircase.

A footman motioned Eliza to follow him to the servants' staircase and she did so, taking care not to trip on the hem of her flimsy skirt. But as she climbed the four flights of the back stairs to the attics, it struck her that, for the first time since they had made their first bargain in his coach, Lord Hartwood was not entirely in control. He *did* need her support here in Brighton—and not only to play out a role.

It would not be easy to help him. The strong feelings he provoked in her were disturbing. She could not entirely trust herself to remain unmoved by them, as she had pledged she would. But overall, the scene that had just taken place in the parlor reassured her: There was work to be done here, just as his horoscope had suggested. He needed her help for much more than just the claiming of his inheritance. Any doubts she had entertained about the wisdom of accompanying him had vanished.

Chapter 7

It had been close to supper time when they
had arrived, so after a footman showed her
the small attic room where her things had been
stowed, Eliza dressed quickly for dinner.

The emerald tiffany gown that Lord Hartwood
had chosen for her to wear to dinner this night
was, if possible, even more daring than the dress
she had worn on her arrival. A band of nearly
transparent openwork ran across the bodice, allowing more than a glimpse of her uncorsetted
bosom to show through the lace's many holes. It
was a good thing it had been summer when she
had agreed to play out this masquerade. To wear
such a gown in an English winter would be to risk
death from pneumonia!

As she put on the fatal necklace Lord Hartwood had decreed she wear, she wondered how

his mother would respond to her presence at dinner. However, when Eliza entered the dining room at eight, doing her best to move across the room with the sinuous motion her protector had taught her and thrusting out her bosom proudly, her hostess showed no overt reaction to her presence. Indeed, the only hint she gave of the displeasure she must feel was that she pointedly did not introduce Eliza to her other guests, but merely gestured to the footman to seat her near the foot of the table.

The empty chairs on both sides of Eliza's place remained empty even after the other guests had been seated. Placed by herself at the far end of the table and subjected to the undisguised curiosity of the others at the table, Eliza felt much like a child who has been sent to sit in front of the class in the dunce's seat. But she was too fascinated by the scene that unfolded before her to waste her energy in responding to the slight. Her experience of elegant living had been hitherto confined to an occasional attendance at the local assembly rooms with her aunt, who did not take much pleasure in social occasions.

She had never before eaten at a table arrayed as lavishly as this one. The huge chandelier hanging from an elaborate plaster rosette set in the ceiling cast its light over the richly gleaming silver utensils, the translucent china, and the sparkling crystal goblets that furnished each place. The center of the table was taken up by a huge silver epergne on which was displayed every kind of fruit to be had at this season. Silver urns filled with flowers dotted the vast expanse of heavy damasked linen.

Lady Hartwood's guests also gave off an air of luxurious wealth. They were dressed in the height of fashion, the women in high-waisted gowns festooned with lace and ribbons, the men in exquisitely tailored suits of superfine, in fashionably muted colors. Though they talked to each other in low voices and cultured accents as they awaited the serving of the first course, Eliza was surprised to note that the bodices of the gowns worn by several of the younger women were hardly less revealing than the scandalous gown in which Lord Hartwood had clothed her. Even so, it was her gown—and what it so barely concealed—attracting the notice of most of the gentlemen, several of whom had fixed her with speculative looks that made her distinctly uncomfortable.

As she felt them devouring her body with their eyes, she was glad her demimondaine status was just a pretense. It would not be pleasant to have men continually looking at one like this. Still, she couldn't help but wonder at how by simply cutting her hair and donning what was, after all, a ridiculous costume, she, Eliza Farrell, long resigned to being a faded spinster, was able to call forth such a strong response from men.

Aunt Celestina had often said it was a mercy Eliza had not inherited the stunning beauty that had tempted her aristocratic father to elope with her mother in the defiant act that had caused her grandfather to disinherit her father and forced him to rely on his gambling for their maintenance. Her aunt had counted it a blessing that Eliza's lack of looks protected her from the disasters that awaited impetuous beauties. But now as she observed the effect she was having on a roomful of gentlemen, aided only by a fashionable hairstyle, a little bit of lace, and very little bodice, Eliza wondered: Could she have turned out more like her mother than she had realized?

Lord Hartwood gazed over at her from time to time with obvious approval, allowing his eyes to linger on her bosom in a way that could not be ignored by anyone in the room. He stared until she could almost feel her nipples burning through the lacy fabric. Then, when she least expected it, he raised his warm brown eyes to meet her own, and when he did so, she felt a burst of uneasiness. Was this what her mother had felt when the fatal connection with her father had first begun? Had his aristocratic blue eyes held the treacherous charm and seductive speculation that she felt now radiating from Lord Hartwood's mahogany gaze?

Hastily, she reminded herself that the passionate, smoldering looks he was sending her were merely part of the calculated performance the two of them had agreed to enact. He was no more attracted to her now than the vicar had been when she had played Lady Teazle to his Sir Peter. And the other men? They stared at her because she was supposed to be a notorious rake's mistress and because Lord Lightning, living up to his outrageous reputation, had compelled his mother to entertain that mistress at her dining table. Most likely they were peering at her so intently because they were trying to imagine why a man as attractive and wealthy as he was would have bothered to take under his protection such a poor excuse for a mistress as herself.

But even so, though she had not touched her wine, Eliza felt almost drunk with the heady sensation of being the focus of so many eyes. What fun it must be to really be a beauty and draw men's attention in this way. And as Lord Hartwood flirted with her so outrageously from his end of the table, she felt how intoxicating it was to meet the electrifying gaze of a handsome, sensuous man and to see approval in his eyes—indeed, something far stronger than approval. It was unsettling, but it was delightful too—as long as she didn't make the mistake of ever forgetting it was all part of a game.

At length, the gentleman who sat the closest to her turned his head in her direction and attempted conversation. He had been introduced to her as a Mr. Snodgrass and, from what she had overheard from his previous conversation, he appeared to be a wealthy button maker whose factory here in Brighton made buttons out of the local seashells.

He was seated with his daughter, a quiet girl she judged to be about the same age as herself. The daughter wore a fashionable turbaned headdress that featured a tall ostrich plume and heavy and expensive jewelry that unfortunately emphasized the dullness of her thin face.

"Quite a lovely necklace you've got there," Mr. Snodgrass said to Eliza in the loud voice of a person whose hearing was starting to go. "I count myself quite a judge of such things. Have to be in the business I'm in. My daughter there has a necklace quite like it, though I must say that I don't think her stones are near as large as yours."

This was the first speech that had been addressed to her since the dinner had begun, and she wondered how best to reply so as to maintain the character she was supposed to be portraying. But before she could answer, Lord Hartwood's voice cut across the table, "Your daughter's jewels could not possibly be anywhere near so large as my mistress's. These were purchased from Rundell and Bridge on Ludgate Hill. They came from some Indian chap, a rajah. Worth a mort of money. Man there told me there was nothing like them to be had anywhere else."

"I shouldn't think there was," said Mr. Snodgrass. "The necklace I bought my daughter was from Neate—he's much cheaper than Rundell and Bridge, though I think the quality comparable. With Neate you're not paying extra for the stylish address. But even so, he charged me a good two thousand pounds for them. Yours must have cost at least that much or more."

"Far more," Lord Hartwood said complacently. "If you were to guess at twenty thousand pounds, you'd be close. But what can we do?" he added with a studied lack of concern. "The women must have their little trinkets."

The heads of all the diners swiveled as one as they stared at Eliza's necklace, until she feared the concentrated power of their regard must soon set her neck ablaze. But she, too, could feel her eyes open wide in amazement. Twenty thousand pounds would have been enough money for she and her aunt to have lived on in comfort for the rest of their lives. To think that Lord Hartwood's father had spent that much on a single gift for a mistress!

No wonder women left the paths of virtue. It struck her anew what an innocent she had been to have demanded only forty-five pounds from Lord Hartwood as the price of her own virtue. No wonder he had seemed so amused when he negotiated with her. She felt a burst of gratitude that he had not gone ahead and truly made her his mistress in return for such a paltry sum. She could not have respected a man who would have taken that kind of advantage of her naïveté.

A low hum of conversation had sprung up after Lord Hartwood's disclosure, but it was cut short when his mother's voice rose, silencing it. "Edward has always had an unfortunate tendency to extravagance." She glared at her son from her place at the head of the table. "My poor dear James used to tell me he would outgrow it, but James was always so kind to his little brother and so willing to overlook his many faults."

"James himself knew nothing of extravagance, Mother, did he?" her son replied coolly. "Yet, I cannot help but remember that it was poor dear

James who introduced me to Rundell and Bridge. They were his favorite jeweler. Do you not remember that set of rubies he gave his wife? They were from that shop, too—" He paused dramatically. "Oh, no, I mistake myself. It was not his wife he gave those rubies to. It was that other woman." And with that he turned his attention back to the plate of turbot before him.

He'd scored a hit. Eliza could see Lady Hartwood flinch, though almost imperceptibly. But it was not polite to stare—though just as she was about to turn her gaze away she remembered that in her role as a vulgar mistress she should stare as rudely as possible. So she raised her eyes again and locked eyes with Lady Hartwood, impudently, until Lady Hartwood herself turned away, visibly shaken.

It was strange to behave so dreadfully in public, but Eliza couldn't help but admit there was a certain thrill of pleasure in doing it. She had always kept a tight rein on her emotions to reassure her aunt, who had given up so much to raise her, that she was not tainted with her mother's or father's failings. Now for a brief two weeks she could be someone else entirely, someone brazen and vulgar, someone who need not control her unruly impulses.

But it wasn't wise to take so much pleasure from this new role. Not only would she have to guard her wayward heart from falling prey to Lord Hartwood's seductive charm, she must also not let herself become too comfortable behaving

brazenly, or how would she return to being a prudent woman when the fortnight was over and she
gave up this new role?

Discomfited by these thoughts, she directed
her attention back to her dinner, which was excellent. There was a delicate sauce on the fish with
a hint of some herb she was unable to identify,
something French perhaps. She'd heard many
of the aristocracy now had French chefs to serve
them. She cut off a piece of the fish and picked it
up carefully with the fish fork, allowing herself a
delicate sniff of the sauce before popping it into
her mouth. Delicious! But as she chewed, she noticed that Lord Hartwood was staring at her fork
with something of disapproval.

What could she have done wrong? Aunt Celestina was something of a Tartar about table manners so she knew hers to be perfect. Of course!
That was it. Her table manners were far too good
for a woman of the class from which a man like
Lord Hartwood would take a mistress. Immediately, she picked up her knife with her left hand,
and pushed a few peas and some sauce onto it
with the fingers of her right, before lifting it to her
mouth. The peas disposed of, she licked the sauce
off her fingers.

A look of pleasure flitted across Lord Hartwood's face. Her gesture had made an impression
on the others, too. The many eyes that had been
following her throughout dinner looked away for
a moment, embarrassed. Her slip had made them
aware again of the unbridgeable gulf that lay be-

tween themselves and a woman of the sort she was supposed to be, no matter how beautiful. She applied herself to the fish with continued pleasure, chewing noisily while displaying her teeth. But as she ate, she sensed that one pair of eyes was still trained on her, a pair of cold gray eyes so very unlike her son's warm brown ones.

Eliza felt herself shrink under their scrutiny. No matter what the others might have concluded about her manners, Lady Hartwood was not entirely taken in.

The dinner was almost over when a small commotion indicated that the last of the guests had arrived. Lord Hartwood rose to greet the new arrival and led her to the table. "Mother," he said languidly, "I believe it has been some time since you have had the pleasure of meeting my father's close friend, Mrs. Atwater, but you surely cannot have forgot her."

Mrs. Atwater. His father's mistress. The woman who had demanded that Hartwood's father buy her the ruinous necklace that now lay around her own neck.

Lord Hartwood seated Mrs. Atwater in the empty chair to Eliza's right. His mother sat like a stone, her eyes flickering from her husband's mistress to her son's, while refusing to acknowledge them in any other way.

Examining Mrs. Atwater, Eliza could barely believe that this was the woman who had played such a fatal role in Lord Hartwood's life. She had

expected to see a glamorous woman. How else
had she been able to demand the extravagant
necklace from her besotted lover that meant his
family's ruin? But the woman beside her reminded
her most forcibly of one of the village women who
had come to clean for her aunt, though upon further examination, she could detect the good bones
buried beneath the fat that framed Mrs. Atwater's
face. In her youth she must, indeed, have been
beautiful. Beautiful enough to ruin Lord Hartwood and his family.

Lord Hartwood turned to one of the ladies who
was seated near his mother. "Lady Hermione, may
I introduce to you my friend, Mrs. Atwater. I believe that Mrs. Atwater was also acquainted with
your ex-husband, the earl, before your divorce."
Lady Hermione's tinkling laugh was replaced
by something more like a nervous giggle as she
nodded to the new visitors.

A portly man wearing a barrister's wig, who
was seated between Lady Hermione and Lady
Hartwood cleared his throat as if preparing to
protest, but Hartwood gave him no time to react
before turning back to his father's mistress. "Mrs.
Atwater," he said. "Let me introduce to you my
dear friend Miss Eliza Farrell. As you can see, like
my father before me, I have a great appreciation of
feminine beauty."

He turned to Eliza. "Mrs. Atwater was once
considered the most beautiful woman in Brighton
and was well known for her fine taste in jewelry.
Indeed, rumor had it at one time that the Regent's

own mistress, Mrs. Fitzherbert, with whom he had contracted a secret marriage, was quite jealous of the attentions our beloved Regent paid Mrs. Atwater. But Mrs. Fitzherbert need not have worried. Mrs. Atwater's regard for my father was quite strong. She was unusual for her kind, not being a fickle woman."

He turned back to his guest. "So how do you find Brighton now, Mrs. Atwater?" he asked smoothly. "Surely it has changed since the days when you formed part of the circle around the Regent and Mrs. Fitzherbert."

Mrs. Atwater nodded. Her face looked strained, indeed, almost as strained as that of his mother. "I don't go out much now, Your Lordship. I'm an old lady, and the world is quite different from what it was in my youth, though seeing you today surely brings back the memories of those days. They were fine times indeed we had back then. The balls there used to be, and the riding about in phaetons with the toffs! It seems like only yesterday." Her voice faded out as she caught sight of the necklace that glittered around Eliza's neck.

"Dear me, I never thought to see those jewels again." She sighed. "I had so hoped I'd never have to sell that necklace, I was that fond of your father, and you know it was he who gave it to me. But it was all I had to give my Charles, and he would insist on going to America. There is so little money to be had from keeping boarders."

The clatter of silverware against china stopped as the diners turned to watch the spectacle unfolding before them. Lord Hartwood turned back toward Eliza, his own supposed mistress. "I say, it is a shame you are not to have the opportunity to observe Mr. Charles Atwater. In his appearance he is most strikingly like my father. Indeed Charles was so like my father, I got a strange thrill the last time I saw him. It was as if my father were alive again. I had to remind myself that Black Neville died in some woman's arms in Paris so it could not have been him in the flesh."

"How quickly all our children grew up," Mrs. Atwater interrupted, the strained look on her face showing how eager she was to change the subject. "Why it seems like only yesterday that you were in short pants, Your Lordship. You had the dearest little sailor suit and you were that proud of it, though you would tear off the neckerchief."

"I had almost forgot that," he said with a laugh. "My father would tie it on so tight I was afraid that I would strangle. I remember him bringing me to visit you once. It was a rare treat. He rarely paid me any mind at all. But I could have only been four or five years old back then. How astonishing of you to remember."

"I could hardly forget. From your father's description of you, I hadn't expected you to be such a darling little boy. And you had such good manners, too."

Eliza saw a look of genuine surprise sweep over Lord Hartwood's face, softening its harsh planes for just a moment.

"Truly, I am glad to see you, Mrs. Atwater," he

replied, the irony that had laced his voice suddenly gone, replaced by a warmth that stood out all the more clearly in contrast to his previous coolness. "We owe gratitude to those who were kind to us as children. You surely do have mine."

And then he stood up from his place at the table and strolled over to the sideboard. He picked up a wineglass and gestured to a footman to fill it with claret. "A toast," he called out, his voice ringing through the silence. "To the women who love us."

"Hear, hear!" a rumble ran through the guests as they lifted their glasses.

"And to hell with those who do not!" He drained his glass and tossed it against the marble mantelpiece where it smashed, spattering drops of the ruby wine on the Turkey carpet. The guests paused, frozen, their glasses still in the air, their voices stilled, unsure of what to do. Then, guiltily, they brought them down. Dead silence filled the room.

Lady Hartwood lifted one hand in a subtle gesture to the footman to pull her bath chair from the table. "I bid you good night," she announced. "I fear my health has proven too weak to sustain the challenge of so joyful a reunion. But please continue to enjoy the evening. My son has gone out of his way to provide you with entertainment. You must stay until the show has concluded. It is not often that we are treated to a circus here in Brighton."

Chapter 8

"**T**he whore must go," his mother snarled. She lay in the huge bed hung in black curtains that dominated the bedroom to which, somewhat to his surprise, she had summoned her son shortly after the last of her guests had decamped. She was playing the Tragic Mother to the hilt, Edward noted. Even her negligee was the black of full mourning.

"I know you brought her here to annoy me, and you have succeeded. But you have done far more. Your insult has made it impossible for Mr. Snodgrass to consider letting his daughter marry you."

"You amaze me. I didn't realize you took such an interest in my future. But pray, why should I wish to marry a whey-faced spinster buried in a cartload of jewelry?"

His mother sniffed. "Spare me your childish attempts at irony. Surely you understand that you must marry wealth. Poor James's final illness left him no time to straighten his affairs. Even when his will is settled there will be precious little left. No other course is open to you but to make a convenient marriage. Snodgrass is a vulgar mushroom but he wants a title for his daughter badly enough that he might have been brought up to scratch despite your wretched reputation—had you not torpedoed that scheme. I am grateful that your poor dear brother did not live to know of the strait we are in now because of you."

He began to reply, but his mother cut him off. "And the way you carried on about those sapphires! It is hard to credit that a son of mine could be so vulgar." Lady Hartwood drew forth a black handkerchief and dabbed at her eyes dramatically before drawing a deep breath and continuing. "To have squandered twenty thousand pounds to buy such a degenerate, wasteful gift and then bestow it on a trollop when I must scrabble each month to pay the house servants!"

"I fail to see how my personal expenditures should have any bearing on the fact you've exceeded the income from your widow's portion."

A wave of anger swept over his mother's face. "The lawyers only send me a few pounds every month. They tell me the income that should have arisen from my marriage portion is gone, sunk in the general ruin of our estate. But of course, you'd know nothing about that, since you've spent the past fifteen years gallivanting around the world giving no care to what was happening to your family here at home."

"If I recall correctly, Mother, I was 'gallivanting,' as you call it, because you'd forbidden me to ever cross your doorstep again."

"As well I should have, after what you did, ruining that poor girl and who knows how many others," his mother sniffed. "But that is neither here nor there. The fact is your poor dear brother, James—" she paused here and dabbed theatrically at her eyes "—suffered so terribly during his last years of life that he was unable to give his attention to the management of the estate. And now there is nothing left."

"And that is why I must find an heiress to marry?"

"As if you didn't know that at the outset."

"When you greeted me you told me I hadn't changed. Now I must return the compliment. It astonishes me to find you still believe that any problem can be smoothed over with an advantageous marriage."

He strode across to the tall window, turning his back to his mother and looking out into the dark where, unseen, ocean waves rolled in over the beach, ending their long journey from France. "How much it must pain you to realize that your precious James gambled away the fifty thousand pounds you got him in Amelia's dowry. How even more painful it must be to have to admit to *me* that he squandered that fortune, when it was my sacrifice that secured her precious dowry to him. And now that James has gone on to his much-deserved reward after destroying the little security you thought to have in your old age, you must start the whole distasteful process again. The Neville coffers must be replenished as always, by enticing yet another victim into the matrimonial bed."

"There is nothing of the victim about it," his mother protested. "I was proud to be able to bring your father a large dowry in exchange for the honor of assuming his noble title."

"And out of the bottomless kindness of your heart you have decided to give the same opportunity to the button maker's faded daughter as you did to the chit you foisted on James." He sneered. "Your life is just one act of charity after another."

He paused for a moment before continuing. "But you needn't exert yourself any further on my account. I'm as fond of the fine traditions of our nobility as the next man, but this is one tradition I'm afraid I must break with. I shall not marry some antidote to restore our family's fortunes."

"Of course you will," his mother said scornfully. "There's no other way. It's the only honorable way open to those of us in the nobility. Your father and his father before him did what they ought. If there is any shame involved, it falls upon Charles II. It was wrong of him to grant your great-grandfather a title without granting him enough land to provide the income needed to sustain it!"

"Yes," he agreed. "Our noble liege was remiss, indeed, not to realize that the men of our line would never get the hang of gambling successfully while in their cups. Your sainted James exceeded even my dear father in his ability to throw away good gold at the gaming table. Fifty thousand pounds in six years! But knowing dear sainted James as I do, I suppose the whole sum cannot have been lost just in gambling. No, there would have been ruby necklaces and diamond bracelets, too. That wealthy wife you found him was an ugly girl and James always had an eye for beauty."

"You will not speak that way of your brother," his mother snapped. "He was worth ten of you, and it was not his fault that Amelia turned out sickly. If you had done your duty, you would have found some way to keep him from gaming. The two of you were close when you were children. You could have stopped him from ruining himself if you had tried."

He fought the impulse to stride out of the room. He had forgot how angry it made him that his mother could always find a way to blame him for anything. "No one could have stopped James from ruining himself," he answered coldly. "He had been spoiled since he was a boy. You and Father never forbade him any pleasure. You paid off his debts and his doxies. I doubt he would have stopped his gambling—or the drinking that made him so inept at it—at a word from me.

"But that is besides the point. Unlike my sainted brother, I do not drink and I do not gamble. And since I had no reason to care what society might think of me, I didn't consider myself too aristocratic to dabble in trade. It may come as something of a surprise to you, Mother, but there are other ways to find a fortune besides marrying one. Unlike my father and brother, I did my gambling sober and confined myself to games of skill. With the money I earned at the tables I invested in India traders. Through their successful voyages I realized a profit of several hundred thousand pounds, which now sits safely in the care of my banker at London."

"Hundreds of thousands of pounds? A fortune earned from *trade*?" His mother's cloudy eyes had opened wide. "How long have you had this fortune?"

"These past three years."

Lady Hartwood opened and closed her mouth twice, as if unable to bring herself to speak. Clearly his news was unexpected. Then she finally spoke. "To think, that with all that money, you did nothing to help out your brother, even when he lay dying. You did nothing to discharge my debts. You *are* a selfish child!"

"Very selfish indeed, Mama. Exactly as you say. But odd as it might seem to you, when I earned my fortune, I believed that I had already fully contributed my share to the family. Without my sacrifice, Amelia would have never married James and the family would have had fifty thousand pounds less to squander. And besides, you had forbidden me to ever cross your doorstep. I didn't think you'd wish to dirty your aristocratic hands with the money I'd earned from trade—though it might interest you to know that the money you've been receiving as your widow's portion these past two years has come from me. The income from James's estate was gobbled up by his unfortunate tendency to pay his debts with post-obits."

He waited for that to settle in. Clearly she'd not known of that, either.

Finally his mother spoke. "What James did or did not do is all water under the bridge. Now that you are Hartwood it's your responsibility to care for the family. You must pay off the mortgages James was forced to put on all his properties, and quickly. If the payments are not made within the month, this house and all the others will be lost."

"I know," he replied languidly. "But there's no point in paying off the mortgages if I'm to forfeit the properties. And that's what will happen if I give in to the temptation to bid you adieu and return to London before the fortnight is over. Remember the terms of James's will. Not only would it cost me a lot to discharge the mortgages, but James made my inheritance dependent on my tolerating you for an entire fortnight."

He had been standing near the foot of her bed, but now he took another step toward her, allowing time for his words to sink in. When he again spoke he made his voice low and threatening. "I have come in response to your most reluctant invitation but I have still not decided if it is worth it to me to remain. If I don't, you'll have to find yourself somewhere else to live—and some source of income to sustain you since the trickle you still get—which I have been paying—will cease."

His mother paled. "I cannot move from here!" she protested. "I have lived here these past fifteen years. I'm a poor sick woman. I can barely walk. How can I possibly find a new home or hope to earn an income?"

"You might have asked your poor dear James the same question, since it was his failure to make any arrangements for your support that put you in these circumstances. However, if you can manage to curb your hostility to me and to the delightful woman I am fortunate to be able to call my *friend*, I am willing to try to last out the fortnight here and secure your home for you."

"So I see. It all comes back to your whore," his mother said with bitter satisfaction. "I cannot fathom what you hope to achieve by flaunting her at me this way. I already know what you are. I have always known it."

"And I madam, could say the same of you. But if you wish me to remain, you must treat Eliza with the same courtesy you would extend to a well-born lady. She may have sold her body to me for money but she had no other choice. Her honesty in doing so is far more pleasing to me than the hypocrisy of the well-raised ladies who'd prostitute themselves to me for a title. Though of course, *I* must pay my sweet Eliza to get her between my sheets, while your gently bred ladies would pay *me* for the privilege—just as you did when you let your father's money buy my father's title for you."

"I should have strangled you with your cord," his mother snarled. "I should like to have the footman throw both of you into the gutter where you so rightly belong, but you have the advantage of me now and have tied my hands. I shall make no more attempts to find you a wife. Go marry your vulgar little whore if it pleases you. The two of you would suit."

"Perhaps we would," he replied carelessly. "I had not considered the idea. But it has some charm. If nothing else, it would be the first time since our ennoblement that a Neville married a woman whom it was not a penitence to bed."

Eliza knew better than to listen at keyholes, but even standing several yards away from Lady Hartwood's door, it had been impossible for her not to overhear Lord Hartwood's angry interview with his mother. She had been making her way down the hallway that led to his bedroom dressed in a scarlet satin night robe, as instructed, when she had heard the sound of argument proceeding from his mother's room. She had not intended to eavesdrop, but once she caught a few words of the conversation she found it impossible to draw herself away. She was shocked by the cruelty of his mother's assault and at the pain fueling Hartwood's snarling attempts to protect himself. He had not lied about his mother's rage, only about his indifference to it. She had become accustomed to his brittle irony, but hearing him express it in this context explained so much more about why he resorted to it.

A sudden rustle behind her in the hallway drew her attention away from the conflict taking place on the other side of the door. Attracted by the same loud voices as herself, a crowd of footmen and maids had suddenly found small tasks that needed to be done in the upstairs hallway. They swept carpets, straightened paintings, and dusted woodwork industriously, keeping as quiet as possible so as not to miss a word of the struggle that was going on between mother and son.

Eliza had barely time to take in Lord Hartwood's last astonishing words—his wild assertion about marrying her—when the man himself burst out of the chamber. His face was pale, except for two spots of bright color that flared under each sharp cheekbone. When he saw her standing so close to the door, his eyes widened. For a moment, she thought that he was going to discharge his fury on her. But he stopped as if balancing on the edge of his rage for a moment, then he let his burning gaze sweep across the hallway. The servants he skewered with his eyes dropped their self-appointed tasks and elbowed each other in their haste to disappear down the back staircase lest they find themselves the target of their master's rage. Only the bravest remained.

A rush of expressions flickered over Lord Hartwood's face, each too fleeting to be interpreted. The fury that had dominated him as he left his mother's room dissolved first into a look of mischief as he watched the servants flee. Then, after his eyes met Eliza's and held them for longer than was almost bearable, she saw something else—the vulnerable look of a scolded child, which vanished as swiftly as it had appeared, and was replaced at last by the cold, ironic expression she had come to know so well.

Eliza tried to imagine what she could possibly say to him, but it was not conversation he wanted. With a swift, fluid movement like a serpent embracing its prey, he took her into his arms and pulled her body close to his. The satin of her negligee rustled as he engulfed her. She could feel his tense, well-muscled body impressing itself along her own. His lips sought hers hungrily, desperately, forcing them open. When he had possessed them he began to suckle gently on them. The pressure of his kiss was so strong that her tongue was drawn quivering but unresisting into the warm, throbbing neediness of his mouth.

Had she not known that this display was only for the sake of the watching servants, she might have been overwhelmed by the depth of need she felt emanating from him. It was as if he was trying to bury himself in her, to lose himself in her softness, to blot out the pain of the interview with his mother with something that only she could give him.

His hunger tore at her, evoking needs she had not, until that very moment, known she had. Though she knew his ardor was just for show, her lips responded to his. Hardly knowing what she did, she found herself drawing his thrusting tongue into her own mouth, moaning, and making tiny, soothing sounds that seemed to be beyond her own control as his arms crushed her against his tall, hardened body. It was a strangely pleasant sensation to be held this way, to be so totally enfolded. There was so much comfort in it, despite his passion, despite his size. As he kissed her, he forced his thigh between her legs, prying them open. She could feel his male hardness yearning against the flimsy satin that was all that separated him from her nearly naked body. She felt herself grow wet in that private place below and yearned to draw him even closer, but ignored the impulse. She must not lose control, not now. Her head fell back and she felt his lips move to her throat. But she must not believe for a moment that the need she felt emanating from him was real.

This show was just for the sake of the watching servants. He felt nothing for her. She must not respond to him with her own unbridled neediness. And yet, as she forced herself back to consciousness fighting to free herself from the wildness he had evoked in her, she saw that the servants were gone, the hallway was empty, and still he held her in this deep embrace.

Her body was afire with sensations she had never before experienced. She might easily lose herself forever in his arms. And with that thought came panic. He did not want her. He had forbidden her to give in to him. He had ordered her not to fall in love with him. But the passion he had sparked in her knew nothing of his orders, it knew only his raw, male magnetism, and the way his warm, throbbing body pressed against hers and demanded she yield to him. If she did not get a grasp upon herself quickly and free herself from him, she knew she would be lost.

Summoning up all her strength, she broke from his embrace, wrenching her quivering thighs from his, and pulling away from his lips.

"No!" she gasped.

A look of shock replaced the yearning in his handsome features. He stood back from her, breathing roughly. The sound echoed in the empty hallway, almost drowned out by the pounding of her heart. Then he rasped, "You're right. We can't couple here. We'll finish this in my bed." But he made no move to leave but instead reached toward her and embraced her again.

A thrill ran through Eliza's body. The memory rushed through her of how he'd coaxed her body that first night and of the startling sensations she'd felt as he'd explored her nakedness. Though when she remembered the alarm that had over-taken her as he'd pushed on farther, it struck her how different things were now. Something had changed. The repeated contact she'd had with him—playacting or not—had calmed the fear she had felt that first time he had held her in his arms. She wanted him now; the warmth and wetness that flooded her womanly organs told her that. He stood locked with her in a passionate embrace, breathing hard, though there was no one there to observe them. Could some of the need that she felt radiating from him be real? Could he want her as much as she wanted him, despite the vehemence with which he'd told her such feelings were forbidden?

But then he spoke, and when he did so, she had her answer. For when he addressed her his voice was far too loud–it wasn't the quiet whisper that was all that was needed to reach her, wrapped as she was in his arms, but something else. Something the actress in her recognized all too well. A stage whisper. His words had not been spoken for her ears, just as the embrace, which had so undone her, had not been meant for her.

She turned away from him and stumbled toward his bedroom, trying to hide the sudden tears that sprang to her eyes. What an idiot she'd been! None of it had been meant for her. How could she have thought that even for a moment? That last embrace had not been for the sake of the servants, no. But it had not been for her, either. It was all an act, as he had intended it to be. Had she not lost herself so shamelessly in the lust his embrace had evoked, she would have noticed a crucial detail: When Lord Hartwood had left his mother's chamber, he had not closed her door.

Chapter 9

"If you learned to kiss like that while acting Lady Teazle with the vicar I will have to change my poor opinion of country life," Lord Hartwood said. He had led Eliza, still stunned from their encounter in the passage, into his bedroom, and after closing the door had flung himself upon the high bed where he lay back upon the cushions. The candlelight amplified the look of mischief that was now in complete possession of his handsome features.

Eliza made no reply. She stood by the doorway, uncertain of how to proceed, eyeing the languid lord sprawled upon the bed with the same degree of caution she might have given a growling mastiff whose owner had assured her that his dog didn't bite. But as surely as if she had been confronting a slavering hound, she knew herself to be in danger.

When she had stood before Lord Hartwood in his office in the bright light of day it had been easy to assure him that she would allow him to take no further liberties with her person, that she would guard herself from any foolish emotional involvement, and that she had joined him in his dubious scheme for reasons both practical and rational.

But it was night now, and the logic that had seemed so compelling in the morning was impossible to follow as the candlelight flickered fitfully over his supine form. The kiss that had seared her with its passion might well mean nothing to him. It might be just another move in the chess game he was playing with his mother. But she could not so easily leave it behind.

With a leap of painful insight, she understood for the very first time why a decent woman should never let herself be found alone with a man. The danger in such an unchaperoned encounter did not lie only in the man, in his handsome, taunting face, in his practiced seducer's tricks, but in herself. Her exposure to Lord Hartwood had changed her in some way she had not expected. It had stripped away a mantle of protection that until now she had not known was guarding her. And without it she felt herself exposed to dangers she could not clearly imagine but whose power she could no longer doubt.

"You are silent, Eliza," Lord Hartwood said, the teasing tone in his voice replaced by one of gentle concern. "Did I frighten you with my display of passion?"

Eliza made no response.

"I did," he said soberly. "It is understandable. I frightened myself, too." He raised his head from the cushions. "I suppose I should scold you, for you promised me you wouldn't again tempt me to violate my principles, and once more you have. But I haven't the heart to scold you. Nor will I threaten you with dismissal—Yes, I saw that fear flit across your face." His face held an unaccustomed look of kindness. "You may hold yourself blameless. You shall earn your money yet, though I will have to tread carefully if I am not to fall prey to your irresistible charms."

Eliza bristled, sensing that he was making fun of her and feeling that his levity did not mix well with the consternation his embrace had caused her. "I gave you my promise that I wouldn't give in to you," Eliza said stiffly. "And I intend to keep that promise. I am a woman of my word."

"I am relieved," Lord Hartwood said, with an ironic lift of his eyebrow. "But how novel it is for me to reproach a woman for her assault upon *my* virtue. I grow more reconciled every hour to my decision to include you in my plans. You are an unending source of pleasure to me."

"And to your mother, too, I would wager."

"Ah, yes. My mother." He sat up in the bed. "Since, along with the rest of the household, you had your ear pressed up against my mother's door, you must have heard her give her blessing to our marriage."

"I heard all she had to say to you."

"Then what think you? Should you like to be my Lady Hartwood?"

Eliza bristled again, his teasing suddenly intolerable. "Marriage is no joking matter. Your mother spoke of it only to insult you, and you responded to her in kind."

"But though our words were said in anger, the argument I made her was compelling. Is it not true that the only difference between the woman who sells her body for one night and the one who sells it for a title is the term of the contract?"

"Perhaps, but that's just one more reason for a woman to stay single."

"Then you will not marry me? I am very rich."

"There is a limit to what I will do, even to disoblige your mother."

Lord Hartwood fixed her with a considering gaze, his mahogany eyes deep and unfathomable. "The surprises, it seems, will never end! I have proposed to my mistress and she has refused me."

"I am not your mistress," Eliza said with sudden annoyance. "Nor were you truly proposing. Save such theatrics for your mother. There is no one here to impress with your outrageousness."

"Only you, my little seeress," said Lord Hartwood quietly. "And you, it seems, I shall never be able to impress."

His warm brown eyes were so open, their expression so transparent, that for a moment Eliza could have believed that there was more to his joking offer than he had let on. But she would not fall for such tricks again. It was all a game to him, a game that was becoming more painful to her by the moment. Uncontrolled, the emotion he had kindled in her boiled up, transforming into something new.

"Do you ever stop playing?" she demanded angrily. "Or is everything a childish game with you?"

"Everything is *always* a game to me," he replied sharply. "I thought I had made that clear from the outset of our connection. It was you who said that my Leo nature made me a man who lived for love, not I."

As he spoke, something in his eyes shut down. The warmth that had filled them only a moment before was hidden behind an icy veil. And as he hid himself from her, it struck her with more force just how foolish she had let herself become. The hurt she had seen in his eyes and their warmth had tricked her into hoping the need she felt emanating from his body was truly a need for her. She had taken it as the first tentative sign that he might, in truth, be learning how to love. But that was only her own need speaking. A Leo need not learn to love. He might just keep on playing—like a mischievous child who would never grow up—playing game after game, as this man before her did, through every moment of every day.

But she could not afford to let him see the extent to which his casual play had transformed her from a sensible woman into a swooning girl. In a tone as cool and ironic as his own she said, "I begin to think I underestimated the power of Sir William's new planet on your Leo Sun. My aunt held that people with Uranian natures had something explosive in their personalities that made them love to shock or surprise. No wonder they call you Lord Lightning! In one evening you have forced your mother to dine with your mistress, and not only with your mistress, but with your father's mistress as well. Then you called your mother a whore and nearly coupled with me on her doorstep. Surely you must have set a new record for playing childish tricks."

"My tricks, as you call them, have hurt no one who did not deserve it."

"No? Well what about the trick that you played on me, Your Lordship?"

"What trick do you accuse me of?"

"You told me the terms of your brother's will forced you to bring your mistress with you. Had that been true, your mother would have known in advance that you would be bringing along a mistress. Yet clearly she did not. She was too offended by my appearance to have had any inkling of what you planned. How foolish you must think me to have believed such a cock-and-bull story as that your brother's will demanded you bring a mistress with you in order to claim your inheritance."

He looked away, his guilty expression confirming that her suspicion had been correct. He toyed with his neck cloth for a moment before replying, "You misunderstood me. I said only that your presence here would help me better *enjoy* my inheritance. And so it has. The will does demand my presence here for a fortnight if I am to inherit and enjoins the same condition on my mother if she is to retain her home, but it put no other conditions on me. Still, you cannot deny that I am *greatly* enjoying the effect you are having on my mother. So you see, what I told you was true. To be able to enjoy myself when forced to spend time with my loving mama, I did need to bring along a mistress."

"So you will defend yourself with casuistry?"

"I have no need to defend myself at all," Lord Hartwood said. "You wished to come, and I let you. You are being paid well for your services. I, in turn, wished to confront my mother with her hypocrisy and could think of no better way to do it."

"Then why did you not trust me with your true intent, instead of deceiving me as to your motive for having me accompany you?"

"I thought you wouldn't come with me if I was more forthright."

"Perhaps I wouldn't. But now that I know that you weren't honest with me, I am troubled. Your mother does seem convinced that it was you and not James who ruined that poor girl. Did you lie to me about that, too, Your Lordship?"

His eyes darkened with fury. "If a man were to call me a liar as you have just done, I would have to call him out and kill him."

"Then it is fortunate that I am a woman, so you do not have to add murder to your list of sins. But you have already admitted you were not truth-

ful with me," Eliza responded with effort keeping her voice even. "So what reason do I have to
believe that it was really James who ruined that
young woman?"

He leaned toward her from the bed, his body
taut. "Surely you more than anyone should have
had ample proof that I do not delight in ruining
innocent young women."

She paused, abashed. That much was true.

"If you cannot believe what I tell you now, we
had best call off this farce," he said, his voice dangerously quiet. "These are the facts: I never met the
girl James ruined. Never. And if I had, I wouldn't
lie about it. Unlike James and my dear departed
father, I do not hide my sins. What I have done, I
have done in public for all the world to see."

The passion in his voice caused Eliza to take an
involuntary step backward. "But if you are innocent," she asked, "why didn't you defend that innocence when first she accused you? Why didn't
you refuse to take the blame?"

"And be the reason James lost his chance to
marry his wealthy heiress and rescue our family
from the morass of debt my father had plunged us
into with the purchase of that damnable necklace?
The damage was done. I did not wish to see my
family ruined. Perhaps it was the wrong decision,
but I was only seventeen when I made it. Besides,
how could I prove my innocence? The girl was
dead. James and I were the only ones who knew
the truth of the situation. James had no compunc-

tions about lying—nor did my mother have any interest in establishing the real truth about who had ruined the girl."

He let out a sigh. "All my life, my mother preferred to believe that it was *I* who was at fault in any situation, rather than her favorite, James. Even when I was a schoolboy she had me whipped for James's misdeeds."

"She did that?"

"Many times. One time, when I was but ten, James stole some firecrackers and set them off in church. He was thirteen, three years older than I, and he ran with a group of wild friends. But still, she blamed me. She whipped me until I bled and then kept whipping me. I still carry the marks of her switch on my back. I can show them to you if you think that I am lying about this, too."

"That won't be necessary!" Eliza protested, appalled. He must have seen the shock in her eyes, for the fury drained out of his own and when he spoke again now it was with a certain desperate sadness.

"You are right when you say that I turn everything into play. I tease my mother with these slight reminders of the way that she has treated me, though I know she will never admit to the truth. I brought you with me and decked you out in that accursed necklace to remind her of who it was who really ruined our family. I paid Mrs. Atwater to come to dinner for I wished my mother to remember that though I may be a libertine, the profligacy that ruined our family wasn't mine."

"And did you trick Mrs. Atwater, too, to get her to come tonight?"

"Damn it, Eliza!" he said, bringing his fist down onto the counterpane. "I made a mistake by not taking you into my entire confidence, but surely my hesitation was understandable. There was no need to trick Mrs. Atwater. She was quite happy to appear here in return for fifty pounds."

"Then why didn't you think your money would be enough to convince me, too, to assist you? You know me to have even more need for money than Mrs. Atwater."

Lord Hartwood's lip curled up in that maddening half smile of his. "You are no more like Mrs. Atwater, a woman bought and paid for ten times over, than I am like that vulgar button maker. I may not begin to understand what motivates you, Eliza, but I've seen enough to know that whatever drives you, it isn't money. More like it is some wan hope of reforming me."

"If that were so, I should find myself sadly disappointed," Eliza replied severely. "You are as you will always be. That is the first lesson of character we learn when we study the astrologer's art. Though the second lesson is that a person need not always express the lineaments of their nature in the lowest possible way."

"As I do now?" His brow raised in an ironic question.

"As you do now. Whatever your feelings about your mother, Mrs. Atwater seemed to me to be a simple, kindly woman. It was cruel to force her to exhibit her shame before the woman who of all people in the world must hate her most. Nor was it right to rub her nose in her son's bastardy by harping on his resemblance to your father."

"You have me there, Eliza. My treatment of Mrs. Atwater was quite wrong. Had I a conscience, it must trouble me now to remember that it was Mrs. Atwater, the person in the room who had the most cause to resent me, who showed me the only bit of family feeling I have experienced these past fifteen years. How strange to think that she still remembers me in my little sailor suit."

His voice had grown wistful and a troubled look had returned to his brooding eyes. But only for a moment. Then that hard look surged back, and his voice grew harsh. "But I do not have a conscience, Eliza, as I have repeatedly told you. And you will not be able to reform me.

"Tax me with being childish all you want—blame Uranus or the Pole Star for my inadequacies. But you haven't seen the end of my childish pranks. Far from it. Would it disgust you to learn that before setting forth on this journey I bought a box of firecrackers to bring along with me? Big, loud Chinese firecrackers? And that I plan to use them, too, before the fortnight is over."

Eliza considered his words before replying. "Are they, too, meant to give your mother another sign that you have forgiven nothing?"

"How implacable you make me sound," he said sinking back against the pillows so his eyes were shadowed from the candlelight. "But I brought them only for sport. As you have so rightly explained to me, I think only of play."

He let his finger trail lazily along the quilted counterpane on the bed. "But is it not a point in my favor that I should think of play at such a time? For when I stand in my mother's presence, in my mind I am always eight years old and she is holding a heavy switch with that look of pleasure on her face that comes on right before she hurts me. Do you not think, my little seeress, that being the case, it is better—far better—that I should think of play when I must face her? Consider, for a moment, my alternatives."

Despite her resolution to let herself feel nothing more for him, Eliza was touched. "Why then could you not simply have told me all this before?"

"And admit I was a coward?" Lord Hartwood's lips clamped shut. "I've had enough of this discussion. You've been alone with me here in my chamber long enough to preserve my reputation as a libertine." He waved one languid hand in dismissal. "Take yourself back to your chamber. Muss up your hair and crinkle your gown in case you meet any curious servants on the stairway. I shall see you in the morning—if you haven't decided to leave me in a fit of insulted virtue because I twisted the truth to get you to be my accomplice."

"I shall still be here in the morning," Eliza assured him quietly. Then she pulled out the combs that secured the back of her new and fashionable hairstyle and grasped a handful of the sensuous satin gown that enfolded her, crushing it until it bore the imprint of her hand. "And I thank you for telling me your story. It is a painful one and it must have been painful for you to share it. But hearing it has convinced me that you really do need my help."

Lord Lightning's eyes gave one last threatening flash. "Perhaps I do, Eliza. And I admit that I should miss you if you were to leave me now. But take care not to let your woman's heart find excuses to fall in love with me. There must be no womanish softness toward me on your part. I am my father's son and my brother's brother, and that makes me a man whom it would be dangerous to love."

"I shall keep that in mind, Your Lordship."

"And so shall I," he said softly to himself as she slipped through the doorway. "And so shall I."

Chapter 10

He'd been a fool not to make her his mistress. Had he done what he ought to have done that first night and not given in to mawkish sentimentality, she would now be firmly under his control. More important, had he made her his mistress, she would not hold the fascination she held for him now. Having had her, he would have satisfied his curiosity and begun the usual process of becoming bored by her.

But he had not, and so Edward found himself lying awake in his bed a good hour after Eliza had made her way upstairs, remembering the enchanting way her freckled cheeks had flushed in response to his gaze during dinner and the charming tendril of copper hair that had fallen forward and framed her honest eyes as she had upbraided him—and trying, too, with very little success, to forget the intense surge of passion that had filled him as he had held her small but luscious body against his own in the hallway.

It must simply be thwarted lust. There was no other explanation for what he was feeling. And lust could be taken care of.

That woman at dinner, Lady Hermione, the one the earl had divorced, had sent more than one significant look in his direction. She'd let her arm brush against his leg at dinner, too, as if by accident and then made sure as she had chattered on about things of no consequence that he might overhear where she lived should he wish to pay her a call. If lust was the problem, it could be taken care of. He knew her type well enough to know how little it would take to bed her.

But that thought brought little comfort. He knew women of her type all too well, knew what she would say after she had sampled his amatory skills and how empty he would feel when it was over. He knew, too, how, within days, all her dearest female friends would get a detailed report about his performance. That was not at all what he wanted.

Nor did he want to find another Violet.

It was Eliza he wanted. Eliza who took his money only to save her books, who asked about his life instead of pouring out torrents of information about her own, who could not be tempted with the lure of marriage; Eliza who had, for a few brief hours, seen good in him where no one else had done so, and, by so doing, caused him to act nobly.

Damn Eliza, and her idiotic claims. It had only taken her spending a second day in his presence for her to take his measure more accurately. She was already beginning to see him for what he truly was and had scolded him soundly. Well, he knew what he was and he'd warned her. If the worst he did to her was confuse her by twisting some words around, she should count herself lucky.

But it stung him that it had been a lie that had caused her to lose her respect for him, for it was not his nature to lie. He bragged that he did in public what other men kept hidden. It was a source of pride to him that he was not a hypocrite but displayed the ugliest parts of his nature proudly, no matter what it cost him. So why had he lied to Eliza? So she would agree to come to Brighton with him? By God, he had almost behaved as if he really needed her!

And that was not the worst of it. He could barely bring himself to remember the way that this evening had concluded. Had he really poured out his heart to her about his childish sufferings like an abused chimney sweep? He was disgusted with himself for having made such a craven pitch for her sympathy just because he could not bear her disgust at his behavior. He had never before told anyone what he had told her tonight about his mother's cruelty. He had never before felt any need to justify his behavior. He was Lord Lightning, fickle and unpredictable. Why should he care what a penniless nobody thought of him?

But he did not like to remember what he'd felt when he'd seen her begin to understand that, as he had maintained all along, he was not a decent man. And he had felt guilt, too, when she'd upbraided him about his thoughtless treatment of Mrs. Atwater, who must, in truth, be wishing by now that she had strangled him with the neck cloth of his little sailor suit.

Well, enough of that. He must pull himself together. He must extricate himself from the connection he had so carelessly entered into. There was no reason to give any woman such power over him, even so unusual a woman as Eliza. Tomorrow he would make it clear that she must give up the over-familiarity with which he had permitted her to behave. He must treat her like the servant she was and caution her to keep her moral judgments to herself. The intimacy that had grown up so swiftly between them—one oddly so much stronger than any he had shared with the women with whom he had enjoyed full sexual congress—must end.

Meanwhile, he must do something to take his mind off the piercing sexual need Eliza had ignited. He must find some woman who would ease it, and quickly. Lady Hermione was certainly not the answer, but as he drifted off into an uneasy sleep, his body still remembering the way Eliza's soft, slight form had felt pressing so close to his own in the passageway and the surprising way that she had responded to his brutal caresses, he thought perhaps a visit to that discreet establishment near the Steyne, which catered to fastidious gentlemen like himself, might be in order.

Eliza, too, was having trouble sleeping. The room assigned to her in the attic was hot and muggy, the bed narrow, and the mattress lumpy, but none of these would have kept her from sleeping had her mind not been in an uproar after her latest interview with Lord Hartwood.

Though she might have fooled him with her recent show of indifference, she could no longer fool herself. She could not trust herself to submit to any more of his embraces unmoved. Despite all his warnings, she was falling in love with him. Having schooled herself for years to be content with the spinster life her aunt had thought best for her, she had believed herself immune to male attraction and trusted herself safe in the company of a man famed for his profligacy. But now she knew better. Had she not recollected herself at the very end of that mortifying kiss she might well have allowed Lord Hartwood to throw up her skirts and complete her ravishment right there in the hallway.

A housemaid who exhibited such behavior would have been turned off without a character. When Aunt Celestina had discovered one of her dairymaids in just such a compromising position with the gardener, Eliza remembered well how the girl had protested in vain that the man loved her. But Lord Hartwood had never given Eliza the slightest reason to believe he felt anything for her except, perhaps, a slightly amused lust. To him she was just an oddity—one more oddity in the life of a man notorious for his taste for the unusual.

How could she have let herself feel such unacceptable emotions, and for such a man? Her aunt would have been appalled. Unable to sleep, she searched through her flowered satchel for the current year's almanac. Perhaps if she looked carefully at the planets' current positions in the heavens she could find something new that would cast more light on what was happening to her.

But she found nothing she didn't already know in the almanac's columns of tiny print. Long before she had let Lord Lightning draw her into his coach she had been well aware that this summer would be the time when the planet Saturn would return to the position in the sky it had occupied at the moment of her birth. This happened every twenty-nine years and was a time when astrologers expected to experience events that reflected the nature of stern malefic planet. Loneliness, poverty, fear, and harsh restraint were the tools Saturn used to teach its hard lessons— though Saturn might also give endurance and the ability to persist in the midst of difficulties. But it depended on the nature of the birth chart how severe the events of the Saturn return might be. If Saturn was well placed, the return might pass with only a shadow of difficulty.

Eliza put down the almanac. She did not need it

to tell her how afflicted her own Natal Saturn was. All astrologers liked to boast that their own charts were more afflicted than those of their peers, as if that conferred some sort of status on them. But her aunt's astrologer friends had been silenced when Aunt Celestina had shown them just how afflicted Eliza's Saturn was. It stood in the evil House of Self-Undoing and made the worst possible aspect—the square—to her optimistic Sagittarius Sun. That ugly square, her aunt had explained, was why her father had abandoned her. Saturn so often signified the Father on a chart.

It was because Eliza had known that her Saturn return was coming that she had not been surprised when her father had come back into her life this spring. That knowledge had helped her bear her father's renewed betrayal. It was exactly what was to be expected when Saturn ruled the hour. But as painful as her father's new betrayal had been, she had known her Saturn return would pass and she would survive, just as she had when her father had abandoned her the first time.

But now she wondered. Would she survive the return unscathed? For something had happened she hadn't anticipated: Saturn, that hard taskmaster, had not been satisfied just to let her father rob her but had found her another unreliable man—one far more attractive than the pathetic wretch her father had become. And true to its placement in her House of Self-Undoing, Saturn would make her love this new man, too.

She would not do it. She would fight that self-undoing with her last breath. But to withstand it, she must face the truth. She was far too attracted by her new protector. She could not afford to allow herself anymore self-deception. She must leave Lord Lightning. She had no other choice.

She put her things back into the flowered satchel and crawled back into the uncomfortable bed. She would need to get some sleep now. Who knew where she might find herself tomorrow night? But even as she sank into a fevered half dream she found herself unable to escape dire Saturn's sway, for as she slipped into the world where dreams took place she found Lord Hartwood waiting for her there, his brown eyes soft, his golden body pulsating. And in her treacherous dream his disturbing embrace continued and she welcomed it. When she awoke, she found herself in tears.

"I shall not be needing you today," Edward announced airily, when he encountered Eliza in the breakfast room. He spoke with the tone of a master addressing a servant. He was proud of himself for engaging her in that tone and for resisting his immediate reaction upon first seeing her, which had been to greet her with the kind of kiss that a man gave to the woman who had kept him up half the night thinking about her charms.

But he had taken himself in hand. She must be put in her place. He would not be stern or forbidding, as there was no point in upsetting her, but he must make the situation clear. No matter how adorable she was when she wrinkled her little freckled nose, Eliza must be taught she could not treat him like an equal. She was a hireling and nothing more. Once she was made to remember that—and more important, he thought wryly, once *he*, too, was made to remember it—they could go on without risking any more scenes like that of the previous night. He shuddered inwardly at the memory of the extent to which he had let himself lose control. It would not happen again.

But why, he wondered, had she taken it into her head to dress herself again in that dreadful gray gown? He cleared his throat and got down to business. "Since I won't be needing you today, Eliza, you may take a maid and walk about the town—after you change out of that hideous gown."

He reached into his pocket and brought forth a golden sovereign. "Here." He tossed it to her. "Use this to buy yourself something pretty from the shops." He turned on his heel, intent on making a speedy exit before she did anything to upset his resolve. It was time to make discreet inquiries among his male friends as to where this year's most charming dollybirds could be found. The seaside air seemed to do unexpected things to a man's need for a woman.

But as he took a step toward the door, Eliza called out his name, and before he could stop her, she hurried over and handed him back the coin.

"I cannot take this, Your Lordship," she said. "After thinking over our conversation last night, I have come to the conclusion that continuing our connection further would be a mistake. I must ask you to release me."

He swung back to face her. He could barely believe what his ears had told him. She had decided to leave *him*? Was that why she had put on her Quaker gown again? His detachment vanished within the instant. "So, that's it, is it? You, too, have decided to abandon me? Merely because of the way that I twisted a few words? It wasn't even a decent lie, Eliza!"

She turned away, unable to look him in the eye. With his angry words he had shown her the way to extricate herself from the trap she had made for herself. She nodded and murmured that, yes, his deception had been the problem, knowing, as she spoke the words, that the lie she was telling was far graver than the one she had chided him for.

What was the alternative? To humiliate herself further? To tell him she was falling in love with him despite his warnings? To see the scorn that must fill his handsome features when he realized just how foolish she had been? She had no choice, but still, she felt ashamed that she, too, had lied. She couldn't bring herself to look at him, but remained standing with her back turned, looking out the window at the hazy morning sunshine, pretending the scene outside the window held some intense fascination for her.

Lord Hartwood made no reply. She heard his boots striking the hard surface of the floor, one sharp staccato tap after another as he paced back and forth behind her. His silence weighed heavily on her. Was it just delaying the explosion, or was he relieved to see her go?

Cornered, she turned back to face him and was shocked by the look of raw anguish she saw displayed on his face in the brief moment before he realized she could see him. It disoriented her, and she found herself unable to do anything but gabble, "I will give you back your money, Your Lordship. Though I must ask you for a couple pounds to live on until I can find some way of maintaining myself. You may trust me for the loan. I will give you my *Tetrabiblos* to secure it. I have no other valuables."

"There is no need for that," he replied, "I trust you, Eliza. Though I don't know why I should since it took so little to change your opinion of me. Was it not but a few short days ago you told me you believed me to be a man with a heart? You saw good in me and braved the scorn of others because you believed in it. But it took only a few hours in my presence, a few unwary words in which I revealed myself to you, for you to become so disgusted with me that you can only think of flight." He shrugged, fully in control of himself again. "I thought you had more resolve. Well, so be it. I warned you what I was."

His voice was cold, as cold as it had been when he had walked in upon Violet disparaging his character in the theater dressing room. But Eliza knew him better now than she had then. She knew that the hardness she heard in his voice was not cold unconcern, far from it.

She had lied to him about why she was leaving and to save herself, she should lie again. She should tell him he had indeed disgusted her. She should stick to her story and make her escape. But despite the coldness in his voice, the eyes he had turned upon her in that one moment when he thought she could not see him were the eyes of an abandoned child. With a shock she realized he cared what she thought of him. It mattered that she had seen good in him where no one else could find it. How could she let him believe she had changed her mind about that, when it meant so much to him?

"You are what I always believed you to be," she said quietly. "A glorious, loyal, and playful man with an immense need for love. The blame does not lie with you but with me. It has nothing to do with your deception about the will. That was not the problem."

"Then what is?" His voice was urgent, his burning eyes haloed by his curling golden hair.

"I am unable to maintain the role you have assigned me," Eliza whispered. "I find it too disturbing to pretend to be your mistress. The scheme was a foolish one. You need a real mistress, not a woman like myself."

So that was the problem! He was overcome by a burst of inexpressible relief. It was only that he'd frightened her with his passion. Well, that was no surprise. He'd damn near thrust his tongue down her throat in the hallway, treating her like a whore, consumed by the pain roused by his interview with his mother. It had been too much for her, even with the help of Lady Teazle. She was still, after all, a country-bred virgin.

But that thought gave him hope. She hadn't lost her fundamental belief in his goodness—as mistaken as it might be. So perhaps he could convince her to stay for another few days. Then, if he was careful and treated her with more delicacy, if he led her step by step, respecting her innocence, perhaps she could be persuaded to—to what? The thought struck him like a slap. What really *did* he want of her? What earthly reason was there to keep her here? He'd made his point with his mother the previous night. Word of the affront he'd offered her would be all around town by this morning. There was no further need to keep a mistress with him, particularly not a mistress who was not a mistress, a virgin who left him burning alone in his bed, yearning for something he would not find in the arms of another, more willing, woman.

What *did* he want of her? He couldn't answer that question. He knew only he could not let her go, not yet. The thought of her leaving was intolerable. He couldn't face it and by God, he would not. He felt his resolve strengthen. He would do whatever it took to make her stay. It wouldn't be that difficult. Who knew better than a practiced rake how to ensnare a woman and bend her to his will? Seduction came naturally to him and women always yielded to his seductive tricks. It was merely a matter of finding the right bait. True, Eliza was not like other women, he'd already learned that, but this would not be like other seductions. It wasn't her body he was after—he'd drawn the line there and he would stick to it. Instead he would use his practiced skills to capture that more elusive part of her, her soul. For just a little while. To make her stay until he tired of her, as inevitably he must. Then he would send her on her way, at some time of his choosing. But not right now. Not yet.

"Come," he said. "We'll find some place where we can speak in private. I ask but a moment more of your time, then I will let you go."

He favored her with his most charming smile. Then he turned and strode out of the breakfast room as if he didn't care a whit whether she followed him or not, though he was relieved to hear her footsteps following behind him. At least he hadn't completely lost his edge. Eliza had responded as he'd hoped. He'd never yet met a woman who could resist that particular smile. He opened the door to the library. Once she had made her way in, he closed the door with a sigh of relief. Now they could speak freely without fear of being overheard.

He gave no sign of the anxiety he felt as he pondered his next step but made her wait as he idly picked up a book that lay open on the round Chippendale table that stood near the heavy leather chair that had been his father's. A book of ser-

mons most likely, and indeed inspection proved it
to be just such a book. His mother's tastes hadn't
changed. He busied himself for a moment leafing
through it, casting about for the best way to begin
his new campaign of chaste seduction. He must
not lie. Not after last night. Eliza must be won
with the truth, so he would tell her the truth. But
very carefully. It only took a moment more until
he began to see exactly how the business could be
done.

He put down the book and favored Eliza with
another smile, cousin to the first and equally ef-
fective, then began. "You have played your part
brilliantly," he said. "But I let myself be carried
away last night. It was wrong and you are right to
be upset. Even a real mistress would have slapped
my face had I forced her to be put on display like
the one I forced you into. I must ask your forgiveness for the way I used you then, though I don't
deserve it."

He put on a humble face as he watched the con-
flicting emotions flicker over Eliza's face. So far, so
good. Women always loved apologies.

Then, still playing for time, he removed his
snuffbox from its pocket and busied himself
taking a pinch. He inhaled, savoring the sensation, his mind working quickly. At last he spoke.
"Last night you accused me of taking nothing seriously and turning everything into a game."

"I am afraid I taxed you with quite a lot last
night."

"But you were right in all you said to me. It's just that I'm not used to being spoken to with such candor."

"Well, that's no wonder if, as you told me last night, you threaten to call out any man who tries to tell you something you don't wish to hear."

"Touché, Eliza!" He winced. "It has been a long time since anyone has had the courage to speak to me with such honesty as yours. My reputation has made most people fearful of me, so they tell me only what they think I want to hear. For that reason I find your candor, though unexpected, most refreshing."

He walked over to the window, and threw back the heavy drapes, letting the sunshine flood into the room, while he thought out the rest of what he would say. He had flattered her a bit about something he knew she prided herself upon—her candor. Now what to do next?

He cast back to other scenes like this with other women, trying to recall what had worked to keep their interest. Perhaps he could appeal to her feminine need to change him. Women always wanted to change him, and as different as she might be from other women, Eliza had already shown quite a taste for doing *that*.

At length he spoke. "You say that you have become tired of playing the role of my mistress after three short days," he said plaintively, with just a hint of a sigh in his voice. "Consider this, Eliza. If you feel like that after playing a role so briefly, can you imagine how I must feel, condemned for the rest of my life to be Lord Lightning? I have been playing him, without a break, these fifteen years."

Eliza said nothing, but he could see he had caught her attention. It was working. As sure as you could catch a trout with a wriggling worm, you could always catch a woman with the suggestion that you needed her help to change.

"It is only with you, who see beyond the surface, that I feel my true self emerging," he added. "It frightens me, Eliza, but with your help, perhaps I can break free."

She made no reply, but merely regarded him steadily with those clear, green eyes.

"You say that I need a real mistress, but I would trade a dozen real mistresses for what you've given me. Don't you see? You've offered me something rare. Something no woman has ever before given me."

"And what is that, Your Lordship?"

"We are long past the point where you should be 'Your Lordshipping' me," he said with an edge of irritation in his voice. "My Christian name is Edward and I would be honored if you would address me with it."

"Edward," Eliza said slowly, as if tasting the syllables. He could sense that the intimacy of saying his name was working its expected magic on her. This was easier than he had thought it might be. Now on to the next step.

"You've offered me your friendship," he said at last. "And your friendship is robust and challenging. I'm not used to having a friend who speaks her mind so forcefully, who chides me for my faults and calls me to account for my deficiencies. But even so, I've come to see the value of such a friendship." He let his voice drop for maximum effect. "Please, Eliza. Don't take it away from me. Not now, when I've only begun to appreciate it."

He stopped his pacing and returned to where she stood. He reached out for her hand and took it gently in his own. How strange it was that though he had already taken so many liberties with her person, he had never before done something as simple as take her hand.

He held it in his for a moment, wordlessly enjoying the feel of her small but strong fingers as they rested against his own, and feeling, too, the involuntary quiver that ran through them. His plea had disturbed her. He could see it in the flush that crept up her graceful neck. Perhaps she was reconsidering her decision. He must keep on talking and not give her time to think. "You also acted the part of a true friend to me last night when you pointed out that I'd treated Mrs. Atwater with indefensible cruelty—perhaps more than you know. The world only saw Lord Lightning displaying his usual disregard for convention, but you saw more—and forced me to look at what I've tried to keep hidden, even from myself."

He paused for effect. What woman could resist an apology coupled with an assurance of her superiority? All that was left to seal her to him, for now, was to share a confidence with her. Women loved to be the repositories of such confidences. It made them feel special and trusted. Fortunately, he had just the confidence to share with her. His voice dropped to barely a whisper. "My cruelty to Mrs. Atwater was all the more inexcusable because I have reason to suspect that it is she, not the woman who calls herself my mother, who actually gave birth to me."

"But how could that be? Your Lordsh— Edward—" she gasped. "Surely if you had been illegitimate you could not have inherited the title."

"I fear it is precisely *because* there was no one to inherit his title except James, who was a sickly child and not expected to live—a title that meant more to him than anything else on earth—that my father prevailed upon my mother to pretend that his bastard was her own child."

"But would it not be a crime, to pass off a bastard as legitimate to preserve a title?"

"It would. Hence if he and Lady Hartwood colluded that way, no matter what their subsequent feelings for each other, everyone involved would have had every motivation to keep it completely secret."

"So you are only guessing, then. But what gave you the idea?"

"Many times during my childhood I heard the servants gossiping. They said that after my mother bore James, the doctors told her that it would be very unwise for her to become pregnant again, as delivering James had almost killed her. But with James so sickly my father needed another heir. Does it not stand to reason that if my mother couldn't give him one he would find someone else who could? Did you not notice how similar to my mother Mrs. Atwater was in her coloring and her looks? If my mother was to claim the child as her own, who was to know the difference?"

"And you believe your mother went along with this?"

"Unwillingly, I wager, but her pride in the title was, if anything, greater than my father's, since she had paid a heavy price—a huge dowry—to acquire the right to bear it. But Eliza, think! If I wasn't foisted on her in that way, what other explanation is there for her lifelong hatred of me?"

What explanation indeed? He was trying to ensnare her by sharing a confidence, but the suspicion he had confessed to her was real enough. It had haunted him all of his life.

Eliza's look of concern deepened. "But if that were true, then the date and time you gave me for your nativity would most likely not be correct. You would have had to be born somewhere else and then brought secretly to your mother's bedroom after the birth."

She paused for a moment, deep in thought, then shook her head. "The horoscope I erected for the date and time you gave me fits your character too well for you to have been born at some other time. It describes your conflict with your mother as perfectly as it does your need to play childish pranks and your explosive, Uranian nature. Had you been born a few hours earlier the Moon would still have been far from Mars, nor would Uranus have stood at your midheaven. The planet that tops the chart describes what the world will think of us, and your Uranian nature matches the birth time you gave me too perfectly. Even an hour earlier would not describe the same man. So it's likely you were born when your mother says you were. It's only because of how painful the relationship has been between you and your mother that you've taken comfort in the thought that you might be your father's bastard."

Had he really taken *comfort* in that thought? Her claim surprised him. He had always kept his fear secret out of shame that he might indeed be an imposter. But it struck him now how little pleasure he would take were he to find proof Lady Hartwood really was his mother. In fact, the thought was horrifying. But of course, Eliza had no proof.

He felt his brow furrowing. "What if your astrologizing is wrong? If I were Mrs. Atwater's child it would explain so much: The way my father never intervened when my mother took out her anger on me. The way he would do anything— even ruin the family—to placate Mrs. Atwater. If I really were her child and he had illegally put me in a position to inherit his title, imagine the power his mistress would have held over him."

As he spoke those words, he realized with horror, that in sharing his suspicion with Eliza he had just transferred that same power to her. With what he had just told her, she could expose him to the world. She could ruin him. He must have gone mad to trust her with a secret so important!

But Eliza appeared oblivious to his gaffe. She cocked her head in that charming way she had and said, "Perhaps if I could examine your mother's nativity, or that of your father, I might be able to determine the truth of the situation better."

"Perhaps, but you just said you would be leaving me," he said in a hollow voice, relieved that she betrayed no hint of recognizing the power he had just given her and remembering why it was he had trusted her with so important a confidence. It was essential now that he use it to bind her to him. So he fixed her with his most languishing gaze and adjusted his features into that look women found so hard to resist, the hurt, Byronic look they always fell for. He let his eyes grow soft and let the hurt flood up into them, gazing into her eyes as if he was showing her his soul.

It was only a stratagem. It was only a trick intended to reinforce the careful groundwork he had prepared for her seduction. But as his eyes locked with Eliza's he felt a sudden loss of control, as if the soul that shone through her flecked green eyes grappled onto his, tore through his ruse, ripped open the tightness that bound his heart and freed within him some spring of inner vitality. He felt his heart pound and sensed her responding with shock to the honesty of what coursed through both of them. They stood together, their eyes joined, feeling the electricity throbbing between them. When at last he couldn't bear another moment of what she had exposed in him, it took all his strength to tear his eyes away. He stepped back, shaken to the core, praying that she would not leave him now.

Eliza was no less perturbed.

If only he had upbraided her, or scolded her, or made her the target of his cynicism. All that she could have withstood, but not the look of agony that had filled his eyes, the real agony that had been so close to the surface throughout his transparent attempts to manipulate her. Oh, he was still acting. He was playing yet another role as he tried to convince her to stay with him. But it was not an act that he needed her. It was not an act how desperately he wanted her to stay.

She must not give in to him! She must make herself turn away from that teasing smile of his, no matter how beautiful it made her feel. She must remind herself how dangerous beauty was to a woman alone and unprotected. She must not let herself become dependent on the electricity she felt in his presence even if it made her feel as if she were alive for the very first time. She must be strong. She must push him away and respond to his enticements with coldness. She must gather herself up and sweep out of the door. She must give him no hint of how hard it would be for her to leave him. He would only use it against her.

He was only pretending. He was a rake, a man who toyed with women. If he needed her at all, it was only to satisfy a momentary surge of lust or because her show of independence challenged him. If she gave in to him now and stayed with him, if she chose to nourish herself on the crumbs of passion he scattered before her, she would end up as doomed as her own poor mother.

What could she look forward to if she stayed with Lord Hartwood except misery? Even if he never again touched her, her heart was becoming more bound to him with every moment, every word, and every gaze. And not just her heart. What his kisses had stirred within her body, the sleeping genie *they* had aroused—she did not dare to let herself remember. But she was no longer the naïve innocent she'd been when Lord Lightning had taken her to his town house. She no longer dreamed that if she gave herself to him, his passion might lead him to love. As much as she sensed him wanting her, she also sensed he did not *wish* to want her. Eventually he would triumph over his need for her. If she stayed with him he would soon tire of her. And when he did, how could she go on, transformed as she would be by what he had taught her to desire?

Perhaps when he claimed he couldn't love, he was telling the truth. Perhaps she had read into his chart what she had wanted to see. Uranus at his midheaven was glorious, yes, like lightning on a summer night—but dangerous and unreliable. She could no more depend on him than she could on her poor obsessive father.

But even as she stood there, struggling to find the words to tell Lord Hartwood that it was no use, that her mind was made up and she must leave him, the words wouldn't come. If only she hadn't gazed into his eyes and seen what she had seen pulsing there. If only he wasn't clinging to her hand as if she was all that stood between him and the fiery pit. If only she herself didn't want to stay with him so badly.

If she were wise she would leave him without a single backward glance. But she could not.

"Will you give me one more day?" he begged softly. "That's all I ask. After that you are free to go."

A single day, when so much could happen in just a single hour? But still, she felt her head nod and was unable to stop it from doing so.

At her wordless capitulation, his grip on her hand relaxed.

"But I shall need some time to myself, Edward," she added. Time to calm herself, time to look once again at his perilous horoscope and learn how she might yet escape.

He let go of her hand. Now that he had got what he wanted, his face had relaxed and a hint of humor quirked up his lip again. "That's a reasonable request, Eliza. We've been very much in each other's pockets these past few days. In any event, some long neglected business must take up my time today. You may make yourself at home in the library or take a stroll with one of the maids—though please, do something about replacing that—that—" he stammered, until giving up on finding a word to describe her old gown, he simply pointed at it with a barely suppressed shudder.

And with that he bowed to her, so very gracefully, the wounded boy replaced once again by the worldly man of the ton, and turning on his impeccably polished heel, he strode out of the library leaving Eliza to wonder how she would survive.

Chapter 11

The house felt strangely empty with Lord Hartwood gone. Eliza retreated to her small attic
room, but the day, though overcast and rainy, was
a warm one and the room most uncomfortably
hot. Her mind was so perturbed she could find no
pleasure in the study of the astrological charts that
were usually so comforting. Even so she forced
herself to spend a good hour reconsidering the
chart she had drawn up for his nativity.

She hunted in vain for some clue that might reinforce his idea that his father's mistress, rather
than Lady Hartwood, was his real mother. But
she could draw no firm conclusions. The chart
drawn for his supposed birth time described him
too well. Born at another time, he would not have
had Uranus atop his midheaven. She couldn't
imagine Lord Lightning without it. And yet, there

was some secret the chart was hiding from her. The square between his Sun and Moon did show a strong conflict between his parents. And what was she to make of how closely Uranus aspected his Moon? Didn't it suggest there was something very unusual about his mother? But of course, she realized with a start, if Lady Hartwood really wasn't his mother, the chart she held in her hand wouldn't have *been* his chart.

It was all too confusing. She had lost her objectivity. She could no longer convince herself that she understood Lord Hartwood's personality. She could no longer translate the cold symbols on the paper before her into flesh and blood. When she tried to consider what a change in his birth time might do to his Mercury, she could hear only his teasing voice so alluring, so irresistible. When she looked at the change it made in his Venus, his handsome face swam up in her imagination, blotting out all thought. And Mars! She couldn't bear to think of Mars, for to think of Mars was to remember what it felt to be clasped in his strong embrace, his hard manhood pressing against her, awakening hungers it was forbidden to satisfy.

Disgusted with herself, Eliza changed into another of Violet's filmy gowns—a translucent cornflower blue muslin which she found surprisingly comfortable in the present heat—and went downstairs, intending to find a maid to accompany her on the walk Lord Hartwood had recommended. But just as she did so, it started to pour again, so she had to abandon any thought of escape.

Regretfully she made her way toward the library, feeling all the more irritated by the need to stay inside. Her annoyance was increased when she found the heavy velvet curtains in the dark paneled room pulled closed so only the dimmest light could filter in. She supposed this was to protect the books from the fading effect of light, but the library's gloom depressed her.

She gazed at the spines of books on the shelves. A gentleman's library, probably purchased by the yard and selected entirely for the richness of the bindings. But as her eyes ran along the books she could not long maintain her dismal mood, for here and there she spotted titles of interest—in particular, some ancient Greek works that she had heard of but never had the pleasure of seeing before.

She removed one volume from the shelf, the *Lysistrata* of Aristophanes in a Flemish edition from the previous century. She stopped for only a moment to appreciate the luxuriant feel of the red morocco binding. Then, after opening the curtains so they admitted enough light to read by, she made her way to a large leather-upholstered armchair by the window and began to page through her find.

Her attentions were quickly engaged by the words of the ancient dramatist and she spent a happy half hour immersed in his comedy, startled by its earthy tone and its frank discussion of those physical relations between men and women that were only whispered about by the moderns.

Perhaps, she thought with sudden understanding, the frankness which the ancients brought to such subjects explained why girls were not encouraged to study the classics.

She had settled into her chair and kicked off her shoes to make herself more comfortable when she was startled to realize she was no longer alone in the library. She had been joined by Lady Hartwood, who had entered surprisingly quietly for a woman of her size. She was dressed as usual in widow's weeds, walking slowly with the aid of a cane. Seeing her make her way across the room on her own so successfully, Eliza wondered why the wheeled chair had been necessary the previous evening. Was Lady Hartwood, like her son, addicted to the use of theatrical display to make a point?

Lady Hartwood's gaze was fixed on the book in Eliza's hand, and, despite herself, Eliza blushed at the thought that the older woman might guess how affected Eliza had been by the play's bawdy dialogue. But she quickly recollected that any embarrassment she might be feeling on that subject was misplaced. Her behavior with Lord Hartwood the previous day had ensured Lady Hartwood must believe that Eliza was not merely reading bawdy scenes but playing them out in real life. So she put the book down and fixed her gaze boldly on the broad expanse of black bombazine enfolding her protector's mother.

"So you can read, can you, girl?" Lady Hartwood said with a sniff, "I wouldn't have thought it. *Your* kind rarely can."

"Of course I can read," Eliza retorted, glad, for once, that her déclassé role allowed her to express the rudeness that Hartwood's mother's statement deserved.

Lady Hartwood came closer until she could clearly see the Greek print that covered the pages of the book that lay open in Eliza's lap. "But of course, you're lying. Don't try to bamboozle me. If you really could read, you would know that the book you hold in your hand isn't even written in English letters."

"It would be very strange, indeed, if it *were* written in English letters," Eliza retorted. "Since it contains a comedy of Aristophanes in the ancient Greek."

"A comedy by Aristophanes?" Lady Hartwood's brows raised in an expression of incredulity. "How would a woman like you have ever heard of Aristophanes? Surely they don't perform his plays at the sort of theater where your kind can be found!" She held out her hand imperiously. "Give me the book."

Wordlessly Eliza handed her the volume.

The older woman examined it for a moment, leafing through the first couple of pages with a sour look, then she snapped it shut and put it down on the table.

"A woman like you, reading a book such as this, is preposterous," she announced. From the way

she'd examined the volume, Eliza suspected that
Lady Hartwood, like most gently raised girls of
her class, couldn't read it, either. Only boys were
taught Greek.

Lady Hartwood turned back to face Eliza. "You
are not at all the sort of woman I would have expected Edward to have chosen as his mistress.
Like most men of his sort, his taste in women
runs to pink, rounded creatures who giggle too
much—creatures he finds it easy to despise. But
perhaps the appeal of such women has waned
and he needs variety to provide the stimulus for
his fading appetites. Tell me, when he first met
you, were you a governess discharged without a
character?"

"Not at all," Eliza said, staring boldly at her interlocutor in a way she knew to be very rude.

"Then you must be some girl from the prov-
inces, lured to the city by some rake, seduced and
then abandoned. You are trying to act the harlot,
but your diction is too good for a woman of the
muslin company, as are your table manners. You
show some signs of good breeding, no matter
how far you might have fallen."

That cursed fish fork. Lady Hartwood had not
been fooled.

"Since you appear to be gently bred," her protector's mother continued, "I shall do you the
courtesy of assuming you find yourself in your
current position through some personal misfortune rather than an inclination toward vice. While

I cannot condone what you have done, I am not lost to Christian charity and I will do my best not to judge too harshly the situation you find yourself in. Especially since you probably don't understand how very dangerous it is."

Lady Hartwood fixed Eliza with one gimlet eye. "You must not delude yourself Hartwood will fall in love with you," she warned. "He is incapable of it."

"So he has told me," Eliza replied. "He seems rather proud of that facet of his nature."

"Your levity is misplaced. My son's crimes are nothing to joke about. He is the most dangerous kind of man—a handsome, charming, lascivious rake who has no concern for damage he does to the women he uses." Lady Hartwood paused, studying the effect of her words.

Though Eliza struggled to maintain her composure, his mother's words disturbed her, echoing as they did, her inmost fears.

"Your paramour is a murderer," Lady Hartwood continued. "You didn't know that, did you? But it's true. He caused the death of a poor deluded creature and thought so little of it, he went out dancing before her body was cold."

Lady Hartwood leaned forward, resting much of her weight on her ebony cane as she continued to speak in a low, conspiratorial voice. "You are not of the ton, and your connection with my son is very recent, so perhaps you weren't aware of his history. But if you are wise, you'll heed my warning. You must not trust Hartwood's promises. He's a very dangerous man. If I, his mother, tell you this, you must assume there's some truth to it."

Eliza struggled to compose herself and shrugged as she imagined Violet might have done upon hearing such news, noticing as she did so how her bosom, scarcely covered by the frilly blue muslin, quivered as a shiver ran through her. But she forced herself to remain calm. She knew there was no truth in Lady Hartwood's accusation. "Why should I believe you?" she demanded. "Edward tells me it is *you* who cannot be trusted."

"Well, he would, wouldn't he? For he must have known I would warn any poor creature who found herself in his power what kind of man he really is."

"I need no such warning," Eliza said stiffly. "Your son loves to shock others and to play at life, but I see nothing vicious in him. Indeed, I find it hard to understand how he has earned such a wretched reputation. I believe he has a good heart and could learn to love given the right circumstances."

"That is only because you choose to ignore the fate of the poor deluded creature he drove to her death."

"There you are wrong," Eliza said vehemently. "I am fully aware of the details. Your son explained the entire situation to me before our arrival."

"Then you are far more hardened than I gave you credit for, and there can be no point in our discussing the matter further."

Eliza knew she should take this opportunity to end this conversation, but the injustice of Lady Hartwood's accusation made that impossible. The blame she had placed on Edward's youthful shoulders had already done him so much damage. She wondered how he had survived it. If she felt this uncomfortable after being the target of Lady Hartwood's contempt for only a few brief moments, what must it have been like for him to have been forced to live with it for a lifetime? And he had been so young when he had first come under such a devastating attack. No one had ever stood up to defend him, not even himself. At that thought, something rose up within her and demanded she be the first. "You are wrong," she protested. "There is more than enough reason to discuss this matter. Consider what your son did for your family—the sacrifice he made for you! I find it strange that you feel no gratitude toward him."

Lady Hartwood had already begun the ponderous process of turning her bulk toward the door, aided by her cane. Now she stopped and again faced Eliza as an unpleasant smile played across her hawk-like features. "Gratitude? You believe I should feel gratitude to him for blackening our family name? For living a life of open vice before the eyes of all the world?"

But who had started him on the path toward vice? "Your words only make me trust Edward more, since they confirm what he had told me. You abhor him not because he has sinned, but because he refuses to hide his sinfulness behind a façade of false respectability."

"I see he has converted you to his Jacobin philosophy. But yes, I should have liked to have my son behave like a gentleman and keep his indiscretions to himself. That is the way a gentleman behaves."

"Or a hypocrite."

Lady Hartwood gave no hint Eliza's bolt had struck home. Instead she took another step toward Eliza. As she drew nearer, Eliza smelled the scent of her perspiration mixed with the heavy perfume that she favored.

"You parrot his words easily, don't you, girl. You think you know it all. But you young girls always do. A man need only turn on you the power of a handsome face, a charming mode of address, and all sense goes out the window. But he is a very dangerous man, that handsome son of mine, with a penchant for destroying the women who love him. Don't you forget it." Lady Hartwood stopped to take a breath. "Or are you too far gone in your own misguided passion to care? If that's the case and you choose to ignore my warning, I'll give you one more warning you would be foolish to ignore." She gestured toward the door with her cane. "I want you out of my home as swiftly as possible. Mark this, my girl, and do not ignore me."

She put the cane down and with only slightly less hostility added, "If you heed my words, I would be willing to help you remove to some shelter for repentant Magdalenes, where you would be taught a useful trade and could begin your life anew. No matter what my son may have told you, I am not a heartless woman."

How could this woman be so self-deluded? "I do not wish to be rescued from Lord Hartwood's protection," Eliza replied haughtily. "I am quite happy in my current situation."

"You will regret it."

But though it was very clear that this was supposed to be Lady Hartwood's parting shot, the older woman would not let Eliza break away from her gaze. Instead, she stood unmoving, fixing Eliza with a glare that grew increasingly troubled, as if she herself wished to break away from their confrontation but could not. Finally a flicker of something akin to confusion passed over Lady Hartwood's face, and she hobbled out the door.

"Well, that takes the cake!" Eliza heard Lord Hartwood exclaim as he threw open the door to the library and bounded toward her. He had just arrived back at the house after completing his errands, and the amusement that filled his features made his normally handsome face even more attractive. "My mother just greeted me with the news that while I was gone, you insulted her beyond bearing by pretending—shameless hussy—to be reading Aristophanes in the original Greek."

"Well, so I was. It was *Lysistrata*. Quite shocking really. I finally understood why my aunt wouldn't allow me to read it."

His warm brown eyes widened in surprise. "Truly? You really *were* reading the play in Greek, not just having a joke at her expense?"

"Of course I was reading it. There was nothing else to do in this wretched weather, and unlike you, I don't fend off boredom by playing tricks on others."

"A hit," he joked. "A palpable hit! But how on earth did you learn to read ancient Greek?"

"Why, from my Aunt Celestina. It is impossible to become a proficient astrologer without some knowledge of the ancient languages. Many of the most important texts haven't been translated, and those that have are translated badly by scholars who don't understand the meanings of the astrological terms."

"My little seeress, you will never cease to amaze me," he said, his amusement showing in his eyes. "But how shall I get over the shame of it if the word gets around the clubs that my mistress is a bluestocking."

"Since the word must already have got around that your mistress is an elderly freckled spinster, the world can have little difficulty adding to its catalog of wonders that she is also a bluestocking, Your Lordship."

"I have told you to call me Edward. You are my friend, Eliza, are you not? That is how my friends address me."

"Very well, *Edward*. But I shall not cease being a spinster, however I address you."

He shook his head. "You are so hard on yourself. And so very wrong. Just now, as I made my way through town I was approached by two acquaintances, men I know from the clubs in London. Both of them made a to-do of wondering why I had been hiding away such a delicious tidbit as they had heard my latest mistress to be."

"And what did you tell them?" Eliza asked, flattered despite herself.

"Oh, merely that I am far too jealous to allow anyone to see my latest treasure. Why risk having some other man steal her?"

"What a bouncer! Truly, Edward, if you want me to believe the things you tell me, you shouldn't admit that you twist the truth so when speaking to others."

"Perhaps what I told them *is* the truth, Eliza. I should very much like to keep you well hidden from the sort of men who make up my circle. Without my protection, you would not be safe with them."

"Would you have me believe that they *all* incline toward ravishing old maids? I am amazed. This is not the picture I have had of the tastes of the men of the ton."

"You are not a homely old maid, Eliza. Not by any stretch of the imagination. And you must know that without my protection you would be in grave danger should you come to the attention of such men. Believing you to be a woman of little virtue, they would quickly move to add you to their list of conquests and they might not be too particular about how they got you to agree to give yourself to them."

"Then I am truly glad to have your protection," Eliza replied with a shudder. The threat he had sketched out had never before occurred to her.

"You have it, indeed. Anyone who dared trifle with you would have to face me at dawn and I am a devilish accurate shot."

"But surely you could not duel to protect the honor of a fallen woman. That would be a contradiction in terms."

"Ah, but I am Lord Lightning! My every act is a contradiction. The world would quickly be brought to understand that a mistress is the *only* woman whose honor I would think it worth defending."

"But since I am not really your mistress, you need not duel to defend a slur against me."

Edward's expression became suddenly serious and his voice fierce. "I should defend you against anyone who offered you the tiniest slight. You may depend on it."

"Because a slight to me touches your inverted sense of honor?"

"Because I care about you, Eliza." The joking tone was completely gone. "And because I couldn't bear to have anyone to threaten you."

"Then I fear you are too late," Eliza said soberly. "When your mother recovered from her surprise at what I was reading, she threatened that if I were not to leave this house immediately, she might take some drastic action."

His face relaxed. "Don't worry about that. It was just an act. She is completely dependent on me for her income. She cannot afford to take action against you. But come, my little seeress," he added, dropping his serious tone. "Let's not waste what is left of the afternoon. I should like to reward you for agreeing to remain with me by furnishing you with some pleasure. Knowing your tastes, I wondered if you would care to accompany me to the lending library. I'm told that Baker's on the Steyne has all the latest books."

Eliza was touched that he had hit upon so perfect a way of pleasing her. It made her feel appreciated and understood. But she cautioned him, teasingly, "If I am to go out with you, Edward, you must give me your solemn promise that you will not make me the occasion for a duel should some pink of the ton be overcome with desire for your freckled spinster of a mistress."

"You have my solemn promise," he replied, taking her arm, "though I cannot answer for what might happen should some bounder take an interest in the auburn-haired beauty who is my latest obsession."

Chapter 12

Because the day was rainy, Baker's Library on the Steyne was crowded with fashionable holiday makers who had come to see and be seen. Ladies dressed in the latest styles leafed through the lending library's large assortment of recently published novels while their partners crowded around the card tables or perused the latest issues of the London newspapers.

Upon their entry, Edward stopped to sign the visitor's book, explaining to Eliza that it was here that members of the ton registered their arrival at Brighton. "Though I doubt I shall receive a visit from Brighton's master of ceremonies as a result of my signing in," he added. "I am most assuredly not considered good ton."

Good ton or not, Eliza could not help but notice that she and her protector were the subject of considerable attention from the ladies and gentlemen filling the room. While they were too well bred to stare, they did seem to find a great deal to interest them in the corner of the room in which she stood with Lord Lightning. Their eyes swept over her, clearly taking in every detail of her looks and her costume.

Over the past few days Eliza had become so used to wearing Violet's revealing garments that she had almost forgot how provocatively she was dressed, but the scrutiny of so many unknown gentlemen—and ladies—brought her attention most painfully to the transparent nature of the sprigged muslin she had chosen to wear this afternoon. Feeling half-naked, she turned away from Edward and made her way toward the corner where the new books were on display. There she could hide her embarrassment while pretending to examine a volume or two.

She had barely begun to browse the beautifully bound books when a young lady a few steps away from her, who was dressed in a simple but elegant white batiste walking dress trimmed in yellow ribbons, reached for a volume and exclaimed to her friend, "Why Amanda, here is Miss Austen's latest effort. I have looked everywhere for it!"

Without thinking, Eliza exclaimed, "Don't say Miss Austen has published another novel. She is my favorite author!"

Upon finding herself so addressed, the lady she had spoken to drew back with an expression of shock. Of course! No properly brought-up young lady of the ton would exchange words with a woman who was clearly a member of the demi-monde. As the lady turned away after administering the cut direct, Eliza observed Edward's face darken and hoped fervently that he wouldn't take offense at the lady's behavior. A woman filling the role of harlot could expect no other treatment from respectable women. But he merely called out to Eliza in an artificially bright voice he clearly intended should carry throughout the reading room. "I would expect a person with your extensive education to enjoy Miss Austen's books. While I personally find her work a bit too constrained in its emotional range, several well-read ladies of my acquaintance consider them the best of their type. Allow me to procure a copy of this latest novel for you."

He motioned her over to meet him at the counter where a scholarly clerk presided, only to discover that the volume the lady had removed from the shelf was the last one to be had.

"I hadn't known that Miss Austen had published anything after *Emma*," Eliza said with some regret. Turning to the clerk, she asked, "What is the title of Miss Austen's new book?"

"*Persuasion*," the clerk replied. "It is bound together with an earlier tale, *Northanger Abbey*. But these volumes are to be her last. A preface in this latest work informs us that the lady has gone on to her final rest."

Eliza felt a burst of sorrow at the news. She had rarely read a book that had entertained her as

much as *Pride and Prejudice* and, though she had
not enjoyed Miss Austen's later works nearly so
well, as none of them had the youthful exuberance
of her favorite, she was sorry to hear there would
be no more of them. Indeed, the news of the au-
thoress's death reminded her how precious—and
how short—life was.

"Perhaps Your Lordship would care to *purchase*
the set," the clerk said unctuously. "Besides our
lending copies, we also have several available for
purchase—in beautiful bindings suitable for the
library of the most discriminating buyer."

To buy a book outright would be a great extravagance. It would cost several guineas—more
money than she and her aunt had spent in a week.
She didn't feel right about asking Edward for such
a costly gift and protested, "That won't be necessary. I'm sure I'll be able to find it some other
time."

But her protector was still playing to the gal-
lery. "I should very much like to buy the book for
you," he said, projecting his voice toward their
audience, but also catching her eyes with his own
and giving her a meaningful glance. "You are sin-
gular among women in that you never ask me for
anything. I should greatly like to give you something that would please you."

Eliza did not protest. She wanted the book too
much. Edward was rich enough the money involved could mean little to him and there was
nothing personal about his gift—nothing that
should make it improper for her to receive it—

since it was clear he had decided to buy it for her
to send a signal to the curious members of the
ton who surrounded them. So she allowed him to
purchase it from the clerk and order, still in that
voice he intended to be heard by everyone in the
room, that the volumes be delivered to his mother's house.

"Hartwood!" a voice called out across the reading room. "They told me I'd find you here, you
devil!" The speaker was a florid man about Edward's age who sported a flamboyant chartreuse
waistcoat. He made his way noisily across the
room and when he reached them threw an overly
familiar arm around Edward's shoulders. Eliza
saw her protector wince.

"It's been a dog's age since I've seen you, Hartwood!" the man exclaimed. "I thought you'd
dropped out of society entirely. Is it true what
they say—that you've given up gaming?"

"I have better things to do with my time than
throw away my money at the tables," Edward replied coolly. His tone made it clear he didn't share
his companion's delight in their encounter. Turning sharply he strode toward the door, leaving
Eliza to trail behind him. But the other man didn't
seem to notice his disdain and followed him outside saying, "Don't try to cozen me that you've
reformed like that brother of yours did on his
deathbed. You're still fit as a fiddle! Anyway I'm
not so downy as to believe that you *could* reform."

The man jabbed an elbow in Edward's side.
"Tell me, is it really true what they say—that you

forced your mother to dine with your mistress in front of a table full of her dearest friends? Foxworthy told me that gem, but I could hardly credit it, even of you."

"My mistress dined with my mother and some friends last night. Yes," Edward replied in a dangerous voice.

"You *are* a devil, then!" his interlocutor exclaimed. "To foist a glorious red-haired vixen on your mother! Foxworthy said she had breasts like ripe peaches. How I should have liked to have seen your mother's face when you introduced the woman to her. Good God, that reminds me—" His florid features suddenly contorted as an idea swept through his mind. "Foxworthy also said he'd had it from his valet that you'd tupped the doxy in full view of the household afterward— stripped off her gown and had her there on the floor." The man's face shone with perspiration and a kind of boyish glee.

"Tamworth, you go too far when you share with me such gems of backstairs gossip," Edward said coldly. "Pray, remember to whom you are talking. I have killed men for giving me less offense."

Eliza braced herself for the inevitable. Would he call the man out then and there, and duel over the honor of a fallen woman? But to her surprise, her protector merely turned on his heel and, after taking her arm and linking it with his own, strode down the street.

It was only when they had walked for several minutes that Edward stopped and turned his handsome face to her, favoring her with an almost humble look she had never seen on it before. "I hope you are pleased with me this time," he said.

"Oh, I am! I so wanted Miss Austen's new book."

"That's not what I refer to. It's that scoundrel Tamworth. I'd have called him out on the spot had you not asked me to keep control of my anger before we set forth. It goes greatly against my nature to let such a slight pass unavenged, but you had just made such a point of telling me it would not please you if I gave in to it."

"So you controlled yourself for me?"

"I did." His eyes held a warmth and luminosity that caused an odd sensation to shoot through her middle. She was not sure she liked it, so strong was it. Yet when his eyes broke contact with hers as he began to speak, she found herself longing to feel it again.

"I told you I wished to give you some pleasure this afternoon and I doubted you'd take pleasure in seeing me give yet another display of temper. I've heard quite enough from you already about how the Moon and Mars—to say nothing of Persephone, Dionysius, and Minerva—have warped my temperament."

She found herself unaccountably moved at this confession. It was as close as a man like himself might come to a real apology. How tempting it was to think it sprang from some deeper emotion than his teasing tone betrayed. Was it possible she was not the only one hiding her true emotions?

It was a dangerous thought. She suppressed it. "Then I am greatly in your debt," she replied, softly, "not only for the generous gift of the book but for your exercise of such self-control."

"Well, don't expect to see much more of it," Edward added testily. "It required immense effort. I should have liked very much to kill Tamworth for the insult he gave you."

He strode a few more paces ahead of her before turning back to Eliza and asking in a plaintive voice, "Are you sure it would disturb you if I killed him?"

"Quite sure."

"Then he shall go free, though he doesn't deserve it."

Again Eliza was touched by Edward's show of consideration. But, though she knew she should let the subject rest, she couldn't keep herself from reminding him that it was precisely to cause this kind of gossip that he had brought her with him to Brighton.

"You're right," Edward agreed, "but I'm beginning to regret I let you persuade me to include you in this scheme."

"You are discovering that you do not like to be gossiped about?"

"On the contrary. I love to be gossiped about. It is my meat and drink. But I do not like to hear an innocent woman described in such insulting terms."

Again she felt a treacherous warmth seep into her heart. His flippant tone could not disguise the real concern he felt for her. And was it just concern, or something more? She felt a burst of annoyance as she caught herself once again wishing for what she must not allow herself to want, and as a result answered him in a tone that came out sharper than she intended. "It's only talk, Edward. It can do me no real harm. I don't know any of these people nor am I ever likely to see them again after I leave Brighton. Besides," she added with the flippancy she would have very much liked to feel, "though I probably should not admit it, I took a certain pleasure in hearing myself described as an alluring vixen."

Edward's eyebrows rose and she allowed herself to savor the look of surprise he had not quite been able to suppress. But it was time to turn his thoughts—and her own—away from the scene that had just concluded. And so, upon noticing that the rain had let up, she took the conversation in another direction.

"If you truly wish to afford me pleasure, Edward, I must tell you I've been longing these past two days to get a closer look at the waves. I've never seen them."

"You've never walked by the ocean?"

"No. This is the first time I've ever visited the seashore."

Edward's face brightened, "Then I shall take you to a place along the shoreline where I used to go in my boyhood when I wished to be alone."

They boarded his carriage and rode some distance along the road that ran along the top of the cliffs until they came to a deserted stretch where Edward told the coachmen to stop. He helped her out of the carriage and conducted her to an outcropping where a narrow path led down the side of the cliff to the beach below.

Standing at the top of the cliff, Eliza found herself looking out over an unbroken expanse of water that stretched to the horizon, its color a mixture of gray and blue under the cloudy sky. Above her, sea birds wheeled in the air, circling and then diving toward the water, their hoarse cries filling the air. She could have easily lost herself in the beauty of the scene, but Edward's slightly amused voice broke into her reverie. "The prospect pleases you?"

"It does! It is so very rare that something one has read about in books lives up to the expectations one has formed of it. But the poets have not lied about the majesty of the ocean."

Edward chuckled softly. "It is impossible to say too much about the beauty of the ocean. But poor jaded Eliza! In what have you been disappointed by the poets?" A look of mischief made his mouth quirk upward. "Surely not their praise of physical love?"

"Oh no," Eliza replied without thinking. "If anything, Ovid underestimates the intensity of pleasure to be found in such experiences—" Then realizing the implications of her words, she stopped, embarrassed. She did not want him to deliver yet another lecture on how she must not fall in love with him.

But no lecture was forthcoming. Instead Edward

only observed in a bemused tone, "So you know your Ovid, too, as well as Aristophanes."

"Of course." She braced herself, expecting that he would tease her about it. Men so often found it ludicrous that a woman should find pleasure in the same studies that delighted them. But Edward merely examined her with a considering look and said, "No wonder you are so quick to stand up for your opinions. It cannot have been easy to pursue such interests in a country village. You must have been considered quite eccentric."

She met his eye and was again surprised at the kindness she saw in his gaze. "I suppose I was," she agreed. "Though I tried not to think about it. Unlike you, I didn't set out on purpose to earn a shocking reputation. Indeed, I should have liked to have been more ordinary—but not at the cost of crippling my mind. My aunt considered the prohibition against formal female education to be the second worst abuse against women of our age."

"And what, in her opinion, was the first?"

"Why, the indissolubility of marriage. She considered the institution of marriage nothing more than a form of slavery and always urged me not to let myself become entrapped by it."

"And how did you feel about that? Did you wish to be rescued from domestic slavery?"

"Well, not at first. I suppose I must have been as foolish as any other girl. When I was seventeen I developed a *tendre* for the curate's oldest son and used to follow him about after church on Sunday. But when I got older, I realized that Aunt Celestina was wise to discourage me from thinking about marriage. I had no dowry and little else to attract a husband. Had I set my hopes in that direction I must certainly have been disappointed."

"Was there no one in your circle who valued your intelligence and wit enough to take you without a fortune?"

"I had no wish to find such a man. I saw little in the marriages of my friends to make me disagree with my aunt's belief that marriage was a trap for women."

"I might argue with you," Hartwood said dryly, "except that you have just echoed my own beliefs about marriage exactly. But I shall not encourage your radicalism any further. I have already corrupted you enough. Let us descend the cliff path and complete your introduction to the sea."

Edward led Eliza down the narrow cliff path, warning her to take care at the steeper points. They had only gone a little way down the path when she accidentally slid several feet and he realized that her delicate silk slippers, designed for ladylike inactivity rather than hard use, posed a serious peril to her.

He reached out to take her hand and held it tightly as they made their way down the cliff. Once again he was surprised by the pleasure he took in the feel of her small, smooth hand clasped in his own. He discovered, too, an unaccustomed pleasure in lending her his physical strength. There was something about Eliza's indomitability that made it that much sweeter to take on the role of protector. The simpering misses of his acquaintance who bragged of their delicacy and fainted at the slightest provocation had never inspired in him the slightest desire to shelter them from harm the way Eliza did now. Perhaps, he mused to himself, it was because he knew if he had left her to make the climb alone, even in those treacherous slippers Eliza would make her way down the cliff undaunted and if she hurt herself, she would show the world no trace of her pain—no more than he would, himself.

Their path led them to a sheltered cove, hidden from the rest of the beach by a projection of the cliff that loomed above them. "May we go near the water?" Eliza asked.

"We can wade here. No one can see us because the cliff hides us." At his reply, her face lit up with happiness like a child offered an unexpected treat, making her so beautiful, he could hardly bear to look at her.

As Eliza bent over to remove her slippers and stripped off Violet's ornate stockings, the sight of her trim calves and ankles stirred him more than made sense. He had already been nearly naked with her in bed that first night, yet the passion he had felt then was so different from the feeling that rose within him now as he caught sight of her five small toes wiggling delightedly against the shingle. He felt a sense of lightness, a happiness, he had never before experienced—never even thought he could experience. But at the sight of

Eliza's face, so filled with anticipation, he snapped out of his reverie. He stripped off his own stockings so he could lead her closer to the water, glad he had dressed in breeches rather than trousers. Then he took her hand and waded resolutely into the icy water, hoping it would cool the heat that was overpowering him.

At the first touch of the frigid water, he felt Eliza's grip tighten and saw how the cold made her nipples thrust up through the thin cloth of her dress. He noticed, too, how her eyes, reflecting back the color of the water, had turned the most astonishing color of green and how the chill had given the skin on her shoulders a rosy glow beneath her enchanting cape of freckles.

Undaunted by the cold, she strode out into the water until it was nearly up to her knees. She reached down to lift a handful to her mouth to taste it. Then, making a face, she spit it out. Just then a sudden swell higher than the rest rolled toward them, and Eliza let out a squeal as she took the brunt of the wave, and the salty water drenched her to the waist.

"I should have warned you," he apologized. "The waves are unpredictable. I'm sorry your gown's been ruined."

"My gown will dry. It's worth the sacrifice of ever so many gowns to experience so intense a sensation."

He had thought it only Violet's gowns that had transformed Eliza from the drab little creature he had found in the theater dressing room into the entrancing woman he couldn't get out of his mind. But now, seeing her standing on the shore, with Violet's brazen dress quite spoiled by the waves, he realized it was not the gown that had given her such appeal.

He could not tear his eyes away from her. She might not be what society called beautiful, but he wanted her more than he had ever wanted a woman. He wanted to run his hands along the rounded buttocks revealed by the damp thin cotton that clung to them like a second skin. He wanted to cup her perfect breasts in his hand and nuzzle against them. He wanted to explore the fiery nether curls whose shadow he saw through the now-transparent fabric. He wanted to—but he made himself stop. What had come over him? He had gone far longer without a woman in the past without descending to such mawkishness.

As she walked back out of the water, Eliza reached down, picked up a long strand of brilliantly colored seaweed, and draped it around her neck.

"A mermaid's necklace," she explained. "Perhaps it has magical powers."

Perhaps it did. For surely she must have enchanted him, as mermaids do the mortal men who come within their sway, for him to feel so besotted with her. There was no other explanation for the way he found himself here fighting an almost irresistible desire to enfold her in his arms and truly make her his.

As she wrung out her ruined skirt, the seaweed

still wrapped around her neck, he was struck by the contrast of her enthusiasm now with the cool disinterest she had shown the night before when he had put around her neck a fortune in gold and jewels.

"You will catch a chill like that," he chided gently, fighting off the urge to warm her by taking her into his arms.

"I'm fine. The sun has come out and it's getting warmer. And anyway, I am used to withstanding chill. My aunt was not a believer in coddling children."

"No one has ever coddled you, have they?" he asked, softly, hoping she could not tell how hard he was fighting off the urge to become the first.

His question made Eliza uncomfortable. The delight she had taken in sporting in the waves—and his unexpected kindness—had caused her to drop her guard. But she must not admit to having needs it would be dangerous to let him fill. "My mother coddled me," she said. "But she died when I was only eight." She paused as she struggled to find something else, safe to say, to dampen the emotion his innocent question had provoked in her. But his words had touched her too deeply. She was not sure she wanted him to understand her so well, so effortlessly. So found herself gabbling. "How often I wish I could speak with my mother now, if only for an hour. There's so much I'd like to ask her, so much I'd want to hear about her life from her own lips."

Edward's dark eyes softened under their pale brows, which glinted briefly as a streak of sun broke through the clouds. "Your words point out to me my selfishness, without your having to utter a single word of reproach."

"What selfishness?"

"The way I've been continually complaining about my mother, who is most definitely alive, when you have long felt the painful absence of your own."

She hastened to reassure him. "That wasn't selfishness on your part. You have every reason to feel the pain of your situation. Though I lost her early, my mother loved me. I can still remember her hugs and kindness. She bought me a beautiful doll once when there was barely enough money in the house to keep us fed. She taught me how to love."

"Which my mother most certainly did not teach me. But you might well reproach me for being a spoiled, petulant, complaining boy."

"No. It isn't petulance on your part that makes you feel so much anger toward your mother," she said, hoping to drive the look of self-reproach from his eyes. "Her hatred of you goes beyond anything I've ever seen. I can well believe she isn't your true mother. It is hard to understand how a mother could feel so much rage toward her own child."

His face lit up with an expression of hope. "Then have you changed your mind? Have you found something in your horoscopes to suggest she's not my real mother?"

She sensed how much the question meant to him and answered him carefully. "I don't know. I spent much time considering it and looking at your chart, but all I can come up with is that there is something unusual there, though I cannot tell what it is."

"Then my suspicion must be true. She must not be my mother."

She was forced to correct him. "A horoscope cannot answer such a question beyond doubt. I wish it could, for it would be such a relief to you to know the truth. But given how important the question is, I don't understand why you haven't simply confronted Mrs. Atwater and demanded to know the truth. It must be torment not to know."

"Not as much torment as what I should feel if my suspicion proved false. It is bad enough to be Black Neville's son and James's brother. To know for a certainty that I am my mother's son—I don't know if I could bear it."

Again his face bore that naked look that was so at odds with his pose of cool unconcern. Eliza turned away and busied herself for a moment with wringing out her damp skirt, fighting the urge to respond to the pain she felt emanating from him with an answering emotion of her own. Whatever it was he wanted from her, it wasn't that. It was her self-control that made him feel safe revealing himself to her. To let her own feelings peep out might damage the fragile bond that had begun to form between them. Better to maintain the façade of wry amusement he expected of her.

She paused, trying to find a way to respond to his admission that would not imperil her own fragile control, then finally spoke. "I can understand why you might not wish to know for certain that Lady Hartwood really is your mother. She shocked me this morning with the intensity of her disgust for you and the degree to which she seems to have confused you with your brother."

"How so?"

"She accused you of being a murderer, of going out dancing the very night you caused a woman's death, when she, of all people, must know it was James who caused that poor girl to die. I cannot understand how a mother could say such a terrible thing about her own son, knowing it wasn't true."

She had not even finished speaking when a startling transformation came over Edward's face. His warm brown eyes, which had glowed with kindness a moment before, hardened. His mouth tightened. She cursed her thoughtlessness in turning the conversation, which had been going so smoothly, onto such a painful topic. But it was too late. His eyes shuttered, Edward demanded, "What exactly did she say?"

"She warned me away from you, saying you were dangerous and that you had driven a poor deluded creature to her death."

"And did you fly to my defense and quote the

authority of the Dog Star and the Pleiades to her?"

"No. There was no need to."

"Thank God for that," Edward said with bitter relief. "For had you done so, you would only have added to the contempt she feels for me."

"What do you mean?" she asked, frightened by the look of anguish that had taken over his face.

"She was not referring to the woman James ruined," Edward said, his voice as dull as lead. "I am guilty of what she accused me of."

"Of driving a woman to her death?"

"Of driving a woman to her death and going dancing when the news of her death was brought to me."

"Oh no, Edward!" She gasped. He could not mean what he'd just said. But if he did—the kinder emotions she had been struggling against feeling the moment before were nothing compared to the crushing fear that gripped her now.

"Your faith in me was misplaced." He spoke in the same deadened voice. "She told you nothing but the truth."

She felt almost physically sick. It could not be true. She could not have felt such attraction to him if it were.

As if responding to her unvoiced thoughts, his tormented face grew harsh. "Don't waste your breath taxing me again with deceiving you," he commanded. "I told you many times I was an evil man. It was you who wouldn't believe me."

The sun came out from behind a cloud. In the stiff breeze from the sea the curling tendrils of his golden hair flared out around his head, glowing like the flames of hell.

Could it be so? Could she have been so self-deluded?

Fear wanted to answer yes, the fear that had controlled her throughout her life until this tormented man had shared some of his strength with her. Weakness chimed in, too, murmuring she'd fallen prey to a delusion just as Lady Hartwood had gloated that she had. But even as fear and weakness contended for her heart, wild courage rose up to meet them—the courage that had been growing within her with each passing hour she had spent in Edward's presence—and protested it *wasn't* true. Lady Hartwood could not be so right and she so wrong.

Fighting the darkness closing in on her, Eliza shouted into the freshening wind, "Edward, I have been with you too long to suppose that you are that evil. You aren't a wicked man. I won't believe it."

He spun around on his heel to face her. "You must believe it," he said, his voice desperate. "I caused a woman to die, just like my brother."

"But surely it was an accident."

"It was no accident. I tell you, Eliza. The woman died and I wanted her to die. I'm not the man you dream of. I am a cold, cruel man who cannot love, and my touch is deadly. You made me wish it weren't true. You made me want to be the man you imagined me to be. But I am not."

He shook the sand from his feet and strode

away from her back toward the path. For a terrifying moment, Eliza wondered if he was going to
abandon her here on the beach. But as he neared
the cliff, he stopped and waited for her.

"At least I haven't ruined you," he said in
a tone of detached satisfaction, his voice once
again under control. He picked up his shoes and
busied himself with putting them on. "Fetch your
things," he said, but the pain Eliza still saw in his
eyes warred with the nonchalance he was trying
to project. She struggled to hold on to the objectivity that was all that could save both of them now.

"You must tell me what happened," she insisted.

"I cannot. I have vowed never to defend myself
for what I've done. You need know only that I am
not worthy of your faith in me."

He smacked his shoe sharply against his hand
to dislodge a small pebble, refusing to meet her
eye. "This morning I gave in to my own weakness
and used my knowledge of how to manipulate
women to trick you into staying with me. But you
had the right of it when you told me you should
go. Thank God you reminded me of what I really
am, before my weakness took complete control.
You are not safe with me. My mother told the
truth. I am dangerous. You must go away quickly
before I harm you further. I will leave the money
I promised you with my man. You may apply to
him for it when it pleases you."

Eliza stood shivering in the cold wind, her fear
contending with another emotion even more difficult to endure, for even as he condemned himself,

she had heard it in his voice: He cared for her. And as her heart opened to the wonder of that knowledge she felt a strange mixture of joy and impending doom. How could she leave him now? She had fought so hard against loving him when she had feared he could not care. How could she leave him now when the agony in his voice told her it was his concern for her that made him condemn himself so harshly? It was not self-delusion to believe that he cared for her—cared so much that he was fighting to overcome the darkness within himself to save her. But that knowledge paralyzed her. What if his self-condemnation was true?

She should flee. She should escape him while he gave her the chance, but she could not. The thought that she meant that much to him gave her the strength to make one last desperate plea.

"You said you needed my friendship, Edward. If that was a trick you played on me, you have tricked yourself, too. For I will behave as a friend must behave. I will go nowhere 'til you tell me the truth about the crime you accuse yourself of. I must judge for myself if you are what you say you are. You owe me that much. You must tell me what really happened."

The dark eyes glowed from beneath the pale gold thatch framing his face. "Go ask my mother for the details. She'll be glad to tell you."

"Your mother hates you. I wish to hear the story from you and from you alone. And I will wait until you tell it to me."

"You'll have a long wait ahead of you, for I've sworn not to tell it."

"Then you must prepare to add oath breaking to the long list of your sins. For I will not leave until I hear the story from your own lips."

He shrugged. His face had become a mask of torment that for once was not an actor's mask. "How like a woman," he said bitterly, "to refuse to leave me 'til you've destroyed my happy memories of our time together and replaced them with one final vision of your face twisted in disgust, after you finally see that, just as I told you, I am an evil man."

Then without another word he took her hand and led her back toward the path.

Chapter 13

He abandoned her when they reached the house, fleeing into his room and calling his man to him there. Eliza made her way alone to her attic room and once again reached into her flowered satchel for Lord Lightning's well-worn chart.

Could it really be true? The certainty that had gripped her by the sea had fled. Could her Edward have really driven a woman to her death and danced when he heard the news? Could he have been that heartless? Had her Sagittarian optimism betrayed her into seeing goodness in him where there was none? The day was taking on the feel of a nightmare. The chart she held in her hand seemed to change as she looked at it, the familiar signs revealing sinister meanings she had never seen there before.

The Moon conjunct his Mars, which she had interpreted as anger against his mother, had other meanings, too. Was it not placed in the House of Death? She had interpreted that to mean that he had a strong sexual nature, for that House was also the place of Sexual Congress. But it also could point to murder. She shivered. Had she simply seen what she wanted to see, seduced by Edward Neville's sensual beauty?

And his Saturn. She had given it little weight in her earlier readings, taking it to mean he'd had a difficult childhood; but now it seemed to glow from the paper with a stark malevolent glare. It was placed in the House that described both childhood and love affairs. So it could also be read as permanent hard-heartedness. As coldness to lovers. And because it opposed his fiery Leo Sun, missing only by a few degrees the damaging square to his Moon and Mars, she had interpreted it to mean that his mother's anger had blocked his ability to express a fundamentally loving nature. But there were other more troubling interpretations of the aspect. It might mean, as he had claimed all along, that he really could not love.

But why would she only see this now?

Had she first read his chart after meeting him, she would have blamed her lack of objectivity on her own involvement with him. But he had been a complete stranger when she had first read his horoscope at Violet's behest. There had been no reason for her to delude herself then when she had seen his need to love.

Or had there been? Overwhelmed by a sense of

foreboding, she heard her inner voice speak the truth she had been hiding from all along. There was a reason why she was looking at *his* chart, not her own. A reason she had been hiding from herself.

She forced herself to extract her own nativity from the satchel. The well-worn parchment was all too familiar. How often had she and her aunt pored over it. How often had her aunt warned her of what now stood out so painfully as she confronted it.

Lord Lightning was not the only one under the sway of unruly Uranus. It conjoined her natal Jupiter, the planet of excess. It stood in the House of Lovers, too, the place where that excess would play itself out in her life. And if that were not bad enough, both Jupiter and Uranus trined her natal Sun—that Sun which was placed in the alarming House of Sexual Relations. How could she view with objectivity a man who excited all that she found most fearful in herself?

"The universe is a mysterious place," Aunt Celestina used to tell her, "and we are not meant to know all."

But she must know all, and swiftly. Was she falling in love with a cold-blooded destroyer? Had her aunt been right that Eliza's impetuous nature would lead her into ruin far worse than that which had befallen her poor mother?

Perhaps she had.

Lord Lightning was everything her Aunt Celestina had feared she might become. Had that been what made him irresistible? Hedged about as she had been by so much constraint, she had been bewitched by the freedom he had appropriated to himself. But under the sway of that enchantment had she overlooked the obvious? That a man who did not feel himself bound by the trivial rules that governed society might easily go further and ignore the serious ones—and cause a woman's death.

The suspicion tortured her. And yet, even as she felt the cold settling around her heart, a voice rose within her and cried out she was being unjust. The man for whom she felt such affection was not just Lord Lightning. He was Edward Neville, too, the sad boy trapped behind the burning eyes that begged her not to leave. And it was not just his willingness to transgress the laws of society that drew her to him. There was much more to him than that.

She must find out the whole truth before she abandoned him forever. Too much was at stake to do anything else. If she was wrong and he was guilty of the crime with which he charged himself, she would accept the judgment of the stars and leave him to live out his life heartless and alone. But only when she was certain. 'Til then, she must find courage and not let her own fears doom the two of them.

She threw herself on the bed, still dressed in the clinging damp clothes she had worn into the sea, but too exhausted to do anything about it. As the evening drew on, knowing she must sleep, she did what she could to calm herself. Breathing deeply, she imagined herself rocked by the ocean's surge, bathed in the light of the cold, implacable stars. But when she finally fell into a troubled sleep her dreams were fitful and disturbing. At long last the light of dawn glimmered at the attic room's small window. She stripped off the salt-stiffened gown and did her best to clean herself off before dressing herself again in one of Violet's silky garments. Though its touch should have repelled her now, oddly, it didn't. It lent her courage.

She would need it.

When she went downstairs an hour later, she discovered that Edward had already left and was not expected back until evening. His man offered her the full purse his master had directed him to give her and offered to attend her to the public coach that departed in an hour for London.

She refused the purse, waved off his offer of assistance, and left him to watch, openmouthed, as she strode out of the house. She was afraid to stay a moment longer and risk hearing any words his master might have commanded him to speak, words that might shake her from her determination to remain. She passed the day walking on the shingle alone, her thoughts in turmoil.

When she returned, near suppertime, she found a gentleman dressed in clerical garb waiting in the vestibule, seated on a side chair. His foot tapped uneasily on the flowered carpet. When he saw her enter, he began to rise and bow politely toward her, but as she came closer, his eyes narrowed as they took in her clinging gown with its low cut front and he sank back onto the bench with a small shudder, as if horrified by how close he had come to treating her with politeness. She hurried past him, too perturbed already to wish to dwell on what he must think of her, but he called out, "Stay, woman. I must have a word with you," and reached out one hand to arrest her further progress. When she stopped, he cleared his throat, blinked his eyes twice and kept them shut for a moment as if he was searching inside their lids for the text of the sermon he was about to preach. Then he addressed her.

"Young woman, do not meddle in the affairs of your betters! You have presumed on Lady Hartwood's goodness. You have gone too far. Yet even now, so great is her Christian charity that she has found it in her heart to give you one last chance. She has asked me to find a place for you, a retreat where in a humble manner appropriate to your station, you might repent of your sins and toil for God's forgiveness. Her kindness to you is inestimable, but her patience is limited. If you would escape the punishment you so richly deserve, I urge you take up her offer, now."

"I have no desire to change my situation."

"Your reply is just as I told her it would be," he said with complacency. "I will no longer lower myself by having further commerce with you. You are a shameless hussy and she will be well rid of you."

Just then Eliza heard footsteps coming toward them down the hallway. The clergyman stood up just as a servant appeared at the doorway and beckoned him into the parlor where Lady Hartwood awaited him. Eliza withdrew into the library, her mood even more somber than when she had arisen. She reminded herself that Edward had promised that no harm could come to her, but the resentful tone of the clergyman's admonition had chilled her. For the first time in a very long time, she found herself wishing she were back in Aunt Celestina's parlor.

She retreated to her own small room in the attic, alone with her uneasy thoughts, until necessity forced her to venture out. She made her way downstairs, where she almost stumbled into Lady Hartwood who was making her way through the foyer, her interview with the clergyman over. Catching sight of Eliza, she smiled a smile that had no good humor in it. Eliza thought of making a dash for the doorway, but it was too late. There was no way to avoid her.

"I see that my son has begun to tire of you already," Lady Hartwood observed with obvious relish. "It is all around the household that he left you here alone last night and made his way to a gambling club that is famed for its accommodating women."

Eliza's face must have shown some of the distress that Lady Hartwood's revelation caused her.

"You have served your purpose," Lady Hartwood continued inexorably. "He has used you to infuriate me and now he will cast you aside. You were a fool to have fallen in love with his handsome face despite my warning. Though it doesn't surprise me. They say there are women who write love letters to the prisoners awaiting execution at Newgate."

Her tormentor's argument, sounding so much like the voice of her own fears, brought out the fight in her. "If your son really was a murderer, would he not be awaiting execution at Newgate, too? Even a nobleman cannot kill and walk free. I cannot believe that your son truly killed anyone, though you seem dearly to wish to believe that he did."

"You *are* in love with him," Lady Hartwood said with satisfaction. "Most foolish of you."

"I cannot believe him guilty of what you accuse him of."

"But he is guilty."

"There must be some explanation. Did the woman you refer to die in childbed?" If he, like his brother, had impregnated some woman only to have her die in childbed, it would be dreadful, but it was not the same as murder.

"You'd like that to be the explanation wouldn't you?" Lady Hartwood snarled. "But it will not serve. I owe you no explanation. You are an unrepentant harlot and deserve the fate that awaits you."

"But I must know what it is that makes you hate

your son so much," Eliza cried out in frustration. "What has he done to put him beyond all hope of forgiveness?"

"Why should you care? You'd be as much in love with him whatever his crimes might be."

"I am *not* in love with him. But I must know what kind of man he is, for my own peace of mind."

"You'll find out soon enough," Lady Hartwood said grimly. "Why not ask him how he enjoyed his visit last night to the brothel."

Eliza looked up and saw a familiar burst of pale golden hair at the doorway, as Edward strode angrily into the foyer. His icy gaze swept from one woman to the other.

"My visit to the brothel was quite pleasant, Mother, thank you. Have you any other questions you would address to me?"

"None! None at all," his mother snapped. Then she slowly turned and made her way out of the foyer, leaning on her ebony cane. As her halting steps vanished down the hallway, Eliza found herself alone with Edward.

He stood by the newel post at the foot of the stairs, observing her with the distant, ironic look she had learned was his defense against showing pain. "Why are you still here?" he demanded. "I left more than enough money for you with my man."

"I told you I wouldn't leave until you tell me the truth about the crime you accuse yourself of."

"Why should it matter? Why isn't it enough that you know I'm guilty of such a crime?"

"Because I must understand you. I cannot

leave with so much unanswered. I may have been wrong about what I saw in your horoscope. I'm willing to accept that. But I must know where I erred, so I may learn from my mistake and not make another like it again."

"So you would force me to divulge my secrets so you might become a wiser astrologer?"

"So that I might become a wiser woman," she replied softly. "If you are truly what you say you are, and if I have made myself blind to it, I *am* in danger, even as your mother claims. I must learn to see the truth, no matter how ugly."

He hunched his broad shoulders as if her words had struck him. "Even now you are the earnest philosopher. Any other woman would be drenching me with tears."

"Why should I shed tears?"

"Why indeed." His voice was controlled, ironic. "You assured my mother that you do not love me, and I know you abhor dishonesty—at least in me. So it must be true. But I told my mother the truth, you know. I *did* visit a brothel last night after I left you."

"What affair of mine is it if you did?"

"Does it not make you jealous?" A look hard to interpret played across his features.

Eliza bit her lip, unwilling to let him know how closely his barb had hit home. She twisted her left hand in the fabric of her skirt, waiting for the pang his words had caused her to die down. "I have no claim upon your fidelity," she said at length. "You are Lord Lightning, famed for your inconstancy.

It is only to be expected that you would tire of a pretend mistress and seek out a real one instead."

Edward reached out and took her hand in his, stroking her fingers softly. "Ah, but you forget, Lord Lightning never does the expected. So your assumption was wrong." He dropped her hand. "Though I did indeed go to the brothel, it was not to ease myself on some poor wretch, but to finish my conversation with Tamworth. It was the one place I could be sure of encountering him." He drew forth his jeweled snuffbox and made a show of busying himself with a pinch of snuff while observing her reaction from the corner of his eye.

Eliza hoped her relief was invisible. "Why did you seek out Tamworth?"

"I wished him to know that though I had spared his miserable life, my patience would be exhausted were he ever to forget himself and speak of you again in such an insulting way."

"And you did that, even though you believed I would be gone this morning?"

"That made it all the more important. Now that you have the reputation of having been my plaything, you would be in the greatest of danger should it become known you were now on your own." He brought his fingers up to his face as if to inhale the snuff and then stopped. "But you have *not* left me," he observed, with a strange look.

"No. I told you I would not leave until I heard the whole of your story."

He blew the snuff from his hand and then slowly put away the glittering snuffbox. "I cannot buy you off," he said in a wondering tone. "I cannot frighten you. I cannot even make you jealous. I suspect you would just stand there and put up with *any* enormity I might serve you with, and just keep staring at me like a Sphinx until you got what you wanted from me."

She nodded, unable to speak.

He sighed. "I have not the energy, then, to outlast you. I suppose I must give you what you want, else you will bribe my mother or interrogate the servants until you find out what you are determined to learn."

She would have called the look on his face amusement, except that the roughness in his voice suggested that he was barely suppressing a much stronger emotion.

He held out his hand to her. "Come," he said. "If you insist on knowing the worst about me, we will walk out along the shore where we can talk in peace, and I will tell you all." He drew in a long breath. "Perhaps then you will leave me alone and I can go back to being the man I used to be."

"If that is truly what you wish, Your Lordship."

He did not correct her use of the distancing honorific, though she had seen him wince when she used it. For a moment their eyes locked, and again she saw the pain that lay hidden under the cool ironic façade.

"I no longer know what I wish," Edward said. "You may take credit for making that much of a change in me."

* * *

They drove in his carriage down the cliff road to the place he had shown her the day before. He gave orders for the coachman to wait for them there. Then he led her down the steep path to the beach.

They walked along the hard-packed shingle in silence. Again the wind was blowing fitfully. His pace was brisk, almost as if he were trying to outpace a pursuer, and Eliza could barely keep up with him. At last, when they had neared the headland, he stopped.

He stared out at the waves for a moment, marshaling his thoughts, then in a calm, measured tone he began to speak.

"I was seventeen when my mother forced me to take the blame for the ruin of the girl who died while attempting to bear James's bastard child," he began. "I told you that. What I didn't tell you was that shortly before that event, I had contracted an informal engagement with the daughter of a neighbor, Estella Hartington.

"Estella was my age and we had grown up together. She was very beautiful and I fancied myself in love with her. Her family was not wealthy and they were not enthusiastic about her attachment to me, as I was only a younger son. But I promised her I would earn enough on my own to make our marriage possible. I even gave her a ring as token of my commitment. We planned to marry when I had attained my majority.

"But when the word of my shame got out, Estella ended our engagement by post, sending me back my ring and refusing to communicate any further with me. I attempted to see her again, to explain the true situation to her. But my efforts were futile. Though she had claimed to love me enough to be my bride, her feelings for me could not withstand the gossip that surrounded the death of James's victim. A few weeks later, I learned she had engaged herself to marry a wealthy viscount—a man far older than herself.

"I was a young man then, and my heart was still tender. I won't bore you with a description of my feelings when Estella cast me off. Suffice it to say that it isn't only women who feel pain at a rejection." He dug into the hard pebbly sand with one booted toe and then kicked the ground savagely.

"I didn't suffer long. I threw myself into the pleasures of the world, as you well know, and then, to get away from my family, I bought a pair of colors and went off with my regiment to fight the French.

"I did not see Estella again until I returned on leave to London some years later. By then some well-chosen investments had made me a wealthy man. As could have been predicted, Estella's marriage had not been a happy one. Her husband had lost interest in her after their first few months together. They had little in common, and she had the further misfortune of discovering she couldn't bear him an heir.

"When she saw me again, after all those years, she professed to have realized the mistake she had made in casting me off and she offered herself to me as a mistress."

Edward stopped. He took a few deep breaths, as if steeling himself to continue. Only then did he resume his story.

"I took her up on her offer. You will not, I pray, make any sentimental excuse for my behavior. I made her my mistress not because I still cherished some fondness for her, for I did not. Far from it. I did so only because for years I had lived with one hope—that someday I could cause Estella as much pain as she had caused me when she had cast me off without giving me the chance to defend myself."

He paused. Eliza could feel him watching to see how she responded to his confession. She schooled her features to betray nothing, afraid that if he saw any reaction there, he would explode into anger, or, worse, laugh that ironic laugh of his and walk away.

He inhaled a deep breath of the sea air, as if inhaling strength with it. Then he plunged back into his story.

"Though I felt nothing for her but contempt, I hid it from her and used what I had learned about women to bind Estella to me. I showered her with gifts. I praised her beauty. I told her I needed her. I gave her a taste of sensual pleasures that she had not known were possible. Then, when I knew she was well and truly mine, I took my revenge upon her.

"One day, when she had been expecting to

depart with me for a weekend in the country, I wrote her that our connection must end. I told her I found it impossible to love her in her new role as a fashionable adulteress. I told her she disgusted me. I said other things, unrepeatable, private things chosen because I knew they would hurt her where she was most vulnerable. I was excessively cruel."

He rounded on his heel, until he was again facing Eliza. "I am *good* at being cruel," he said with savage satisfaction. "Don't fool yourself that I'm not."

Eliza bowed her head so that her expression might give him no hint of the compassion she felt rising within her. Despite the way he condemned himself, a heartless man would have told this story very differently.

As he continued, his voice grew more rough and uneven. "My rejection had its expected consequence. Estella was made to feel what she had lost. But I wasn't prepared for what happened next. She began to follow me about, to haunt me wherever I went, begging me to give her another chance. I refused to respond to any of her communications, but that only drove her to more excess. She stood outside my window at night, shouting for me to come down. She followed me into my club, begging for one more interview. Disgusted with the shame she had brought upon his ancient name, her husband cast her out, and there were rumors he was preparing to sue her for divorce.

"By then I had long since tired of my revenge.

Indeed, I wished I had never undertaken it. I could go nowhere without her following me. She behaved like a madwoman. When she cornered me in public she made wild scenes filled with violent accusations. I was sick of the whole affair but there was nothing I could do to end it.

"Finally, one day, a note was brought to me by one of her servants who urged me with great vehemence to read it. When I refused, he told me that Estella had threatened to kill herself if I did not. I threw it in my desk, unopened, and told him to tell her to kill herself and be damned for it."

The pale hair on his forehead was slicked down now by sweat and tendrils of it bracketed his tormented eyes. He was breathing fast, as if outrunning a pursuer. Only after a visible struggle did he resume.

"The next morning, her body was fished out of the Thames. She had thrown herself from Tower Bridge, after loading up her pockets with stones to make herself sink. When the news was brought to me of what she'd done, I opened the note she had sent me, and saw that in it she had begged me to meet with her at a given hour at that selfsame bridge.

"In her note she told me she repented of how cruelly she had treated me when we were eighteen. She said she wanted only one last chance to explain herself, and that should I give it to her, she would leave me alone forever. She said she could not live with the knowledge of how her earlier treatment had twisted my nature into cruelty.

Clearly she expected me to read the note and prevent her from destroying herself. But of course, I didn't read the note until she was dead."

Edward stopped in his painful recitation and looked Eliza fully in the face. "You are thinking I must have been consumed with regret that I had not read the note. You are thinking it was a tragic mistake that I was not able to go to the bridge that night and allow her to make her confession to me. You are relieved to hear that if I abetted her murder, it was only through an act of omission. You are already making excuses for me, relieved that I had no part in Estella's murder, that I did not brandish an axe or give her a drink of poison. But I tell you, Eliza, you are wrong."

His voice cracked. "My only reaction to hearing of her death was relief. Never again would she trouble me with her importunities. I *rejoiced* that I had not opened her note. I was *glad* she had died. And it was at that moment, when I felt that burst of utterly selfish relief that I knew myself to be no different from my father or my brother. I *had* killed Estella with my selfishness, just as thoroughly as if I had forced her to drink some poison, and I was glad of it. It was with a light heart indeed, or perhaps I should say completely without a heart, that, just as my mother told you, I celebrated her death by attending a ball that very night."

He stopped and stood silent before her, his face rigid with self-control, daring her to assure him she could forgive him and ready to leave her forever if she did.

But Eliza said nothing. Her ability to forgive him could mean nothing to him if he could not forgive himself. That he could feel such guilt told her that he was not heartless. But the pain in his eyes told her he would not be able to hear any words that might absolve him until they came from his own heart. So she simply stayed silent, regarding him with a calm, open look, as his damning words, as hateful as anything his mother could have said to him, flowed through her, unmolested, like the sound of the waves that broke upon the shore.

His eyes continued to bore into her, daring her to protest his innocence, still waiting to discharge on her the fury such a protestation would unleash. But as the silence stretched out between them in the gathering dusk, a new look began to replace the bleakness in his eyes.

The words of condemnation he had lived with, unspoken for so long, had finally been spoken out loud. She had listened to them but no words of hers had tried to push his own words back into the gaping wound they had issued from. She had said nothing that needed to be argued with, nothing that might force him to insist that he was guilty. And now, those damning words, once spoken, were fading away into the evening air. He had told her all, pouring it into the healing womb of her silence, and in that silence the words had begun to lose their power, and she sensed that, for the first time since he had unfolded Estella's note, Edward Neville felt a touch of hope.

"Thank you, Eliza," he said, at last, brushing

away something that glittered at the corner of one eye. "You are wiser than you know."

With no further word, he began walking slowly down the beach, drawing her along with him. They walked along the hard-packed shingle in silence as the sun set. As its last beams faded, the moon shone forth from behind a bank of towering clouds, illuminating their edges. The water was still, except for the slightest gentle ripple. They walked along the pebbly shore and Edward took her hand and held it gently, his palm firm and warm against her own.

As they stood drenched in that ghostly light, feelings rose within her, but it had become impossible to speak. Edward, too, seemed to be feeling the same way. He lifted her fingers to his lips and kissed them tenderly. Then, as if he had heard something passing between them unsaid, he breathed her name just once and leaned over and brushed her lips with his.

Warmth coursed through Eliza's body as if a current had begun to flow between the two of them. She felt hunger gnaw at her very core as his lips lingered and then pressed more roughly against her own. As if he'd heard her silent need, his lips parted and she felt his tongue dance gently toward hers. She opened herself to him, her whole body tingling as she gave herself up to the intoxication of his kiss. She wrapped her arms around his chest, pulling him closer, thrilling as she felt his hard muscles tense beneath her touch.

He had kissed her this way once before, in

the hallway, when he'd been trying to annoy his mother with his lust, and she had thought then that he had taught her what a kiss could be. But now, the tenderness that flowed through her at the touch of his gentle lips showed her how little she had ever truly known. *This* must be what her aunt had feared for her so desperately, this haunting softness that crept under all her defenses and made her feel the aching pang of love. But it was too late for her aunt's warnings. With the tenderness of his kiss Edward had swept away the last of her resistance. Now that he'd dragged out his painful story and laid it at her feet he was no longer hiding from her. He was not playing a role. His soul was in his lips and as it met hers she throbbed with the need to meld herself with him, to draw him into herself and give him the final healing he so needed. As their kiss deepened, he enfolded her in his arm and pulled her even closer, claiming her for his own. She breathed in the powerful male scent of him, hungry as she had never been hungry before. The urgency in his ragged breath told her she was not the only one whose hunger was more than they could bear.

But that realization brought with it a new terror. There was nothing feigned in the passion with which he was responding to her embrace. He was no longer holding her at a distance. She was no longer protected by the barrier he'd erected around his own heart. The long-buried guilt that had made him live as an outcast had been exposed to the light. His healing had begun. If she gave herself to him now, he would receive her. She would lose herself in him. She would be at his mercy, unsafe, as lost in her love for him as her poor mother had been when she'd given herself to Eliza's father. But even knowing that, she could not break free.

Edward finally broke the connection, releasing her lips and stepping away from her.

"I shouldn't have done that, but I couldn't stop myself."

Eliza said nothing. Her mind was in an uproar. She, too, had not been able to stop herself. Her body was still filled with the tingling craving he had awakened. She wanted to fling herself against him and cling to him as a drowning man might cling to a spar after a shipwreck. She wanted to feel his lips again, to feel his hard length pressed against her body. She wanted to lose herself in the completeness of the union she felt glimmering between them. But she wanted to flee from him, too, far away, where she would not be tormented by his touch. She hoped it was not too late, that she could still live without him, that she could get back to being the way she'd been before he'd made her crave his touch and yearn to fill herself with him, back when she'd needed no one and felt nothing. She yearned to blot out the longing he had awakened in her and knew that she could not.

She loved him. She would always love him. She could not deny it.

To her dismay, she began to weep. The tears coursed down her cheeks, unstoppable, as if they

were the only outlet for the passion that had built
up within her.

"Oh no, Eliza," he said, "I didn't mean to hurt
you."

"It wasn't that," she said when she could speak
again. "I didn't know a kiss could be like that."

"Have you only read about kisses in your books
then, too?"

She nodded.

"It does not go into words well, kissing," he
said, gently stroking her cheek.

Eliza dried her eyes, rubbing them with the
back of her hand. "Was it like that for you, too,
when we kissed, or did it overwhelm me only because I'm so old and have never been kissed with
such tenderness before?"

"It wasn't just you. I have never before felt like
that with anyone. I don't know how I shall keep
from kissing you again."

"But you must keep from doing it," she said
sadly. "It is part of our agreement, is it not?"

"It is. Though I regret it."

He broke from her and strode on ahead of her
down the beach. As he moved away she felt as if
something inside her was being tugged after him.
Some connection had been made that could not
be broken. She wondered if she would still feel it
if he were out of sight. If he were gone. If he were
dead. It was frightening to feel herself so bound to
him. So at his mercy.

She suddenly felt a chill. The breeze had sprung
up and was blowing in to shore from across the

water. It pushed the clouds swiftly across the sky, until they obscured the face of the moon. The sky darkened. Only a diffused dim glow remained of the moonlight. She hurried to catch up with him, suddenly afraid of the dark. His face was turned away from her when she came up beside him, his expression impossible to read. She shivered.

"We must go back. It's going to rain," he said. "The weather changes so quickly by the sea." As he spoke a thick drop spattered against her cheek, and then another.

By the time they reached the carriage they were soaked. The coachman said nothing as they got in but merely flicked his whip at the horses and started them on their journey home.

Edward held her close as they rode back, enfolding her in his arms to protect her from the cold, but even so she could not stop shivering. Though they were safely out of the rain, sheltered in the carriage, drops still spattered down her cheeks, and when she tasted them as they rolled down to her lips the taste was sharp with salt.

Chapter 14

It was quite late when they arrived back at the house. Lady Hartwood had retired and the servants had gone to their beds. Eliza, too, would have gone upstairs had Edward not begged her to rejoin him in the library when she had changed out of her wet clothing. After some hesitation, she had agreed. He was not sure why it seemed so important to him that she spend the rest of the evening with him. He had given her what she had demanded. He'd told her his shameful story. He had given in to the emotion that had risen within him in the aftermath of his confession, but he had controlled himself admirably and somehow avoided disaster.

There was no further reason for her to remain. And there were all too many reasons why, if he knew what was good for him, he would go into

his room, bolt the door, and not come out until he
knew for certain Eliza had returned to London.

He knew himself too well to doubt what would
happen if he didn't. Like any accomplished rake,
he recognized the subtle signs that indicated
a woman had lost her ability to withstand him.
Eliza had given him those signs in their last long,
searing kiss by the shore. It was too much to
expect him to hold back now. Like a dog trained
to the sound of the horn, he would respond. He
would close in on her and finally make her his.
He doubted he could withstand the temptation of
Eliza's pulsing lips and fervent body much longer.
But as unprincipled as he was, he must withstand
it. Rake though he was, he was determined to
adhere to that one principle he had left. The one
that had hitherto kept her safe from him.

But it wouldn't be easy. The scene on the beach
where he had uncovered his shame to her re-
played itself over and over again in his mind. He
kept remembering the warmth in her eyes, how
open and accepting they had been, and the beauty
of her silence. He wondered still at how she had
refused to judge him, how she had just stayed
with him and accepted him for who he was with
all his failings—all! How with her silence she had
shown him, as no words could ever have, what
love might be. That love she had insisted he was
born for.

He twisted in his chair, trying to retreat to that
comfortable place within himself where he didn't
care and everything was a joke. But he could not.

Hope had entered his heart. It whispered that he *could* learn to love and begged him to explore the possibility.

It was wrong! Like Eliza. Dangerously wrong.

He leaped up out of his chair, unwilling to think about it any longer. He would go up to his room. He would bolt the door. He would give instructions that Eliza leave on the morrow and, by God, this time he would make sure they were carried out. He would not give Black Neville's son the chance to seduce and abandon her.

But before he could put any of his plans in train, his valet interrupted him to deliver the parcel containing the volumes he had bought for Eliza at the lending library and hand him some letters that had come by the late post. One letter in particular caught his attention with its unfamiliar seal.

It was written on a cheap paper that contrasted strongly with the imprint of the heraldic crest with which it was sealed. The handwriting was that of an educated man, but the letter was written as if in haste, and the hand was difficult to read. Even when he managed to make it out, the words were disjointed and confused. He had to read the letter through twice before he felt he truly understood it.

When he did, he was aghast.

The letter was from Eliza's father. He sent his compliments and explained that he had only recently discovered from Lord Hartwood's man of business the identity of his benefactor and the further circumstance that that benefactor had taken his daughter, Eliza, under his protection.

Edward read these words with irritation. What could his man of business have been thinking of to let Eliza's father know she had gone off with him? He would have thought the man had more sense.

He read on, expecting unpleasantness. But the fear that he was about to find himself involved in an affair of honor with an enraged father gave way to astonishment as he read on. Instead of demanding that Lord Hartwood make an honest woman of his daughter, or meet him at dawn with pistols, Eliza's father had taken quite a different tack.

Writing that after learning of His Lordship's fondness for his daughter and bearing in mind that such a girl, had her father's luck not turned so abominably bad, might have had considerably brighter prospects, but of course, understanding fully, as he did, that such things happened, as unfortunate as they might appear to those who looked only at surface considerations, which a life of philosophy had taught him to ignore, Eliza's father finally rambled to the point: Might His Lordship be prevailed upon to make himself a small loan, a trifle of some several hundred pounds to be repaid when his circumstances improved? He had every reason to believe this might occur in the very near future. Meanwhile, he hastened to assure Lord Hartwood, if such a loan were made, His Lordship could rest comfortably in the assurance that Eliza's father would not trouble him again.

Edward sat, stunned. Eliza's father's only concern was to extract some financial profit from his daughter's ruin.

Such things were not unheard of. One could not be a man of the world without knowing that in the degenerate classes men did sometimes sell their daughters when there was no other way to keep body and soul together.

But the letter that he held in front of him, with its heraldic seal and casually scrawled signature, left no possibility that Eliza's father might be such a miserable brute. For at the sight of the seal Edward had realized he knew the man. Everyone knew him. He was a fixture of the gaming hells. Robert Farrell, third son of the Marquess of Evesbury, the man they nicknamed Pythagoras because of his lifelong obsession with working out a mathematical system with which to beat the house.

Quickly he scanned his memory for what else he might know about the man. He remembered something about a runaway marriage and that Farrell had been disinherited. But all else he knew for certain about the man was that his bad luck at the gaming tables was legendary and that no one, no matter how far gone in his cups, would ever lend Pythagoras Farrell a penny.

But if Eliza was Pythagoras Farrell's daughter, she was also the granddaughter of a marquess and a woman whose social rank was equal to his own. She was a gentlewoman, an innocent gentlewoman who had borne her untold sufferings with exactly the kind of quiet, uncomplaining fortitude that embodied what was best about the English aristocracy.

Edward rubbed his forehead in distress. How could he have been so oblivious to the signs she was a woman of his own class? Her accent might be rural, but that was only because she had been raised far from the metropolis. He blessed whatever good angel it was who had taken him under its protection that he had been spared the horror of discovering too late that, like the man he despised above all others—his brother, James—he had ruined a girl of gentle birth.

But his feeling of complacency on that account did not last more than a few moments. Though Eliza retained her maidenhead, his behavior had ruined her as thoroughly as if he had raped her that first night at his town house. Whether or not he had made her his mistress in fact, the polite world *believed* he had, and in that world—in which she deserved to move—the appearance was as important as the fact.

A quiet voice whispered that there was no remedy for what he had done to Eliza except to marry her. The thought stopped him dead. He had never wished to be married. He had seen nothing in the marriages of his peers to convince him that marriage was anything more than a trap every bit as deadly as Eliza's aunt had suggested. But barely had that thought completed when he remembered what he had felt when Eliza had nestled in his embrace in the carriage as they had made their way back from the shore, and for the first time in a long and eccentric life, the unpredictability of his nature shot home and Lord Lightning astonished himself.

He wanted to marry her.

Marriage might be a trap, but he wanted her trapped—in his arms, in his bed, in his heart. The realization that his own twisted sense of honor demanded that he marry her unleashed a ferocious desire to keep her in his life. Though the more rational part of him knew he could not succeed at marriage any more than that he could fly off a cliff by flapping man-made wings, he knew he must make the attempt, even if it killed him.

His train of thought was interrupted as Eliza entered the room. She had changed out of her wet clothes as he had instructed her to do, but rather than donning another gown as he had expected her to do, she had wrapped herself in nothing more than a dressing gown of the thinnest silk. Its peach-like tone brought out the beauty of her auburn hair. Its soft folds emphasized the curve of her breasts. Was she wearing anything underneath it at all? He would have sworn she wasn't. With difficulty he forced himself to ignore the provocation she presented, wondering all the while what she meant by appearing this way. Coming from any other woman the message would have been unmistakable. But this was Eliza, so he knew not what to make of it.

Unsure how to proceed, he reached for the gift he had bought for her earlier, Miss Austen's book.

Considering what he was about to offer her—his hand in marriage—the gift was of trivial importance, and yet, as he handed her the fat parcel containing the four volumes, he could not help but feel anxiety as to how she would receive it. He wanted so much for it to please her.

She took the parcel from him with a smile that seemed to him, oversensitive as he was at this particular moment, a trifle forced.

"You were too kind to purchase so extravagant a gift for me, "she said as she set about unwrapping the brown paper in which it was covered.

He thought he detected a slight hesitation in her voice. Perhaps it was only his guilty imagination that made him think it, but she seemed to be avoiding his eye, too, which was unusual, given how fearlessly she was wont to gaze at him. The absence of her regard made him aware of how accustomed he had become to losing himself in the sea green depths of her open gaze whenever they were together.

Still wishing to avoid conversation, he strolled over to a small desk and picked up a paper knife with a gold and onyx handle and brought it over to her. She would need it to cut the pages of the new book. "This was my father's, so I expect it's mine now," he said. "You may consider it, too, a gift."

Again she thanked him. Again he had the feeling she was holding herself apart from him. Had he frightened her that much with their seaside embrace? But if so, why had she appeared wearing nothing but that provocative dressing gown?

Finally she spoke. "I should like to begin reading my new book immediately, but that would be rude, and a very poor way of thanking you for my gift."

"On the contrary, I should take your enthusiasm as proof that my gift pleased you." He was glad to find a neutral topic with which he could converse with her.

Eliza gave him a wary, considering look. Then she seated herself in the tall brown leather chair across from where he already was seated, and for a good half hour they sat in companionable silence, Eliza reading and Edward pretending to do so.

How could he bring up the subject of marriage with her? And how could he do it without revealing that he had received her father's shameful letter? He wished to spare her any knowledge of that— indeed he must. He did not wish her to know how the letter had catalyzed his desire to wed her. He knew Eliza well enough by now to guess how she would respond to any hint that he wished to marry her out of pity.

It was unfortunate that the subject of marriage had come up the previous afternoon and that he had told Eliza that he shared her Radical aunt's disapproval of the institution. It would be hard to suggest marriage now without seeming like the worst sort of hypocrite. On the other hand, she did seem fond of him, and the way her body had responded to his during that lingering kiss by the seaside had certainly confirmed that however unusual a creature she might be, she was still, at heart, a woman. So perhaps, though her theories condemned matrimony, she might respond more favorably were she to receive an actual proposal. Perhaps she had declared her disdain for marriage because she thought it was what he wished to hear.

But a moment's reflection brought home to him that Eliza had never shown the slightest inclination to say what he wanted to hear. Her disdain for marriage was real, so he must move carefully. If he were to make her a formal proposal only to have it thrown back in his face, he couldn't answer for what might happen. He could not bear to lose control of himself again and make her his victim as he had done to Estella. So before he could risk making a proposal, he must determine exactly the true state of her feelings on the subject.

It was time to interrupt her reading.

"Does Miss Austen live up to your expectations?" he inquired.

Eliza looked up from her book. As she cocked her head in that irresistible way of hers he saw the slightest trace of a blush infuse the adorable freckles scattered over her cheek, almost as if he had interrupted *her* in some guilty thought, but she quickly responded to his question. "The story begins with some selfish relatives, rather like the beginning of *Sense and Sensibility*, but the heroine is out of the common way."

"How so?"

"She isn't a young girl, like the heroines of most novels, but an older lady of some seven-and-twenty years, well past her prime. She has turned away a suitor in her youth because he had no prospects. Now he is to return to the neighborhood after having earned himself a fortune."

"And does he pay her his addresses, despite having been previously rejected?"

"I haven't read that far, but as it is a novel, and as she appears to be the heroine, one has to assume they will eventually be happy, though not before a good deal of suffering is got through. One doesn't expect the story in a novel to work out as it would in real life."

Hoping to turn the conversation from such polite generalities to the subject that now filled his mind, he ventured, "Perhaps now that her objection to him has been removed, her suitor will propose to her again."

"That would be unlikely. What wealthy man would want a faded woman of twenty-seven when he could have a beauty of eighteen?"

This had possibilities. "At twenty-seven a woman may still have much to recommend her. I can't imagine having the conversations I have with you with some chit of eighteen, nor can I imagine turning to her, as I have to you, for advice."

If only he could get the benefit of that advice in his current situation! Then it struck him how he could. He need only pretend that the advice he was seeking was for someone other than himself.

He cleared his throat, "Speaking of advice,

I had a letter today from a good friend of mine in town who has got himself into something of a pickle with a young lady. I had meant to ask you what you thought might be the best thing for him to do, but it slipped my mind until now."

Eliza's face lit up. Like all women she *did* love to give advice. "What are his circumstances?"

He tented his fingers before him and plunged on. "My friend is, not to put too fine a point on it, something of a rake—not at all the sort of man a decent woman would consort with. But with one thing and another he's managed to compromise a girl of good birth. The thing to do, of course, would be to offer for her. But my friend is having a great deal of trouble bringing himself to the point. He writes to me for advice, probably assuming I will talk him out of it. Still, I find myself somewhat at a loss to know what it is I should tell him."

"Has he got her with child?" Eliza demanded.

"Oh nothing like that. The damage is only to her reputation. But people are talking, and my friend has unwisely given them something rather juicy to talk about, though he has not, in fact, violated her. My friend is not utterly lost to honor. Indeed, it is because he still has some shreds of honor left that he wonders if he must marry her."

"Well, the answer seems perfectly clear to me," Eliza said forcefully. "Such a marriage would be a terrible mistake. Were there the possibility of a child, marriage would be a necessity. It's not right to bring a child into the world knowing it will have to live with the shame of bastardy. But if there's no possibility of a child, the woman would be a fool to marry such a man simply to stop wagging tongues. Why should she condemn herself to spend a lifetime with a libertine, simply because people with nothing better to do might gossip about her?"

This was not what he had hoped to hear.

He tried again. "What of the injury to my friend's honor? If he doesn't offer for her, he must go through life burdened with the reputation of being a man who has ruined a woman of good birth."

"I cannot see why that should matter to him," Eliza retorted. "If he's as great a rake as you say, I would assume he's already ruined his share of less fortunate women. Why should one more matter just because she's of gentle birth?"

"Your aunt *did* fill you up with radical notions," he observed. "But surely you know society takes such distinctions seriously. My friend hasn't ruined a servant girl, but a woman of his own class."

"I see," Eliza said in that tone that meant she didn't. "But I still cannot comprehend why that should condemn the lady to a lifetime chained to a rake."

Worse and worse! Still, he could not give up. "There is some possibility that the lady might be fond of him, but the devil of it is that my friend is not certain of her feelings. And he has his pride. He does not wish to offer and be rejected."

"What a loathsome man!" Eliza said firmly. "To think of his own pride at such a moment."

Edward sighed. This was not turning out at all the way he had hoped. "I think you're being too hard on my friend. At least he is trying to do the decent thing. Indeed I'm rather proud of him. I wouldn't have expected him to do it."

"Well," said Eliza, softening, "perhaps I am jumping a bit too hastily to a conclusion. My aunt always warned me that doing just that would be my downfall. And if she were here, I know she would tell me I must not assume that everyone thinks the way that I do. Just because *I* would not like to be forced to marry a rake to please some foolish idea of propriety, it does not follow that your friend's lady might not be very glad to have him make her an offer."

Edward found himself speechless, but Eliza did not seem to notice. Instead she asked, "I don't suppose you know when your friend was born, do you?"

"No, I'm afraid your astrologizing is not an option here; there is no way to get any birth information about the couple."

"Well, there is a way of casting a horoscope that could be helpful, even without birth information. Have you got your watch?"

Edward pulled his gold hunter out of its pocket, wondering what Eliza was up to now.

She consulted it, made note of the time, and then explained there was a kind of chart she could erect whose purpose was to answer a specific question. That kind of chart required nothing except knowledge of the time when the question had arisen.

With little else to give him encouragement, Edward urged her to draw up the chart, hoping that whatever she saw in it might support his cause. So Eliza went upstairs, fetched her flowered satchel, and then, when she had returned to the library, settled herself at the desk to begin her calculations.

As she worked, he strolled over to see what it was that she was doing. He looked over her books, one of which he recognized as being a table of latitudes designed for the use of mariners. Then she made numerous mathematical calculations, the purpose of which he could not begin to guess.

As he watched her, he realized that if he had paid a little more attention to how she constructed her horoscopes when he had first met her, he might have avoided mistaking her for a woman of the lower classes. Clearly she was a very competent mathematician, which implied a degree of education no woman of the lower classes could have received. This discovery only depressed him further. He cursed the lamentable self-absorption that had led him to miss so important a clue.

At length, Eliza looked up and announced that the chart was finished and she would now have to ask him some questions to make sure it would serve their purpose and answer his question.

"Ask away. I am at your service."

Eliza took a deep breath and began. "The Ascendant describes the questioner—you—well. It is in Aries, which shows a fiery, energetic man prone to anger. The subject is marriage, which we place in the Seventh House. Libra lies on the cusp of that house, so the lord of the matter is Venus, goddess of love, which confirms the suitability of the chart to a question concerning a marriage. All this suggests that the chart is indeed fit to read."

She paused for a moment, then turned back to the chart. "Looking now at the Sun which is co-lord of the querent, we see it lies in the Sixth House, the House of Duty. That, too, fits. The Moon co-rules the question and it lies in the First House and has just made an aspect to Venus, planet of love, which fits again. The question is definitely one of marriage."

She looked up at him and smiled a warm, delighted smile. "Edward, I am *so* glad you asked me to do this chart for you, for it does suggest that perhaps I was too hasty in my original judgment. I asked you many questions but forgot the most important one. You told me that you thought the lady might be fond of him, but you said nothing of your friend's feelings. Does he perhaps love her, too?"

"I couldn't say," he said quietly. "My friend did not confide in me that far, which is understandable, given what the world knows about my feelings about love."

"Then there is your answer, for clearly he does. This chart reveals their marriage would be a matter of love, not merely one of propriety. But to get our final answer of whether it will actually take place we must look at the next aspect that will occur between the lord of the questioner, Mars, and the lord of the question, Venus. The relationship between the two will give us our answer about whether they should marry—"

Eliza paused abruptly. "Oh no! I have muddled it."

Edward's hopes which had been on the rise, deflated. "Why, what is wrong?"

"*You* asked the question, so the ascendant describes you, but I forgot that the question was about your *friend*'s marriage, not your own. So I must read the chart for the friend, not you, and that changes all the houses! She leaned her head against her hand. "It is so vexing! I am never sure whether a friend is a Third House relationship or an Eleventh House one, so I am in doubt as to which planet to assign to your friend. And now I am reminded most forcibly why it is I don't like casting this kind of horoscope. There is far too much to remember!"

She cocked her head up in that endearing way of hers. "Perhaps you can help me decide which house to use for your friend. Is he an older, serious man?"

"No, I should say he was quite frivolous," Edward replied.

"Is he fond of talking?"

"Quite."

"Then the Third House must describe him, being ruled by Mercury. But Mercury is afflicted on this chart by Mars. Is your friend prone to speak without thinking?"

"At times."

"Or perhaps it is that he is prone to speak falsehoods, especially where women are concerned. Oh, of course," she added, answering her own question. "That must be true, as you already told me he is a sad rake."

He was glad Eliza's eyes were on the chart and could not see his struggle to maintain his composure. But he also found himself gaining a new respect for Eliza's abilities. He had not expected the chart to reveal quite so much of the truth.

Eliza pondered a little longer then said, "It is, after all, as I had thought. When we ask the question about your friend, rather than yourself, his marriage would be described by the Ninth House whose lord, Jupiter, is in the Tenth. That means that the marriage would indeed be only for the sake of reputation." She pointed her pen toward the paper. "And the outcome is clear, too. Mercury's next aspect will be a square with Jupiter."

Edward interrupted, "The outcome is clear to *you* perhaps, but I am at sea with all your houses and lordships. What is the final judgment?"

"Why just what I told you before. Your friend should not marry the lady. If he does, only problems will ensue. But I am so glad I caught my error in time! Had I continued to read the chart as if the question was about you instead of your friend I should have thought it a love match and one I should have recommended."

Edward said no more. He had learned a valuable lesson about attempting to manipulate Eliza with the stars. But as he sat in silence while Eliza packed her books and charts back into the flowered satchel, he realized that his clumsy appeal for help had not, after all, been a waste of time. She *had* told him what he needed to know.

She believed that a marriage would only be justified if there was the possibility of a child. And in saying that, she had, unwittingly, shown him exactly what it was that he must do if he were to gain her assent to the proposal of marriage his honor required him to offer her.

So that was that.

He rose abruptly and strode over to the armchair where Eliza had seated herself after finishing her consultation with him. "It's getting late," he said. "I'll help you bring your things upstairs." Then he snuffed the candles, all except for one branch, which he picked up with one hand. Wordlessly he reached his other hand for hers, knowing, sad rake that he was, that her response to this simple gesture would dictate all that came next.

If she did not take it, the path ahead was uncertain, but if she did—all would move in the direction his ludicrously rejuvenated sense of honor decreed it must.

He gazed into her eyes, remembering the power of the kiss they had shared in the moonlight. Had it just been the power of the waves that had moved her then, or was she almost his? As he waited, an overpowering longing for her swept through him. He dragged himself back to rationality. It was she who must be swept away, not him. And indeed, he sensed her even now teetering on the edge of making her decision. His hand lingered just out of her reach, then brushed against hers. He willed her to take it, feeling his need for her welling up inside again. At last, she gave him her hand. He squeezed it gently, letting all he felt for her flow into the softness of her touch. Then she stood up.

The kiss had not been just a trick of the moon.

Chapter 15

As she let Edward lead her up the stairs, Eliza wondered at the calm with which she had behaved throughout the past hour. For upstairs, in the same room to which he was leading her, lay that poisonous letter she had buried at the bottom of Violet's trunk—the letter she had found on her bed when she had gone upstairs to change her rain-dampened clothing. Immediately upon seeing her father's seal on its cheap paper, she had known she would have to leave Edward immediately—and she must do it without giving him any hint of why it was she was leaving.

Her father could sniff out money like a bloodhound. Hadn't he managed to show up on her doorstep only days after the solicitor had handed over her Aunt Celestina's carefully hoarded bequest—despite his having let years go by in which she hadn't heard a single word from him? And now he had tracked her down again, writing so coolly that although word had come to him that she had given herself to Lord Hartwood without benefit of marriage, he would leave it to others to judge her, for he was on the brink of an enormous break-through. The potential for gain was immense—but only if she convinced her wealthy protector to make a heavy investment in his doomed and damnable scheme.

Her father hadn't changed. She knew he never would, but still, the truth slashed through her like a knife. She must leave Edward now, before her father could make his way to Brighton. There was no alternative. She would not let Edward become yet another victim of her father's obsession. She couldn't bear watching his regard for her turn into contempt and then disgust.

She wondered how she had managed to con-verse so coolly with Edward tonight after read-ing that poisonous letter. How had she been able to discuss Miss Austen's book and advise him on his friend's predicament? She must be as good an actor as he was, for she had carried it off so well, without ever letting him suspect that her heart was breaking with every word he spoke to her and every liquid glance of his warm brown eyes.

Her sadness had made her stupid, of course. How else to account for the mess she had made when reading that chart for his friend? But he had not noticed. Sometimes his self-absorption came in useful.

But no matter what she felt. Now that her father had tracked her down, she must leave Edward, though it would be so hard to do so. Though it would be intolerable.

Perhaps that was why she had dressed herself in the most scandalous of all of Violet's garments, the peach silk dressing gown. And nothing else. She was no longer the innocent she had been when she had first opened Violet's trunk. She knew very well the response such a garment would provoke in him. But as she had tried to accept that she must leave Edward forever her sadness had turned to hunger and something fierce had risen up within her and declared that if this last night with him was all she had left, she would enjoy it to the utmost.

She would open herself to life. She would give herself up to what he had made her yearn for with all the teasing foretastes of joy he had given her already. Not just the pleasures of the body he had awakened her to, but the rest of it: The way he listened to her and valued her opinion. The way he respected her intelligence and brought out in her the playfulness she had so long suppressed. He had given her so much. Her heart swelled as she remembered the way he had shown her how much he needed what she alone could give him, no matter how hard he might try to hide it behind that ironic façade. Perhaps it was fate that the book he had bought for her spoke of the regrets of a woman her own age who had turned away from love. She would not make that mistake.

So it had been with only the faintest tremble that she had given her hand to Edward in the library and let him lead her up the stairs to her small room in the attic. When they reached the landing, she stood at the doorway, uncertainly fumbling with the knob, hoping he would not turn away and leave her there alone. That he had forbidden her to do this was no longer a concern. She would leave him the next morning, anyway, before he had a chance to send her away. Still, she half expected him to make some protest as she pushed open the heavy, squeaking door and drew him into the room after her. But he, too, seemed to have forgot his prohibition, for he had followed her into the tiny bedroom and closed the door behind them with a decisive click.

He put the branch of candles he was carrying down on the table. He dropped her satchel and placed her new book on the side table where the gold stamping on the bindings glowed dimly in the candlelight. Then he stopped and looked at her with a questioning look that made her feel all the more how devastated she would be if he were to leave her now. Still clutching his hand, she led him silently toward the bed and motioned him to sit down beside her.

As he seated himself beside her on the bed his eyes met hers, and she saw that, inexplicably, they were filled with a look of determination. For a moment, again, she expected him to rise and flee. But he did not. So she would make the most of it. He was here with her tonight, and though tomorrow she must leave him, before she left she would learn what it was that happened next between two people who had been drawn together as strongly as the two of them had been.

As if he had heard her thoughts, he leaned over, whispered her name, and then kissed her.

It was not like the kiss by the shore. Then they had been outside, and the energy of their kiss had risen with the wind and been quenched by the sound of the sea. But there was no sea here. There was no wind here. There was only the rising feeling of something inside her as old as the sea and as fleeting as the wind that reached out toward him in the silent privacy of the small bedroom and waited for him to show the way.

And he knew it. His kiss was long and slow. As his lips parted, taking hers with them, the soft, delicate probing of his tongue met hers, and she felt an agony as something opened within her she had not known was there. It was as if a current of yearning flowed from his tongue to the pulsing center of her body. And then his hands began their dance.

His fingers glided over her silk-covered breasts, teasing and treasuring them, gently and then harder, as if he had heard her need and responded to it almost before she'd become aware of it. The current flowed stronger as she soaked in the exquisite sensations. He pulled loose the sash of her scandalous dressing gown, and it gave way, falling open before him and revealing her naked body. His deep brown eyes widened and became even more beautiful as he regarded her in the candlelight. His pupils were black and immense. There was nothing between the two of them now but skin and energy.

His fingertips found her nipples and twirled them into madness. Sensations flooded her, almost too much to take in. Overwhelmed, she lay back against the thin pillow on the bed. His lips broke contact with hers, filling her with disappointment until, moments later, they found the hollow of her neck, and his feather-light kisses sent electric shivers pulsing through her body. Almost before she knew it, his lips had moved on and licked and nibbled at her ear. The sound of his quickening breath ignited a yearning deep within her.

He pulled himself upright. As his hands grasped the bottom of his shirt, she hungrily took in the flash of his cool pale skin against the darkness as he peeled off the shirt and tossed it aside. The golden hairs that spread down the center of his chest gleamed faintly in the candlelight, gilding him with dancing sparks.

Then he embraced her again. His flesh against hers was warm and comforting. The hard muscles of his naked chest sank into the resilient softness of her breasts. As he pulled her closer the touch of his wiry curls as they brushed against her sensitive skin inflamed her. Still clasping her in his warm embrace, he gently adjusted her position until she was lying on her side. Then his hands roved up and down her back, pressing on muscles that luxuriated in the release brought about by his touch.

He kneaded them harder, making tension melt and sending waves of pleasure coursing down her spine. As he drew spirals on her shoulder blades with the tips of his fingernails, she gripped him convulsively, filled with need for him.

Then again, he released her, but this time she felt no fear he would not return. She watched as he drew off his breeches and stood before her as nature had made him, proudly erect, massive and beautiful in a way she had not known a man could be. Though there was something frightening, too, about the power that now radiated from him.

As if he had sensed how new this was to her, when he took his place beside her again in the bed, he stroked her cheek. He made little comforting noises with his mouth and moved his hands slowly down her flanks with a gentle teasing touch. Again the hunger built within her, even stronger than before. She raised her lips to his and kissed him fiercely, pouring into her kiss all the desire he had made her feel. Her tongue throbbed as it explored the taste of him. She felt herself becoming moist inside.

She needed so much more of him. Still locked in their kiss, she drew his naked body closer, pressing herself against his long, luxuriant flank, and writhing against him as she rejoiced in the feel of his hardness. Releasing his lips, she nibbled at the base of his neck and heard him moan softly. The sound of his need for her drove her to near desperation.

Yet even as she felt herself being swept away,

one small part of herself stood aside and watched, struggling to store each fleeting moment of bliss in her memory for after it was over, saving it for that time, so impossible to imagine now, when her memories would be all she'd have to console herself with, after he was gone.

Edward's mind reeled. The woman beneath him wanted him as no woman had ever wanted him. His demure Eliza! What was going on?

He tried to get control of himself. Despite the way she was arousing him, she was still a virgin, and nothing about her newfound passion suggested otherwise. He struggled to keep his control as her lips nibbled at the sensitive skin at the base of his neck. He must not overwhelm her. But when her small, even teeth nipped at the tender flesh there, sending a shock throughout his body, he knew it was not she who was in danger of being overwhelmed. Her hands raked through the mat of hair on his chest. Her scent enveloped him. He'd never smelled anything as enticing as her spicy clean skin and the fainter, maddening musk of her desire for him. Her hands drifted downward below his navel, exploring the sensitive skin above his pubic hair with fingertips that seemed to know exactly what he needed at the exact moment he felt his need. He moaned at the pleasure her dancing touch evoked, until she silenced him with her lips, kissing him hungrily, pulling his tongue into her warm, moist, hungry mouth, and driving him almost to the brink.

But two could play this game. Taking control again, he let his hand drift over her taut belly. Her breathing quickened. He thrilled at the tiny shivers that went through her at his touch. He brushed against the auburn curls that awaited him below. Feeling her startle, he paused, then circled her navel playfully yet tenderly, until she relaxed again. He glanced up at her face and saw the blissful way her ginger lashes fluttered as her eyes drifted closed. He kissed her gently on her lightly parted lips. No woman had ever been so beautiful.

He let his fingers drift back to her sumptuous mound and found her silky curls. He teased them until he felt her rise to meet him. Gently his prob- ing hand explored the open, welcoming cleft he found awaiting him below. He heard her breath- ing grow harsh as he kneaded the tight ridge of her excitement, rolling its slickness between his two fingers.

She arched against him and cried out. The pressure in his manhood grew as her wetness gushed forth in response to his determined prob- ing. He longed to kiss her there and learn the taste of her, but held back not wishing to frighten her. Only when he felt her full and swollen beneath his hand, did he part her legs and kneel between them. Gently, oh so gently, he placed himself against her opening, sliding against the wetness there. He gave her time to adjust then gently in- creased the pressure until the tip of his manhood entered her. He felt her stretch and stopped. He must not hurt her. But her face still held that look of bliss. She widened her legs and the movement almost brought him to the edge. He froze, waited a moment, then pressed harder against the slippery membrane until her sharp intake of breath made him stop again. He pulled back, delaying for one last instant whatever it was that would happen when she changed from maid to woman. But just at that moment her arms tightened around his back. She pulled him closer, forced him deep within her and he slid home. At last, she was his.

He paused, luxuriating in the slickness of her. He hoped he had not hurt her.

"I'm all right," she said, as if reading his mind. "Don't stop. I couldn't bear it."

He didn't stop. He couldn't have stopped now, even if he'd wanted to. He embraced her and whispered her name as he plunged into her silky depths. He felt her tighten around him as her desire grew. At each thrust, her hips arched to meet him. Her breath quickened with his. Her moans of pleasure echoed his own. Their breathing rose together. Yes, she was his, but he was hers, too. Entirely hers, lost in the wonder of her. Then she shuddered, and he felt her convulsing around him. She gave one last gasp of pleasure, and he exploded in ecstasy inside her.

When it was over, he was afraid to look at her. He had never bedded a virgin. He had never bedded a friend. He had just done both and he wasn't sure if he could bear the aftermath. If she were to cry, if she were to berate him for seducing her, he didn't know how he would face it.

He would marry her, of course, and perhaps this was the time to make her his offer when they were both still overwhelmed with the passion they had just shared. But something held him back. Her words describing the horror of being tied to a rake came back to him, more devastating now that it was too late for him to heed them. Would she hate him because he'd maneuvered things so she would be tied to him whether she wanted it or not?

He felt a hollow feeling well up. Perhaps she would never forgive him what he'd just done to her. No, this was not the time to bring up marriage. He was still too full of happiness from what he'd just shared with her to risk it. Better to wait a little longer before letting her learn how grievously he had manipulated her. He couldn't bear to destroy the delicate joy that had blossomed in his heart when they had made love.

It was Eliza who was the first to speak. "It was my fault," she said gently. "I broke my promise to you."

A wave of compassion swept over him. That she should blame herself, when she had only been responding as he had known she would to his well-honed skills of seduction! But it would be easier on both of them and bode better for their future, if he let her believe it had been she who had made the decision that had ended her independence.

"How could I be angry?" he reassured her. "No,

I am moved more deeply than I can express that you have chosen to honor me this way."

Eliza laughed. "Honor seems a very strange word to apply to our situation." When he made no reply she continued. "Is it always like this, when making love? Or did it seem that way to me because I waited so long before experiencing it."

What way? Edward felt a stab of uncertainty. Had he hurt her or given her pleasure? He lifted himself up on one elbow and gazed down into the depths of her sparkling green eyes to see if he could find any hint there of what she had experienced, but he could not. So he said only, "I cannot tell you without knowing what you felt."

"There's no way to describe it. Pleasure is such a weak word. It was so much more than pleasure. It felt for a while as if light was rising up inside me and then it seemed as if I became inestimably beautiful with every touch of yours."

"You are beautiful," he said softly.

"And then—I don't know how to describe it— but all there was, was you, and you and me together. It felt so right to be doing what we were doing. It seemed a holy thing to me—" Eliza stopped, suddenly embarrassed at what she had just said. "I suppose it seemed that way to me only because I am not a woman of the world and have no experience of such things. Perhaps one gets used to it, and it is just another pleasure that one takes, like dining at a restaurant."

"I think not," Edward said with a laugh. "Unless you know of restaurants far superior to any I've ever dined in. But no, it *was* a rare and precious thing we experienced."

"Then it was that way for you, too?"

"It was."

"Though you are a man of the world who has been with hundreds of women—"

"My reputation is far worse than I imagined," he said, shutting off her words by laying a finger on her lips. "I've been with perhaps a dozen women in my life, not hundreds."

"I am glad to hear that," Eliza said. "It would be hard to be jealous of a hundred women."

"You need be jealous of none of them. No one has ever moved me as you have, Eliza." He spoke the truth.

But even as he spoke he felt the old familiar fear. He didn't need to have been with a hundred women to know what she would say next. First she would tell him she loved him. Then she would beg him to tell her he loved her, too, and that he'd be faithful and never leave. He would have to make promises, not knowing if there was any way he could keep them, knowing that as much as he might treasure what they had shared he was still his father's son, his brother's brother.

Though he felt he would die if he could not make love to her again, he couldn't trust himself to tell her he would always love her. He couldn't trust himself to live up to such a terrifying claim. And as that fear rose up within him, he felt the joy that had filled him only moments before dissipate as he waited tensely for her to say the words he knew must come next, the words that would echo through the memories of all the other nights he had spent with all those other women he had just told her meant nothing to him.

But Eliza said nothing.

Instead, her eyes broke contact with his and she looked away with something in her heart-shaped face that shocked him, something that looked to him like guilt. He felt a tug of pain. What did *she* have to be guilty about?

He took her hand again, but it felt cold and life-less. The warmth had fled. She was pulling away from him, severing the connection—she, not he—was retreating.

He felt himself crash back to earth as the magic seeped away. She reached a hand down to where he had just spent himself and brought it back to her face. "I'm bleeding," she said plaintively. He longed to embrace her and tell her it would be all right, but his fears were too strong. He was not sure it *would* be all right.

So he merely got up and searched through the pockets of his breeches for a handkerchief and handed it to her so that she could staunch the flow. "It's normal to bleed like that the first time," he said, wondering if it really was. He had never before bedded a virgin. "There won't be pain the next time."

At his words, her eyes slid away from his again and he realized with a pang that she did not want to think about a next time. A wall had sprung up between them. The openness and joy that he had felt was replaced by cold terror. Then she turned back to him one last time and asked, "Is it normal to feel this sleepy, too?"

He told her it was. Then, unable to bear the bleakness in her gaze, he got up and dressed himself clumsily, preparing to return to his own room. Bidding her good night, softly, he kissed her one last time and received a sleepy kiss from those lips of hers that had just filled him with such ecstasy, learning as he drew away from her, that there was only one fear more terrible than the thought of what his uncontrollable fickleness might do to Eliza: the fear that *she* would be the one to leave him first.

Chapter 16

When Eliza awoke the next morning, her first thought was that the events of the previous evening had been a dream. Then she saw Edward's handkerchief lying beside her on the bed still stained with the faint pink evidence of their lovemaking. She crumpled it and shoved it deep under the covers, realizing as she did so how futile the gesture was. There was no way of hiding from what she had done.

She felt no regret for having done it. It would be impossible to regret last night. She would treasure the memory of what they had shared for the rest of her life. But she was in peril now. Having tasted the pleasure of her lover's touch, she could barely imagine how she was to leave him. Her animal nature, which had slumbered for so long, was fully awake. It cried out for him, urging her to run down the stairway to his room and fling herself on him. It was so hungry for more.

But there could be no more. The power of what she had opened herself to was far stronger than she had expected. She understood now exactly why the woman Edward had abandoned had drowned herself. She understood now, as she never had before, what had caused her mother's ruin. If she didn't sever the bond that connected her with Edward now, while she still possessed a shred of her self-control, she would never be able to leave him. And if she stayed only disaster could follow.

Not because of what her father might do. She faced the fact squarely that she had deceived herself. She had used her fear of her father's reappearance as an excuse to justify giving in to the impulse she could no longer resist, the longing to give herself to Edward. Her father's machinations were not the disaster that loomed over her. She had dealt with him before and knew she could survive the worst he could do to her. No, the true disaster waited where it had always waited: in her own wanton heart and the ungovernable passion hiding there, which her aunt had tried so fruitlessly to protect her from.

She had given herself to a rake and she had done it on purpose. She had done it knowing that he didn't want her love. She had done it after listening to him explain how he used women and discarded them, after letting him prove that the wounds he had suffered made it impossible for him not to hurt the women who exposed their hearts to him. She had given herself to him anyway, convinced she was strong enough to change him. But that had been self-deception. He would not change. His resentment was too strong. Yet still she had fallen in love with him—just as her mother had fallen for her wastrel father.

Desperate to find some hidden cause for hope, she arose and fetched his horoscope, much smudged now from all her pawing over it. But there was nothing new there. The chart had not changed. The man had not changed. All that had changed was herself. She had finally lost control.

She flung his horoscope on the bed, wishing she had never seen it. She wished for once that its symbols didn't speak to her so clearly or, that if they must, she could drown out what they had to say. But she could not. Mars still squared his Leo Sun. Saturn still opposed it. Her Edward had a huge capacity to love, but it was thwarted. So instead of expressing his Leo nature as love, he expressed it as playacting. He played role after role, burying the man who was Edward Neville beneath the glorious creation who was Lord Lightning, letting Edward peep out from time to time and show his human need for love only when it might give piquancy to the role.

She would not change him. She didn't even want to. Though she loved what she had seen of Edward Neville, she couldn't deny it was Lord Lightning she had fallen for first, Lord Lightning who had swept her up into his exciting life and lent her some of his own magnificence so she could free herself from the role of faded spinster her aunt had insisted she take on and replace it, if only briefly, with that of his glorious vixen.

It was only now, when it was too late, that she was forced to remember *why* she had taken on that spinster's role. She had been safe in her drab gray gown, safe from the urgings of her own impetuous heart. But her pride had been her downfall. She had been so proud of how she had detected the man, Edward, who hid behind the façade that was Lord Lightning, that she had allowed him to strip her of the role she, too, was playing—the role that was all that kept her true self in check. Now it had burst through, and she had become the person she had always known she was: impulsive, sensual, and doomed.

It would only be a matter of hours until he would send her away. She had felt him begin to withdraw in the aftermath of their lovemaking. When he saw her next in the cold light of morning, he would remind her how she had broken the compact they had made at the beginning of this ill-advised adventure and send her away.

She sighed. It was all so difficult. She had *meant* to leave him. She had made love with him knowing she *would* leave him. She had made love only *because* she must leave him. But now that she faced the necessity of actually leaving him, it was more than she could bear.

She got up and washed herself carefully using water from the cracked pitcher on the washstand, wondering at the strange secretions that their bodies had produced together. Then she went through the trunk, laying aside the flamboyant garments in which she had clothed herself over the past week. She was done with them. She hunted through the contents of the trunk until she found her plain gray dress and with shaking fingers she put it on. She would never again feel safe in it, no, not when she knew the full power of what lay coiled within her and what her long-hidden inner nature really wanted. But she could no longer wear Violet's tawdry gowns and play the parody role of mistress, now that she knew the real power of what it meant to be Edward's lover.

She went through the rest of the things in the trunk, packing into her flowered satchel only the things she would need to survive. As much as she wished she did not have to, she must also keep the fifty pounds Edward had given her after that first night. She couldn't afford to be melodramatic. It was all the money she had in the world, and she would need it to establish herself wherever she could find herself a home.

She debated what to do with the book he had given her, that tale of a woman like herself who thought she had grown too old for love. Had the heroine found love with the man she had scorned in her youth or did Miss Austen have some other tale to tell? It didn't matter. Eliza had parted ways with her heroine last night. There were many ways Miss Austen might tell her story, but none, she was certain, would turn out like her own.

But though she knew she should leave the book behind, she couldn't bring herself to do so. Edward had given it to her as a gift. It had been part of the playacting they had indulged in, but still, it would be her only concrete memento of what they had shared. So she took the book and tenderly placed it with her other books in the satchel. After another moment's thought, she also took the gold and onyx paper knife he had given her with the book. It, too, had been a gift. Then she seated herself at the desk one last time to write him the note that would tell him she was leaving.

The words were hard to find. She didn't want him to think his honesty on the beach had driven her away. Sharing his story with her had allowed him to begin to heal from the heavy burden he had carried for so long. She had no wish to destroy that. So she took her time, carefully composing a note that would do the least harm. When she had finished it, she looked around one last time at the small room where she had learned so much. Then she tiptoed to the landing of the back staircase the servants used. She waited until she could hear no voices or footsteps and descended, letting herself out of the back door.

When she reached the street Eliza regretted she had brought no umbrella with her. It was raining again and she had no idea where she would go, though she knew she must leave Brighton if she were to have any hope of avoiding seeing

Edward Neville again. Fortunately, she knew public coaches left the town center every hour for London where it would be easy to vanish into the anonymity of the metropolis.

She hastened along the sidewalk, feeling quite irrationally as if she were being pursued, but dismissed that thought as a trick of a mind that yearned for Edward to come after her and beg her to remain. But any idea that the pursuit existed only in her imagination was cut short as a voice called out, "Stop!" She heard the unmistakable sound of heavy footsteps behind her. A rough hand grasped her arm, and she smelled the sour smell of old tobacco and gin. A rough voice demanded, "Be ye the woman residing at the Hartwood residence calling herself Eliza Farrell?"

"I am," she whispered.

"I have a writ for your arrest," the man barked. "Don't try no tricks, no running away. We had the house watched. My men are all around you."

Eliza stared. Had her father got back into debt that quickly? "What am I accused of?"

"That's for the magistrate to tell you. Now shut yer gob and don't make me have to shut it for you. Will you be coming along without a struggle, or will I have to tie you up?"

Without waiting for a reply the man removed a thick piece of rope from his pocket and used it to bind up her hands with a speed that suggested much practice in the maneuver. He tossed her satchel to a younger man and then dragged her down the street behind him using the rope like a leash until they came to a large gray house where an older man with an old-fashioned bagwig came to the door and after conferring with her captor, motioned for Eliza to come inside.

She was led to a small bare room at the back of the house that contained only a deal table and a couple of chairs she could not help but notice were nailed down to the floor. The man in the wig told her curtly to sit down, then both men left, locking the door behind them.

She sat for what seemed like hours, wondering what was to come next. Was she to go to prison for her father's debts after all? Or was it something worse? Had he moved on to swindling? She thought of the letter he had sent her and his veiled threat to come to Edward for more money. Blackmail, too, was a crime.

Finally she heard a key turn in the lock and the man in the bagwig came in followed by another man who carried a small writing desk. The man in the wig introduced himself curtly as the chief magistrate of Brighton, but she realized with a shock she had met him before. He had been seated next to Lady Hartwood at her fatal dinner party.

"Is your name Eliza Farrell?" he demanded.

Eliza answered, "Yes." The clerk's pen scratched across the paper.

"And is that the name under which you were baptized?"

"Yes." The pen scratched again.

"And in what parish was your birth registered and on what date?"

"St. Giles parish, London. I was born November 29th in the year 1788," Eliza replied.

"And have you been residing in the house of Lady Hartwood since this Saturday past?"

"Yes."

"And did you carry on there an irregular connection with her son, Edward Neville, Lord Hartwood, in defiance of Lady Hartwood's demand that you leave her home?"

Eliza said nothing, but she could feel her face flushing. What could these questions possibly be leading up to?

"Answer me!" the man insisted. "Did you remain in the house of said Lady Hartwood pursuing carnal relations with her son in defiance of her demand that you should leave her home?"

Eliza whispered, "I did."

"And is it true that you present yourself to the public as a fortune-teller, drawing up astrological horoscopes and claiming to foretell the future with them?"

"I am an astrologer. That is no crime!" Eliza protested.

"And did you take money from Lord Hartwood both for the granting of sexual favors to him and for the telling of his fortune?"

"I did not!" Eliza cried out. "But this is monstrous! What am I charged with? I have a right to know! It cannot possibly be illegal to be a man's mistress."

"It is not the time to discuss the charge. Our purpose now is only to establish the facts in the matter, though I will inform you that it *is* against the law to tell fortunes for money in Brighton."

"But, I did no such thing—"

"Hold your tongue, woman. You are only to answer my questions. Did you remove any fixtures or jewelry belonging to Lady Hartwood from the house?"

"I am not a thief!"

He gestured to a clerk before grunting, "Bring over the evidence." The younger man handed over her satchel. Item by item, the magistrate removed all her things from it, calling out a description of each one for the benefit of the recording clerk. All her precious books and almanacs as well as her collection of horoscopes were pulled out and placed on the table, followed by the purse, which contained the fifty pounds in bank notes. The last thing the magistrate removed from the satchel was the paper knife Edward had given her the previous night. He held it up to view it more closely and noted, "One paper knife in gold and onyx, decorated with the Hartwood crest."

"This concludes the taking of your statement," the magistrate intoned. "Your belongings, to wit the contents of the flowered yellow satchel with which you were apprehended in the act of leaving the Neville residence, have been entered into evidence and will be retained by the court.

"That being concluded, you have the right to know what you are accused of. The plaintiff, Lady Hartwood, of 31 Marine Parade, accuses you of illegal trespass, lewd behavior, fortune-telling, and theft. Your case will be heard at the Michaelmas quarter sessions in Lewes. Until then, you will be held in Brighton as a prisoner. In deference to your sex you will not be held in the gaol but will be entrusted to the custody of the constable, to be cared for in his home at your own expense."

Lady Hartwood had had her arrested! Though Edward had been so certain of his control over his mother, so sure she would put up with whatever he dished out to her, he had been wrong. Fatally wrong. Even the financial hold he had over his mother had not been enough to keep her from retaliating. He had humiliated his mother beyond bearing and she had struck back.

Eliza's stomach lurched. What else had she expected, putting her trust in a man whose character was indelibly flawed? She had paid for her father's foolishness, now she would suffer for the fecklessness of another charming man.

Despair swept over her. It would be six long weeks until her case would come up at the quarter sessions. It might be five more months until she was tried at the January assizes. She had no money with which to pay for her keep during the long months of imprisonment, so she could expect to receive only enough food and warmth to keep her alive. If she was convicted of lewd behavior, the penalty would be transportation. She had no idea what the laws were against fortune-telling. But if they accused her of stealing the paper knife with the Hartwood crest, the penalty for the theft of an item costing over one shilling was hanging.

Edward had said he thought the paper knife was part of his inheritance, but that was only a guess. Perhaps he was wrong. Perhaps in law it belonged to his father's widow.

If only she had never met Edward Neville or seen his accursed chart! If only she had heeded the warning of her own afflicted horoscope where evil Saturn stood in the Twelfth House—an indicator of imprisonment—and had avoided the Uranian temptations her aunt had always said would turn her life into an ongoing disaster.

But it was too late for regrets. She had thrown her lot in with Lord Lightning and let his unpredictability give license to her own impulsive nature. Worst of all, despite every warning he had given her, she had let herself fall in love with him.

Now she would suffer the consequences.

Chapter 17

When Edward awoke from his own, untroubled slumbers, he knew it was going to be a beautiful day. His body felt wonderful and he quickly remembered why. As he rose and went over to the washstand to begin his morning ablutions, he noticed that his fingers still held Eliza's scent. A kaleidoscope of sensations washed through his memory as he inhaled her richness. Eliza! He'd never known how deeply a woman could move him. He felt rejuvenated and revived.

He rang for his valet and spent an inordinate amount of time on the selection of his wardrobe for the day. It was foolish, but he wanted to appear at his best when next he saw her.

He hoped that Eliza had arisen this morning feeling something akin to his own excitement. But that thought brought with it a burst of uneasiness as he remembered the way, when their lovemaking had been over, he had felt her retreat from the closeness they had shared. Coldness settled on his heart. He remembered feeling that coldness before—the one other time he'd opened his heart to a woman in his youth. But he shrugged off his fear. Why make problems where there were none? Eliza must marry him. She had no choice. She might fancy herself free and independent, but in the end she must know there was only one outcome possible after the connection they had forged the previous night. If she were feeling any morning-after regrets they would quickly be dispelled when he made her his offer of marriage.

Certainly there had been nothing in their lovemaking to prejudice her against him. He might be mistaken about her feelings for him—women's feelings were a complex area that no man ever truly understood—but he *did* understand women's bodies and he knew that he'd never before evoked such an overwhelming response from a woman. So it was time to settle the matter and put an end to this turmoil in his own heart. Once Eliza had accepted his offer, their connection would fall back into a comforting routine, and he could get on with his life.

But when he knocked at Eliza's door there was no answer.

Perhaps she was still asleep. He knocked again and after still receiving no answer, he began to feel a faint irritation at having his plans go awry so soon. Seeing no other choice, he opened the door.

The room was empty.

His immediate thought was that Eliza must have gone downstairs to breakfast, but as he looked around the empty room he knew she hadn't. There was no sign of the flowered yellow satchel that usually stood by her bed, and the pile of books that had covered the small table beside the bed was gone. The table was completely empty, except for a single sheet of writing paper that had been carefully folded over with his name written on the outside.

A quiver of fear ran through him. Happy women did not express themselves in notes. With shaking fingers he opened it and read the contents.

Eliza wrote that she understood completely that he must send her away, now that she had broken their contract. She had chosen to spare him the unpleasantness of a final interview by leaving before he awoke. She thanked him for his kindness to her and absolved him of blame, as brave to the last as he had always known her to be.

Poor Eliza! Her suffering had been so unnecessary! He cursed himself for having given in to his own weakness and not proposing to her last night. He had acted selfishly. He had not thought she would still feel bound by the terms of that silly contract he had made with her. Not after what they had shared last night. So he must find her and set things straight. Though she gave no hint of where she was going, perhaps he could trace her through the coaching services. Most likely she would

head to London or to her home village—Bishops
something. He cursed himself for not having paid
more attention to the name. But whatever it took,
he would track her down. They would marry. But
meanwhile his heart ached as he imagined her
alone somewhere, thinking herself seduced and
abandoned when she was not.

He strode down the stairs and ordered his best
horse saddled immediately. Then he went up to
his room to change into riding clothes and pack
the things he might need if he were forced to stay
somewhere overnight. When he was done he went
downstairs. But just as he was about to leave, his
path was blocked by his mother.

He was tempted to brush her aside but something in her look made him stop.

"She's gone," his mother said in a tone that
could only be described as gloating.

"How could you know?" Surely Eliza had not
taken his mother into her confidence about the
events of the previous night?

His mother took a deep, self-satisfied breath.
"I know because I have had her arrested. I grew
tired of your childish games, Edward. I decided it
was time to end them. Your whore has been taken
up for trespass, lewd behavior, fortune-telling,
and theft. If the charges stick, she will be on her
way to New South Wales or the gallows. If not,
she will at least spend some months in gaol awaiting trial."

He barely restrained himself from flinging

himself at his mother and throttling the life out
of her but he knew that he must maintain the appearance of calm if he was to have any hope of
saving Eliza.

"This is still my house," his mother continued, "though you seem to have forgot that. And
I warned her to leave though she chose to ignore
it." His mother was enjoying her victory. "When
you made me a laughingstock among the people
whose good regard means everything to me, you
left me with no other choice. She is gone now, and
I will no longer be forced to share the same roof
with your whore."

"That whore, as you call her, is the woman who
is soon to be my wife," he snarled.

"Then you are even more depraved than I
credited," his mother replied. "But by all means,
marry her. You will be well matched: a rake and
a whore. I only hope your children shall not be
born poxed."

Edward just stared at her, as the enormity of the
move she had made in their lifelong battle sank
in. Surely she couldn't have done such a thing,
not when the terms of James's will obliged her to
put up with him or lose her home! But the confidence she radiated told him louder than words
he had missed something. Something important.
She was too clever a woman to have taken such
an action if she had not found a way to neutralize
the power he had held over her. As this realization swept over him all his hard won confidence

evaporated. He was at her mercy again, as help-less as he had been as a small child. And he didn't even know why.

A stabbing pain shot through his gut. "You cannot be my real mother," he whispered. "I would rather have been born to the dirtiest whore who works the docks than think that I owed my existence to you."

Then he slammed the door in her face and rushed out to find Eliza.

It took longer than he expected to find out who served as the magistrate in Brighton. He had to go several places before he found the man's di-rection. Once he had it, he made his way to the magistrate's house driven by a fury stronger than any he had ever experienced. He pounded on the magistrate's door and when he was let in by a large, muscular, liveried flunky, announced, "Tell your master Lord Hartwood is here. I must see him directly. The matter is urgent."

As if he had not heard him, the flunky gestured to a bench in the hallway, muttering, "Take a seat," and adding as if it were an afterthought, "m'lord."

He ignored the man's insolence. "Perhaps you did not understand me. I am *Hartwood*. And I demand you take me to the magistrate at once. I will brook no delay. The matter is of the utmost importance!"

The flunky merely waved him toward the bench. "Take a seat, m'lord. His Honor will see you when he's ready." He showed no sign of being impressed, indeed, his response suggested that dealing with angry noblemen was a regular part of his job.

Perhaps it was. Brighton had more than its share of noble visitors. Or perhaps this was simply the magistrate's way of reminding supplicants of his power. But that power was real. He would get nowhere ignoring it. His mother had started the heavy wheel of justice in motion, and once it started moving it could easily crush a man beneath its weight. So he must calm himself down and speak mildly and reasonably. He would not advance Eliza's cause by punching out the magistrate's minion. He must win the magistrate over and convince him of his mother's irrationality. He must flatter him. He must do whatever it took to get him to release Eliza.

After what seemed like hours another flunky entered the room and called out his name. Edward rose and accompanied the man into an inner office where he found the bewigged magistrate sitting behind an enormous desk. He had the sense that he'd seen the man somewhere, but exactly where escaped him.

"What is your business, Lord Hartwood?" the man asked in a weary voice. "Your mother has already contacted me twice this morning about our interrogation of her prisoner, and I have sent my man over to her twice with my report. I should hope that my diligence in this matter would have given her satisfaction and that she need not send you to inquire into the matter yet again."

"My mother is a vicious, meddling bitch," Edward said, "and I come to tell you that you have erred gravely in doing her bidding."

Only when the words were out did he remember that he had intended to be mild and reasonable. Too late, he attempted to modulate his voice. "I apologize for my vehemence, Your Honor, but my mother is indulging in an ill-conceived vendetta with me. I am partly at fault, I confess it freely. But there is no true basis for her charges. Miss Farrell is blameless and should not have to suffer because of our family quarrel. I intend to do whatever it will take to have you release Miss Farrell immediately."

The magistrate looked uncomfortable and made a great show of shuffling the papers on his desk. "Please, calm yourself, my lord," he begged him. "The vast edifice of English law provides many protections for those who are unjustly charged. If Miss Farrell is innocent, she shall surely be found so by the court and released. But the matter is out of my hands. A charge has been brought, and depositions have been taken, and the process is underway. Once a case is entered into the system, the stipulations of the law must be adhered to. Unless Lady Hartwood is willing to withdraw her charges, the only way I can release Miss Farrell is if Miss Farrell's counsel can convince the judges that the charges should be dropped when her case comes up at the Michaelmas quarter sessions. Until then I must keep her under confinement."

"But that's monstrous! The quarter sessions aren't for another month! There's no basis to Lady Hartwood's charges except spite. And her spite is causing an innocent woman to suffer."

"Innocent?" The magistrate coughed discreetly. "I must advise you that there has been evidence introduced into the record which would contradict your assertions. And indeed, Hartwood—" the magistrate's voice dropped conspiratorially, "With all respect, I myself attended the dinner at which you imposed the society of this Farrell person most inappropriately upon people of unblemished respectability. My mother has been Lady Hartwood's confidant these twenty years. There can be no doubt as to the justness of her complaint, and with all respect, I must caution you that you do Miss Farrell's case no good by applying to me in this way. I must take down your words as evidence, you see, and given that the prisoner is the subject of a charge of lewdness, which I must advise you involves Your Lordship materially, the showing of too much partiality by yourself may weigh heavily against her."

So that was where he had seen the man. At his mother's dinner party. Though it was with difficulty that Edward restrained himself from telling the magistrate what he thought of his laws and into which physical aperture he could shove them, he was not a complete fool, and the man's words brought home to him the danger into which his unthinking impulsiveness had put Eliza.

"I take your point," he said at last in a steely voice. "How much will it cost me to end this unpleasantness?"

The magistrate frowned. "There is no question of bail in a case where the charges are this serious."

"I'm not talking about bail. I'll pay you whatever it takes to end the matter. You would be well advised to heed me. *I* can afford to be generous, while my mother, whatever she might have told you, has no funds except for those I choose to give her."

The magistrate stood up. "This interview must be at an end, Your Lordship. Strong emotion appears to have made you forget the respect due to my office."

So bribery would not work. Edward cursed silently. Now he must undo the damage he'd caused by attempting it. He put on his most penitent face. "Your Honor, I was carried away by my passions. You must forgive me. I meant no insult to yourself or your office. But before I leave can you tell me, is there some way, at least, that I may visit with Miss Farrell and bring her some promise of help? Can you tell me where she might be imprisoned?"

The magistrate nodded. "You may visit with her, subject to the regulations that apply to the general public. You will find her at 27 Camelford Street, in the custody of Mr. Cuthbertson. She will remain there, maintained at her own expense, until the quarter sessions." The magistrate stood up signaling that the interview was at an end.

* * *

Fortunately, Edward found Mr. Cuthbertson far less resistant to bribery than the magistrate. A sovereign was all it took to get him to remember a loophole to the regulation preventing the general public from consorting privately with a prisoner.

Having secured the money in his pocket, the man led Edward down a dingy corridor to a steep flight of stone steps that led to a basement room that had been set aside for the keeping of prisoners. He removed a heavy key from a ring on his belt and made a great show of opening the lock. Then he motioned Edward into the cell, and after locking the door behind him, informed him through a peephole in the door that he would be back to free him in half an hour.

Edward did not think it was possible for him to feel any worse about the peril in which his unthinking behavior had placed Eliza. But he was not prepared for the impact on his heart of the misery he saw flood into her eyes when she saw it was him.

"So you have come," she said in a voice so dull he could barely recognize it as hers. "And you will apologize and tell me how terrible you feel and promise it will never happen again. Then you will leave, and I will still be here in gaol."

"I will free you!" he protested.

"Yes. Of course," she said, much too quietly. "You will free me, just as my father will buy me a coach and four when he has earned back all his losses at the gaming table."

"Eliza," he said, feeling his temper rise. "I'm

not your father. You were right about my mother,
and I was wrong to ignore your warnings. But I
will not leave you here! I will do whatever it takes
to free you and when I have freed you I will make
it up to you for what you have suffered. You have
my word on it."

Still speaking in that dangerously soft tone,
Eliza ignored him. "I should have known better
than to let myself fall prey to your fatal charm.
You warned me, but I wouldn't listen. It seems I
am fated to love men who cannot see beyond their
own obsessions. My father's is high play, yours,
another kind of playing. Was it not just a game
to you, beguiling me while thinking up ways to
annoy your mother as you pushed past every
limit she set for you? You were enjoying yourself
so much, thinking only of how she had wronged
you, never caring that real people were involved,
that real people could get hurt."

Her words cut him to the heart. But he was not
as bad as she thought. He stretched out one hand
toward her. "Eliza," he began, "I deserve every
angry word you can heap on my head. I've been
a fool and you are paying for my foolishness. But
I will get you out of here. And when I do, please,
Eliza, tell me you will forgive me."

Eliza sat stiffly across from him, her head
bowed. "Why should it matter to you what I think
of you? You warned me that it would be dangerous to give my heart to you, but I ignored your
warning. I am my own victim, not yours."

The pain in her eyes tore through the last shreds

of his self-control. "I cannot bear to have you hate me, Eliza. Not after last night. I found the letter that you left for me this morning, and it horrified me to realize that because I had not the courage to speak up then, you'd been left believing you would be abandoned. I should have asked you to marry me as soon as you gave me the precious gift of yourself. I meant to, but I was a coward. I can only beg your forgiveness for that, too."

He dropped to his knees, feeling the cold dampness of the stone floor seep through the silk of his breeches. "This isn't how I'd hoped it would be when I made my proposal but I cannot bear to delay another moment. Eliza, I would consider myself the most fortunate of men if you would consent to be my wife."

Eliza's eyes opened wide and for a moment he thought he saw surprise flash through them. Then she cocked her head and laughed sourly.

"Marry you?" she said. "And ensure myself a lifetime of misery, instead of just a single episode of disaster? You must be mad."

Edward said nothing, aghast at how much pain had been hiding behind Eliza's own fearsome self-control.

"It is all a game to you, isn't it?" she said bitterly. "Playing tricks on your mother, making me fall in love with you. And now you think you can fix everything just by assigning me a new role."

Edward wanted to protest that she was wrong, but he was silenced by the heavy realization that every word she said was true.

"I, too, have been a fool," Eliza said. "But I finally understand my own danger. After you'd awakened me to all the excitement I'd missed in life that evening at your town house, I pretended I could stay objective. I convinced myself I stayed with you so I could offer you help. But I was self-deluded. I fell in love with Lord Lightning. I let myself succumb to the charms of a practiced rake. My aunt tried to keep me sheltered and protect me from my own impetuous nature, but it was no use. I am too much my mother's daughter. She married a charming man whose only flaw was that he couldn't think past his own desires. She, too, thought she could change him."

Her words stung, but he forced himself to silence, knowing he must not try to justify himself to her. The pent-up anger in her words was so familiar to him, so like his own. But perhaps all was not lost. Had she not just said that she loved him? It had frightened him yesterday to think Eliza might love a man as flawed as he knew himself to be. But now, with a sudden awakening he knew her love for him was all that stood between himself and total devastation.

Eliza's dull voice went on relentlessly. "My father was a charming man when my mother first met him, just as you are now. She was far his inferior in rank. They might not have married except that, as my aunt told me, she behaved as imprudently with him as I have with you. She gave herself to him thinking she loved him and when she discovered she was to bear me, she was forced to marry him or face society's judgment upon her."

Eliza stopped and took a ragged breath. "By the time I was born she had learned the extent of her mistake. My father was out gambling the night of my birth. He didn't come home for three days, and, when he did, it was to tell her he had gambled away the last of her dowry. I don't think her love for him long outlived my birth, but by then it was too late for her to free herself." Eliza toyed nervously with the edge of her sleeve. "At least I am fortunate to find myself the full victim of your thoughtlessness before I was swayed by my passions to accept your offer. I've been reminded of what a lifetime with you would mean before I was condemned to live through it. I will not make the mistake my mother made."

Edward wanted to protest that he was not so entirely lost in his own selfish desires as her dreadful father had been. But his protests died unspoken. He had been so obsessed with his own wounds he hadn't noticed hers, though life had hurt her as badly as it had hurt him. Perhaps worse.

Why else would she have chosen to be a spinster despite her beauty and her lively nature? Why else had she maintained that schoolmistress's air of cold emotional control? It had been that control of hers which had so attracted him—the thought that she could remain unaffected by the surging anger and pain that so often filled his own heart. It had been her relentless control which had goaded him to use all his skills to penetrate her defenses.

As he had done, oh so successfully, last night.

He felt terror now as he became aware of how little he could trust himself. Did he really know where the games ended and where reality began? Last night, when he had seduced her, had he really meant to marry her? He remembered how his body had burned for her and how easy it had been to convince himself her seduction was necessary. And though he had justified taking her with the belief he must marry her, had he not ripped through the last of her defenses when he had kissed her by the sea, *before* he'd seen her father's damning letter with its revelation of who she really was?

It *had* been a game to him, a novel game filled with tenderness and desire rather than coldness and disdain, but a game nonetheless, like the game he played with his mother, the game that kept him from feeling the anger that otherwise might overwhelm him. Playing Lord Lightning kept him safe, but at what cost?

As he saw how hard Eliza was fighting the tears threatening to overwhelm her, and the emotions she, too, had tried so hard to deny, something shifted within him. It was as if he could feel the chain break that had kept his own feelings safely bound. As his control snapped, he felt tears welling up within him, as he waited for the catastrophe that must follow as his feelings, finally liberated, overwhelmed him.

But it did not come. Pain surged up in him, and need, and raging anger so violent it must soon consume him, but as he stood in the center of the storm that was his own heart he was steadied by the beauty that radiated from Eliza. She stood so wholly exposed as she grappled with her own annihilating fear, and the fury within him retreated. It slunk off like some wounded animal, the broken chain clanking behind it as it dragged itself off to die. And as the anger ebbed, another emotion flooded into him.

Love.

As he watched Eliza's dear freckled face flush as she contended with the release of her own long buried terror, he realized with painful clarity how much he loved her. How he loved her more than he loved himself. And he knew beyond question he was willing to make whatever sacrifice it took to heal her wounds the way she had tried to heal his. She deserved better than the man that he had been. But he was all she had. So there was nothing left to do but rescue her from the predicament that man had put her in.

"I have been all that you say I am," he said, his head bowed. "My words can do nothing for you now, so I will spare you them. But know this: I am not like your father. I will free you from this imprisonment. I am not completely without influence, and I will not rest until you are free."

Eliza nodded, but her eyes when they met his were dull with misery.

He bit his tongue and stopped himself from

pouring out words that would tell her of the love now filling his heart. That would only be more selfishness. It wasn't what she needed. Instead he just stood silently before her, opening himself up to the fullness of what he felt for her. As he did, tears coursed down Eliza's face, and she began to shake. He put his arms around her and drew her close, comforting her like a dearly beloved child, patting her on the back, and making feeble soothing sounds. As he held her, he felt once again that indescribable flow of energy that arose between them when they embraced.

This must be love, he thought with wonder, *this joy that arises when I am close to her, even when there is no reason to feel joy, this hope that fills me when there is no reason to hope.*

Eventually she calmed. She said nothing more but did not push him away, and simply clung to him, as if she, too, knew they were bound by something beyond words, until they heard the clatter of the gaoler's key as it turned in the cell door.

She sprang back, and Edward was forced to leave her.

Chapter 18

"**Q**uite a tasty piece," Mr. Cuthbertson remarked as he led Edward up the stairway away from Eliza's prison cell. "Wouldn't mind sampling a bit of what she's been peddling meself." He smacked his lips together in anticipation.

Edward resisted the temptation to kill the man where he stood. It would solve nothing. Instead he drew him aside and hissed, "There's another five guineas waiting for you when she leaves here, but only if she leaves here untouched by you or any man."

"So it's like that, is it?" the man said, suddenly remembering to tug his forelock respectfully. "Fond of the lady, are you? Well, take no offense, Your Lordship. It was only my little way o' jokin', not meaning any disrespect to the lady."

"See that you remember that," Edward commanded.

He hoped the hefty bribe would be enough to keep Eliza safe, but he was troubled. He knew what happened to women imprisoned for prostitution. It was essential that he find some way of getting her released immediately. Every hour she spent in custody increased the danger to her. But how to free her?

Appealing to his mother to withdraw the charges would be useless. Clearly she felt it was safe for her to challenge him and until he understood why, he must move carefully. Whatever the explanation, she was far too pleased with the advantage her latest move had given her in their battle to give it up now. *He* might have seen the futility of such game playing, but why should she quit the game, when at last she was ahead? He must find some other way to rescue Eliza.

Mentally he went through the list of his acquaintances, trying to find one who might have enough influence to get her freed, but they were a frippery lot, and besides, it would take more than wealth and titles to free Eliza. Only the Regent had the kind of power that could interfere with the majestic grinding of the law. But Edward had never run in the Regent's circles and doubted that his name would mean anything to him—unless he was aware of Lord Lightning's terrible reputation.

There was only one person of his acquaintance who had been a familiar of the Regent: Mrs. Atwater. His heart sank when he remembered the shameful scene in which he had just compelled her to play a role. Once again his thoughtless play-acting had made Eliza's situation more difficult. He had almost dismissed as worthless the idea of appealing to her, when it occurred to him that though Mrs. Atwater might not wish him well, perhaps he could sway her by making it clear that the favor he asked was not for himself but for Eliza, a woman, after all, whose situation must remind her of her own, and one, moreover, who was a victim of her own protector's hateful wife.

It was worth a try.

He turned his steps toward the modest street in an unfashionable part of town where Mrs. Atwater had her dwelling and when he reached it, knocked decisively on her door. When she opened it herself, he breathed a sigh of relief. He not been certain she would have agreed to speak to him had he been forced to relay his message to her through a servant.

He suspected he had woken her from slumber. She was dressed in an old-fashioned pink silk wrapper that had clearly seen better days and her graying hair was still braided for sleep. She was blinking, blearily, and her posture told him she wished to get rid of him as quickly as possible. Still, she took his hat and led him into the small parlor whose walls were lined with richly framed faded prints depicting the scenes of her former triumphs.

He quickly explained the situation to her and asked her if she would be willing to use whatever influence she had with the Regent to ask him to effect Eliza's release.

A look of annoyance crossed her face. "So your mother has taken away your latest toy, has she? Surely with what I've heard of your tastes, Your Lordship, you can easily replace her."

"What you hear of me is much exaggerated. But she is not my toy, nor could anyone ever replace Eliza in my life. My mother sensed that and chose to strike back at me by harming an innocent woman whose only fault was to have seen good in me where none existed."

"I'm not surprised to hear that your mother did strike back, nor should you have been. She was never one to leave an insult unavenged. And the insult you offered her was beyond anything. Had I known what you had planned for her that night you bid me to her home, I shouldn't have gone, no matter how much money you offered me. Truly, Your Lordships I was ashamed to have been part of it."

"I deserve your reproach. Eliza has opened my eyes to many things, not the least of which is the inexcusability of the way in which I treated you. But she didn't do it soon enough to save herself from becoming my victim."

Mrs. Atwater's eyebrows lifted and he sensed that his words might have gone some way toward winning her over to his cause. "Would you pay me to speak to the Regent for her, too?" she asked.

"If that was what it took to convince you to help her, yes."

"How much?"

"Name your figure. I will not haggle over it. I must free Eliza."

She let out a long, slow whistle, "So, you really do care about the girl. More's the pity for you, for I cannot take your money. It's been many a year since I've run in Prinny's circle. Why, I doubt he would recognize me now, looking like this." She gestured ruefully toward her ruined face. "Besides, you of all men should know how little note men of the world take of women like me. After all this time, I doubt he would recall my name, far less wish to hear me ask him for some favor. I'm just a face in the crowd to him, now, I am, whatever I might have once been to him."

"You won't even try?"

"And humiliate myself again for your sake? I'm not that hard up, thank God!"

Edward's shoulders sagged. "Then I must take my leave of you and look for help elsewhere. I'm sorry if I've offended you with my request."

She went to get his hat. When she returned, she favored him with a long, examining look. "This Eliza of yours *is* more than a passing fancy, isn't she?"

"Far more. I have asked her to be my wife."

"Well fancy that! That will get the world a-talking. Lord Lightning's to marry his mistress!"

"No. He will not. She's turned me down," he

said quietly. "And I do not expect to be able to change her mind."

"Yet you still are willing to pay whatever it takes to free her. Why I believe you do care for the girl."

"I do, though it would have been better for her had I lived up to my reputation for heartlessness. Had I not cared for her, she would not have become my mother's victim."

Without handing him his hat, which she still held in her hand, Mrs. Atwater said, "I must think very well of this Eliza of yours, as she seems to have taught you some humility. And for her sake, I must tell you this: I've just remembered something quite troubling, Your Lordship. I've heard distressing stories about the magistrate."

"What have you heard?"

Mrs. Atwater's voice dropped. "Only that he likes to examine the girls privately."

"Privately?" he repeated.

"Yes. Privately. Late into the night." She shook her head, making her long gray braids shake. "And after he is done with them quite a few of them are reported as having escaped."

"You mean he lets them go in return for sexual favors?"

"It's worse than that. The girls are never seen again. The rumors are that he sells them to a brothel keeper in London who caters to the sort of men who like to hurt women."

Edward's stomach clenched. "If this is known, why is nothing done to stop it?"

Mrs. Atwater sighed and smoothed one age-spotted hand over her heart. "They're fallen women. No one cares a fig what happens to them. And there are powerful men who find such perversions pleasing. They wouldn't like to see the supply of criminals to the brothel stopped."

He felt as if ice were forming around his heart. The danger to Eliza was far worse than he had imagined. Could he threaten to expose the magistrate? It was unlikely. He had no proof but the wild assertions of an aging demimondaine. No, his usual theatrics would be no use in this situation.

He turned back to Mrs. Atwater. "My behavior to you has robbed me of any claim on your kindness," he said. "But I beg of you, for Eliza's sake, if there is anyone else you know who might be able to effect Eliza's release, tell me who it might be."

Mrs. Atwater fixed him with a stern gaze. "There is only one person who can free her, Your Lordship," she said. "And you must know already who it is—though your pride might keep you from addressing her."

"And who is that?"

"Lady Hartwood."

His heart sank. Lady Hartwood. Who hated him. Who had always hated him. Who could not *really* be his mother. But even as the old familiar protest flashed through his mind he realized with a shock that perhaps this, too, was only another game—a game he had played with himself since he was young, because if she really were his mother, the pain of her rejection would be too great to bear.

Meeting his father's mistress's once beautiful blue eyes, their color faded now with age, he said, "You are right. I have no choice but to appeal to Lady Hartwood. But before I do, there is one thing I must know."

The knuckles on his tightly clenched fist had gone white with strain.

"What is that, Your Lordship?"

"Is she really my mother, or are you?"

Mrs. Atwater's small hand flew to her mouth in surprise. "Me, your mother? You must be joking."

"I have never been more serious in my life."

Mrs. Atwater peered closely at him. "Me, your mother! Whatever put that into your head?"

"I'd always heard my mother had much difficulty birthing James and how the doctors told her she must not bear another child. But James was sickly. So I thought my father had forced my mother to pretend your child was hers to ensure he might have another heir."

"He never would have done that. Your father was a very proud man. He would have been horrified at the idea of polluting his noble line with the blood of the likes of me. He wouldn't even acknowledge my poor Charles, though he had no doubt his own blood ran in Charles's veins. Why as you said, he looks just like him!"

Edward struggled to breathe. "But you were so kind to me when I was small. I used to think it was because you were my real mother—I used to hope you were." He fought against the tears that threatened to unman him.

"Well, I'm not your mother, Your Lordship. I was kind to you because you were a sweet little bit of a lad, and because, well, your birth made my life far easier. But you must get over that idea that I am your mother. It is not true. Lady Hartwood is your mother, as much as she might have wished she weren't."

"But if I am her child, why has she always hated me?"

"Do you really not know the answer to that?" Mrs. Atwater asked. "I should have thought by now someone would have told you."

"Told me what?" More fear gripped him at the realization that, as mistaken as he had been, there was still some secret here, even if it was not the one he had expected.

Mrs. Atwater turned away and put down his hat on a chair. When she turned back to face him he saw that she seemed to be struggling with some strong emotion. "If you really don't know the truth, it's not my place to tell it to you," she said at length. "I owe that much to Black Neville. He wouldn't have wanted it known, and even though he's been gone these many years, I owe it to him to keep his secret now."

"Your loyalty does you credit, but it is misplaced. My father wasn't faithful to you any more than he was to my mother. And why should you owe anything to him, when he wouldn't acknowledge your son, Charles, who looks just like him?"

The warring emotions flitted across her face. He'd struck a nerve.

"He was a proud man, Black Neville was. But he didn't abandon Charles, even if he wouldn't claim him his own. He gave me that necklace for Charles, didn't he? And when he gave me that necklace, he gave me every penny he had command of. He couldn't have done more for any son."

"I always wondered why he gave it to you. James was still alive and he was his heir. I always thought my father did it to pay for your silence because he'd passed off your child as his own, but if that was not the case, why did my father beggar his heir and give everything he had to Charles?"

"James was always sickly. You could see that just by looking at him. It was a wonder he lived long enough to marry that poor girl. Black Neville didn't think James would live to inherit his title."

"But James was not his only child," Edward said softly. "He had me. I was strong and healthy."

"Oh yes," Mrs. Atwater agreed. "He did have you. But he wanted his *real* son to get his money."

His real son? It took a moment for her words to sink in. Then, as Mrs. Atwater saw understanding flood into his eyes, her hand flew up to her face in dismay. "Oh I am such a blabbermouth! I meant to keep his secret. He cared so much that no one should ever know."

"Know what?"

"That your mother had betrayed him with another man. What else could it be?"

What else indeed.

"You can see why I felt fond of you, now, can't you. Once your mother had fallen pregnant with another man's brat, he had no more care for her, and I had him all to myself. But I felt sorry for you, poor child, because none of them gave a snap for you, and it wasn't as if you'd had any say in it."

Then another realization dawned. "But if I'm not my father's son, then I'm also not Lord Hartwood!"

"Oh, but you are, for he did acknowledge you. That was part of the bargain he made with your mother. It makes no matter to the law whose swiving did the work when a child is born to a woman joined in lawful matrimony. Not if the father won't raise a stink about it. And he didn't, even though he'd been in Paris with me from Michaelmas to New Year's the year before your birth. You are his son in the eyes of the law and no one can challenge your title."

"But why didn't he raise a stink?"

"Pride. What else? He couldn't bear the shame of going through a divorce, nor could he bear to be exposed in the press as a cuckold, as he would have been had he gone forward. So he agreed to acknowledge you as his son and let your mother remain his wife in the eyes of the world, though he told her were she ever to make another misstep, he would divorce her. He let her know, too, that she could never again utter a word of complaint about anything he did or he would reveal her shame to the world. So she lived with that hanging over her, and I imagine that is what pushed her to become the way she is now, obsessed with reputation and propriety."

"So *that* was why she would never denounce anything he did, even when he ruined us by giving you that necklace."

"It was. She knew what was due to her husband for giving her that second chance. Many another man would have cast her out when the truth had become known."

"But if Black Neville was not my real father," he whispered, "who was?"

"That was the worst part of it for him. Had your mother dallied with someone of his own rank, I think your father could have borne it. Lord knows he'd left his own cuckoo's eggs in many another nobleman's nest. But when he forced the truth out of your mother, he learned your father was some strolling player who had come through town, a handsome devil who had the reputation for playing Romeo on the stage and off."

An actor. Of course.

Mrs. Atwater added, "I always thought she did it to get back at him for running off to Paris with me. Those women of the ton, they're expected to ignore that kind of thing, but your mother was a woman of spirit and she rebelled, though she should have known better. Even a woman as strong as your mother wasn't going to change a man like Black Neville. He liked his pleasures, and he didn't like them interfered with. But if she had hoped to make him jealous by dallying with that actor, or thought it might bring him back to her, she was sorely mistaken. Her infidelity made him hate her. He never forgave her, and when he saw you growing up so healthy and strong while James was such a weakling it enraged him further. That's why he gave me that necklace for Charles. It was her dowry money, and it pleased him greatly to give me all of it, to punish her for forcing him to leave his title away from his blood."

Mrs. Atwater was still talking, but he could no longer hear her words. They were drowned out by the cacophony that rose within his heart. He was not Black Neville's son. He was not the damned son of a damned race. He could not blame his nature on his father. He did not even know the man who'd been his father. And his mother's life-long hatred, the hatred that had poisoned his life, was no longer inexplicable. It was all too easily understood. It had nothing to do with his own character at all, only with the way that his very existence must remind her till she died of her one life-ruining mistake.

He thanked Mrs. Atwater for her frankness and stood up. When she handed him his hat and he put it on, he was almost afraid to look at himself in the glass hanging in the hallway. He hardly knew who he would find looking back at him. He no longer knew anything except he had let his own pain drive him to hurt his mother where she was most vulnerable. Now Eliza would pay a terrible price for his blindness, unless he could somehow find a way to get his mother to relent.

Chapter 19

"Her Ladyship left no word as to when she will return," the butler informed him on his return to the house, dashing his hopes that the situation could be resolved quickly. The butler believed Lady Hartwood had gone to visit Dr. Abercrombie, perhaps to receive one of his famous hydrotherapeutic treatments, but he was not certain.

There was no point in attempting to follow her to the doctor's bathhouse. His mother would not thank him for interrupting her session, so he made his way down the passage to the library intending to wait for her there, only to find that it was already occupied by the Reverend Mr. Hoskins, the clergyman who had attended his brother on his deathbed.

The clergyman seemed surprised to see him. Addressing him in a low voice, he inquired as to why Lord Hartwood had not already returned to town.

"Surely you of all people must know the answer to that," Edward replied. "You were present when my brother made his will. There is more than a week left to the term of the visit his will compelled. If I were to leave now, my mother must lose her home."

"How very odd," the Reverend Mr. Hoskins replied, screwing his face into an expression of surprise. "It has been two days at least since I informed Lady Hartwood that James's will could not hold up in court."

"Not hold up in court, but why?"

The clergyman assumed a solemn expression. "Alas, though it is hard for a man of the cloth such as I am to admit that religious sentiments such as those James Neville entertained at the end of his life might proceed from any but the most elevated of causes, I was forced to conclude that by the time he drew up the will in question, the balance of your brother's mind was disturbed."

"But how could you prove it?"

"Why, by citing the impropriety of the terms he included in that will—the terms that brought you here. Though your brother, looking into the abyss, saw too late the sinfulness of his previous life and hoped to atone for it by forcing a reconciliation between the sole members of his family he'd leave behind to mourn him, it was unconscionable that he attempted to force your mother, a virtuous woman, to associate with a son whose behavior

has been such as yours has been. And had there
been any further question of it being improper,
your subsequent behavior upon your arrival here
would answer it."

The clergyman licked his lips nervously before
continuing. "After discussing the situation with
Lady Hartwood last week and being made privy
to her understandable dismay at the situation into
which James's will had forced her, I informed the
family's solicitor I would be willing to testify in
court as to the unsoundness of James's mind in
his final hours." The clergyman's voice grew conspiratorial. "I was in attendance, as you know, and
was in a position to make a definitive assessment
of his condition. Her solicitor then advised Lady
Hartwood that, in view of my testimony, there
could be no question that the court must set aside
that will, and that James's earlier will, which was
drawn up at the time of his marriage would go
into effect."

"So there was no need for us to play out this
travesty," Edward said bitterly.

"None at all," Mr. Hoskins assured him. "The
earlier will leaves this house and its contents to
Lady Hartwood for the term of her life, as well as
any income from what was left of your brother's
personal estate. The rest reverts to you. But I confess myself astonished that your mother has not
yet informed you of this."

He was not at all astonished. This was the explanation for why his mother had moved against
Eliza. Had he been informed that the will would

be set aside, he would have left for town immediately, taking Eliza with him, and his mother
would have lost the opportunity of retaliating
against him. No wonder she had kept it secret.

But what was he to do now? If the will had been
set aside, he had lost the last hold he had over his
mother. His heart failed him when he considered
the coming confrontation. He had nothing left to
bargain with and she knew it.

Eventually his mother returned home and
after a brief consultation with the Reverend Mr.
Hoskins, who scurried away back to his burrow
when it was done, she invited Edward into the
front parlor. She took her old accustomed place in
her armchair, but made no motion for him to sit
down, so he was left standing in front of her feeling the way he'd felt when he had been a small
boy sent to her for punishment. Fear, longing, and
a dull unnamed pain warred for possession of his
attention. He felt her loathing for him radiating
out from her, as he always did in her presence. He
felt, too, her pleasure in having finally got the best
of him. It took all his control to stand before her,
knowing he no longer had any control over her.

And yet, as the force of her anger washed over
him, and he braced himself as if for a blow, something within him surged up and reminded him he
was no longer a helpless child. He was a man. Nor
was he the damned and evil man she'd always
insisted he was. Eliza had shown him that. The
loathing he felt for himself in his mother's pres-

ence flowed through him, but now that he knew whence it sprang, he no longer fought it and he resisted the temptation to respond to her anger with his own.

She was his mother. He could no longer doubt it.

She had made a single foolish mistake out of thwarted love, and in so doing had lost what she held most dear. As he regarded her now, no longer peering through the distorting lens of his own anger, he saw for the first time a woman who had once been young and headstrong, who had loved a rake and failed disastrously in her attempt to make him love her back. Her lifelong hatred for himself had nothing to do with who he was or anything he'd done. It was only her response to the disaster she'd made of her own life. And as he saw this, a surge of joy rose within him and he knew that he was free.

Lady Hartwood motioned him to be seated, but he remained standing for a moment longer, still stunned by what he saw in her. Then it struck him that she might take his inaction as more rudeness. He could not afford to alienate her further, so he sat down.

"I have received a very strange letter," she said after the silence had grown nearly unbearable.

"A letter?"

"From the creature who calls herself Mrs. Atwater."

He said nothing, but anxiety rose within him. Why had Mrs. Atwater written to his mother?

"It appears she believes your doxy to be in

some danger of being kidnapped and sent into a
bordello. She makes wild accusations against the
magistrate, a man I have entertained here in my
own home. I find it difficult to credit such a thing.
He is a man from the finest of families. Why, I've
known his mother for years."

Edward spoke carefully, not sure what else
might be written in the letter. "I've heard such
rumors, too. But you of all people should know
that a son might have morals quite different from
those of his mother."

His mother nodded, not quite suppressing a
look of triumph. She made a show of consulting
the letter again, then put it down in her lap. He
might be done with game playing, but she most
assuredly was not. He would have to play this last
hand with the greatest skill he'd ever employed.
He considered his next move, reviewing every
possible way he might sway her, before rejecting
them all as useless, until like a gamester counting
on one last throw to save him, he finally spoke.

"I don't know what else Mrs. Atwater has written you," he said quietly. "But you should know
that I went to her to see if she could use her influence with the Regent to save Eliza. She told me
she could not. She upbraided me for my behavior
to you and told me you and you alone could save
Eliza. She spoke the truth. I only ask that you let
the punishment fall where it should, on my shoulders, and not on Eliza, whose only fault was to
think her woman's love could help me become a
better man."

"Women always think they can reform men like you," his mother said bitterly. "I trust she has learned of her error."

"I believe she has," he replied quietly. "You should also know that I have offered for her and she has rejected me."

His mother looked at him with renewed interest. "She has more sense than I credited her with." She brushed away an imaginary speck on her cuff. "It would be no pleasure even for a woman like her to be married to a rake like you."

"That was exactly the sentiment she expressed in response to my proposal," Edward said. "I don't know that I shall be able to change her mind. I have done many things I'm not proud of, as you very well know, and they cannot be undone. But if there is any way I can prevent harm from coming to Eliza, I will do it, no matter what it might cost me."

"It is easy to speak such words." His mother sneered. "But they are only words—and you are a master of words. What are you willing to *do* to save her?"

He skewered her with his eyes. "Whatever it takes."

A look of satisfaction spread over his mother's face. "If you are truly willing to do what it takes, then perhaps we may deal together, at last, you and I. James's previous will—the one the court will accept—doesn't leave me nearly enough to live upon."

Chapter 20

An hour later, Edward left his mother's house clutching the paper she had signed, which announced her intention of withdrawing her charges against Eliza. The paper had not been bought cheaply, but he had given her all she asked for without argument. His money would mean nothing to him if Eliza suffered more harm.

He hurried to the magistrate's house and pounded on the door. But the man who let him in informed him that His Honor had gone to a meeting of legal gentlemen and could not be reached until the morrow. Edward demanded to know where the meeting was being held but the man was close-lipped and would give him no further information. There was nothing for it except to come back the next morning.

But at least he could go and tell Eliza the news.

The constable's house was only a few streets away. He ran the whole distance.

The lights were off when he reached the house, as if the household were already asleep. He knocked on the door. It seemed like hours passed until it was opened. He was glad to see it was the constable who faced him and not a servant to whom he'd have to explain his mission. But when the constable realized who had summoned him an expression of dismay swept across his face.

"She's gone, Your Lordship. You're too late. There was nothing I could do to stop it. I am only the constable and it's not my place to tell His Honor how to conduct his business."

His blood ran cold. "What are you talking about, man?"

"His Honor's servant came and took the woman away with him for questioning."

"Now? But it's almost night!"

The man shifted from foot to foot. "Such is the custom when they have a woman accused of that kind of crime," he muttered. "The magistrate likes to question them in private. In the nighttime, if you get my meaning."

So Mrs. Atwater's suspicion had been true! He tried not to let his panic show.

"But where does he take them? I have just come from the magistrate's house. I had an order for the woman's release, but they told me he was not there!"

"Aye. They wouldn't be at his house," Cuthbertson said with a meaningful look. "But I don't know as that I can tell you where it is they go."

Edward pulled out a fistful of golden coins and held it out to him, saying, "Don't waste my time, man. I know you can be bought. Tell me where she is. If you won't tell me, I'll shake it out of you."

Cowed by his fury, the man made no effort to negotiate but merely said, "Calm yourself, Your Lordship, calm yourself. I always like to help a gent in trouble. They are most likely in a little room at the back of the old town hall. That's where he goes when there's a woman to be examined."

"How long ago did they take her?"

"It could not be more than half an hour."

Thank God it was not longer than that. Perhaps there was still time to save her. He tossed a sovereign toward the man contemptuously, letting it fall onto the street, and then turned away from him without another word.

It was almost dark by the time he reached the market square. The rambling half-timbered town hall stretched along one side of the cobblestoned marketplace. He looked up at the windows looking for a sign that someone was there, but they were all dark. He tried the door, found it locked, and pounded on the heavy oak timbers, but no one came to open it.

Perhaps the constable was wrong? Perhaps this was not where Eliza had been taken? The light was tricky as the long summer twilight still lingered. It would be hard to see the flicker of a dim candle shining from inside. He went around to the side of the building where the shadows might make it easier to detect light coming from inside.

Yes. There was a flicker in an upstairs window. Someone was there. The man had told him the truth.

He ran back to the front of the building and pounded on the door again, but again no one answered. It was hardly likely they would interrupt themselves if they were up to the kind of mischief the constable had suggested.

If he could just somehow get in and speak to the magistrate. The man would be forced to release Eliza once presented with the paper his mother had signed. He could hardly ignore it. But if the magistrate had taken Eliza for illicit purposes of his own, he would not wish to be detected.

Edward pounded on the door again, though by now he expected no answer. He thought of smashing in a window but dismissed the idea. He would hardly do Eliza's cause any good by breaking the law himself. And if he were to burst in on the magistrate and find him in a compromising situation—he forced his thoughts away from the image; it was too painful to think of Eliza that way.

There must be some way to rescue her. Something that wasn't illegal. He had military training. Surely there must be some strategy he'd learned that would solve this problem.

Think, Edward, he told himself, think! He went deep within himself, forcing his mind to become calm, cleared of everything except the need to come up with a solution, just as he had done during the war when he and his men had been lost in the Spanish swamp. He remembered feeling the same stillness, as if time slowed down, and the sudden clarity that had shown him the way out. He focused on Eliza, opening himself to her and feeling her love, until, it was as if he could hear her voice within him, calling out to him, telling him that the answer lay in himself, in being true to his own Uranian nature.

Despite his distress, he almost laughed, realizing that the way Eliza used that astrological imagery of hers was such a part of her nature that even in a crisis he could not imagine her without it. His Uranian nature indeed! He could barely even remember what she had meant by "Uranian." What was it? Something to do with surprises. That was part of it. And new things. He tried to remember what else she had said to him, and recalled her laughing at what she called his explosive Uranian nature—

And with that thought he realized that he had found his answer.

It was so very simple. It would have to work. He turned away and rushed back toward his mother's house. He had no time to lose, but if he could act quickly Eliza could still be saved.

Chapter 21

"**T**he prisoner will answer the questions put to her by the court!" The voice was harsh and the words slurred.

Eliza stood in the center of the room, in front of a plain oak table, her hands bound together by a rope. A man wearing a solicitor's wig and robe sat on a bench before her, clearly much gone in his cups, while the magistrate, who was dressed in a long black gown and barrister's wig, stood before her demanding that she answer his questions.

But the questions were obscene.

Eliza stood silent, unwilling to show the fear that the men had aroused in her, unable to understand how they could act this way. She was afraid to guess where their drunken interrogation was going and more afraid that she already knew.

It had all started earlier, just as night had begun

to fall. She had been resting in her cell, unable to get Edward's offer of marriage out of her mind, fighting against the treacherous urges that made her regret having to refuse it, and loving him all the more for having made it to her—as impossible as it must be for her to accept it—when she had heard her gaoler and another man joking rudely in the hallway. The two of them had laughed raucously at something and then unlatched her door. Once it was open, the new man, a well-muscled brute who smelled of onions and weeks without a washing, had smiled suggestively and said that he hoped she was not tired as she'd have a busy night ahead of her, his arms making a vulgar gesture as he spoke.

Eliza could not help but shudder at such crudeness, but their crudeness was only a dim foretaste of what awaited her when the brute delivered her to the back room in the town hall.

She had recognized the magistrate immediately. He was the man who had presided over her arrest—the man who had sat beside Lady Hartwood at her dinner party. At first she'd felt relief when she recognized him. Surely his presence meant she had indeed been called in for more interrogation and nothing worse. But then his companion had come over to inspect her, his wig askew, his breath heavy with the smell of alcohol.

"I say, Brillingsworth, you've outdone yourself this time, by Gad! You've brought us Hartwood's fancy piece. It will be a treat to examine such a specimen. The man is famed as a connoisseur of the frailer sex." The man's eyes raked over her body, making her feel as if she had already been stripped. "I say, let us proceed at once to the examination of the physical evidence." The man was slavering in anticipation.

"Control yourself, Stenbury," the magistrate admonished. "We'll get to that in good time. But we must follow the proper protocols. Procedure must be followed in all things, as surely a judge like yourself should know. First we must have the questioning of the prisoner. Then we may move on to the examination of the physical evidence."

She had never imagined that respectable men could do such a thing. What little she knew of depravity, she knew from the novels she had read. But the novelists who wrote the books she had read were writing for polite readers and their imaginations had not been equal to a scene like this. And of course, in books, the heroine was protected. There was always some rescue. The hero would burst in and save the girl. But this was real. And real life, she'd learned, was where rescue did not come. Real life was her father losing every penny she'd given him and then demanding more. Real life was Edward regretting the mischief he had done her, declaring his love, and leaving her behind in the cell unprotected. And real life, too, was what she saw lending an anticipatory sparkle to the bleary eyes of the drunken men before her. And knowing that, she felt sheer, unalloyed terror. She was alone and helpless. Nothing could save her but her wits. And at the moment her wits were completely addled.

"Objection sustained, Y'r Ludship," the other man replied with a drunken smirk. "Let us move without delay to the questioning."

"Eliza Farrell," the man intoned, "you are here on a charge of lewdness. You must answer all questions to the best of your ability, being completely truthful in all things. If you lie, it will go hard with you." The man coughed and then continued. "You are known to have associated with Edward Neville, Lord Hartwood, a man known for his lascivious life. Is that not true?"

Eliza said nothing.

"What kind of a cocksman is Lord Hartwood?" the magistrate interrupted. "Is it true as I have heard, that the women like him because he has a rod of prodigious length?"

Eliza again was rendered speechless, but the way that the man referred to Edward infuriated her. "Lord Hartwood is a decent man. Unlike you," she said through clenched teeth. "And his sexual abilities can be of no interest to the law."

"The prisoner will answer the questions!" the magistrate snapped. "How old were you when first you had sexual congress with a man?"

Eliza said nothing.

The other man made some adjustment to his pants, loosening them and sliding a hand inside. "How many men have you had in one night?" he asked.

"How many men have you served at a single time?" cried the magistrate.

"Have you ever taken on two men at once?" the other man demanded. His eyes glittered with anticipation. "There is no point in playing the innocent with us. We know what you are and are well able to appreciate your talents. Surely you won't begrudge us our bit of fun when you've given plenty of it to other men! Or do you like to have the truth tormented out of you? That could be interesting, too, though I had not thought that such was Hartwood's taste."

Eliza stared at them. This was true corruption and profligacy. Yet it was Edward who had earned the reputation as a rake, not these men who held respected offices. She felt a pang as she remembered Edward's kindness, the care he had taken to lead her to pleasure on that one night they had shared together. The world called him a libertine—a world that ignored the hidden perversity of the men who held her here, pillars of the community, entrusted with the administration of the law. No wonder Edward was filled with rage at the world's hypocrisy.

A wave of tenderness swept over her as she recalled the warmth Edward had kept so well hidden from everyone but herself. But she must not waste her energy on futile longings. She must think of some way to save herself. But her mind was frozen, and when she tried to silence it and sink deep down to the place where answers came from, all she saw was Edward Neville's face. All she heard was his voice, begging her to trust him, promising her everything would be all right.

As if Edward Neville could save her! As if anyone could.

"We shall have no sport at this rate," the other man complained. "The woman acts like a mute and will tell us nothing."

"Nay, there is sport still to be had of her," said the magistrate. "Proceed to the physical examination of the evidence." The other man murmured his agreement, and the magistrate lunged toward her, lifting her up and pushing her down on the table. She struggled fiercely despite the ropes that bound her hands but she could do nothing.

"Hear, hear," the other man agreed. "We must do something about those legs, the woman kicks!" Her skirt was pushed aside and she felt a rope wrapped around her left ankle and then pulled tight as it was secured to one leg of the table beneath her. The magistrate grabbed at her right ankle and arms and repeated the procedure.

"She won't fight us any longer," he said, and it was true. She had fought all she could, but it had been useless. Now she numbed herself to endure what she must. The struggle was over.

Suddenly the air was filled with the sound of crackling explosions. A lurid glow lit the room. The light from the window flickered orange and gold.

"I say, Brillingsworth, what's that?"

Eliza swam back into consciousness to realize that the men had rushed over to the window.

One of them pried a pane open and the room was filled with an acrid smell. Thick smoke billowed into the room.

"Gunpowder! There's some disturbance in the square!"

There were more explosions.

"Gunshots!" the magistrate shouted. "Radicals! By God. We are under attack!"

"They've set the building on fire," the other man exclaimed. Then a look of terror crossed his face. "There's no time to spare. The militia stores its black powder in the basement. We must make haste before the fire gets to it or we shall all be blown sky-high."

The men rushed to the door. She could hear their footsteps clattering on the stone stairs, then nothing. They were gone. But what little consolation that might give her was undone by the knowledge that they had not stopped to untie her before they left.

The smell of acrid smoke was getting stronger. She tugged against the ropes that held her hands and feet, but it was futile. She could not move. She could do nothing but lie tied to the table helplessly awaiting the final explosion.

How many seconds of life remained to her? Ten? Five? Soon she would know beyond a doubt what lay on the other side of death. She tried to pray in this, her last moment, but again she was tormented by the thought of Edward Neville. Instead of the peace she had hoped for, she gave herself up to the longing to see him one last time. There was no point in fighting it. She closed her eyes, letting her last moments be filled with the memory of the comfort she had felt in his arms. She imagined his lips on hers. She imagined him gently calming her and smoothing her hair with one hand. Edward, her love, whom she would never see again. Edward.

There was one last huge explosion. Then she thought she had died and was on her way to heaven, for when she opened her eyes she saw Edward, slashing through the ropes that bound her. Then his knife nicked her wrist, and the blade's sharp sting told her that her body was still miraculously alive. It *was* Edward beside her, real and not imagined, and he was holding her tightly as she clung to him, unable to speak, wanting the moment to last forever—but it could not last, for now they were both in peril.

"We must flee," she cried. "This building will explode!"

"No. We are safe. No harm will come to us here."

"But the shots! Any one of them must have set the building aflame. There is black powder in the basement. We must get out now while we can!"

"The building is not on fire," Edward said mildly with a hint of a smile. "There were no shots. You can trust me on this."

Eliza pulled away from him, barely comprehending what he had told her. "But wasn't the building under attack? What of the gunshots I heard?"

"You heard no gunshots, merely the sounds of a mischievous boy playing. With fireworks."

He enfolded her in his arms, holding her as if he would pull her back from death itself. "You are safe, Eliza. The explosions were Chinese firecrackers and Roman candles, the work of a single troublesome boy, a boy who is overly fond of games, games for which you have many times reproved him."

Her eyes widened. "The explosions were *your* fireworks? The ones you had in your trunk?" Amazement dawned on her. "Then you rescued me!"

"Of course. You didn't think I would leave you at the mercy of swine like that?"

"I can scarcely believe it."

"I rescued you, though I shall regret for the rest of my life that my stupidity led to your needing to be rescued in the first place."

"But we must still leave here quickly, before those men come back," she said with a shudder. "Or they'll arrest both of us."

"For what? I am but a blameless spectator who happened to be walking through the square after some unknown boys got up to some mischief. The law can find no fault with that."

"But I am under arrest for—" Eliza could not bring herself to name the charge, her memories of the past half hour were still too raw.

"You are under arrest for nothing," Edward said fiercely. "I have obtained a letter from my mother withdrawing all her charges."

So she was really safe. Incomprehensibly, safe. "But how?"

"I apologized to her for my ill treatment of her and convinced her to withdraw her charges."

"You humbled yourself to your mother for me? You really let her win?"

"Eliza, you taxed me with being like your father, unable to cease playing. But I have never let the intoxication of play so dominate my life that I lost sight of what was important. You have been thoroughly rescued. You are a free woman. The charges against you have been dropped, and you are truly safe."

She let herself go limp and nestled deeper into the shelter of his embracing arms. Nowhere else had ever felt so safe, so right for her. She drew the moment out as long as she could, luxuriating in the feel of his warm breath on her cheek, soaking in the perfection of the moment, fighting desperately to remember why it was she must not allow herself to love him though her soul cried out that she must.

And then she did remember. Slowly the flashes of self-awareness she had experienced in the gaol forced their way back into her consciousness and it came back to her why the game she had been playing with Lord Lightning now must end. As stern reason dragged her back to earth, the brightness fell from the air. She felt herself clear her

throat as she struggled to reassume the air of nonchalance which was all she had ever had to protect her against Edward's irresistible appeal.

In a tone that gave no hint of the sadness that
had swept over her, she said, "It wasn't your fault
alone that I found myself in peril. It was, after all,
my idea to come here with you and play your mistress." As she pulled herself upright, he dropped
her hand, responding to the harshness with which
she had broken out of their embrace. As he withdrew, she felt herself bereft. Still, she forced herself
to keep on speaking in a light tone. "You cannot
take full credit for all that happened, Edward.
Much as I should like to blame you, I, too, have
an impossibly impetuous nature. Uranus rules us
both, which you would have learned if you'd ever
asked about *my* nativity. Indeed, my own natal
Uranus is conjunct Jupiter, which makes me even
more impulsive than you are."

As she gabbled on, she saw him study her face
as if seeking the answer to an unasked question.
When he had found it, he stood up and adjusted
his rumpled coat. She saw him bite his lip. Then
he took a deep breath, and his expression hardened. He, too, was recovering his self-possession.

"I am much at fault for not inquiring more
deeply into much else that concerns you," he said
in a sober tone. "And not just about your nativity.
But I can well believe you, too, are ruled by the
planet of surprises. For my life has been in a continual uproar since the moment I first drew you
into my carriage."

"I am sorry for that," she said. "But you may take comfort in knowing it must all be at an end now."

"I suppose I must," he said, his eyes hooded, their expression once again impenetrable. "Come, Eliza, my carriage waits below."

Chapter 22

Only when they were out on the street, making their way through the crowd of people who milled around, drawn by curiosity to know what the noise and smoke had been about, did Eliza realize she had no idea what she would do next. It was fortunate that Edward moved with a decisiveness that reassured her he had some plan in mind. After they had walked only a short distance she saw his carriage. She clambered into it and, as he gently wrapped her in the fur he had found resting on the seat, she realized that despite the warmth of the evening, she had been shivering.

At length he spoke. "I will never forgive myself for what you've been forced to undergo in the past hour." His voice was once again unnaturally formal, and she sensed what it was costing him to maintain such rigid control. But whatever effort he was expending, it could scarcely be more than what it took for her to keep from flinging herself into his arms and seeking her comfort there. But she must not. She did not dare.

What future was there for her if she gave in to her reckless love for him? He had rescued her as he had promised, but that was a far cry from pledging to love her forever. The events of the past day had snapped her out of the dream in which she had been living.

She had known him for less than a fortnight. How could she possibly imagine they could be happy, bound together in marriage for a lifetime? Passion had brought them together and it might keep them together for as long as such passions might last. But she was too wise to think it would last for a lifetime. It took love, not passion, to make a lifelong union work, the kind of unselfish love that could forgive a partner's failures. She had no reason to think Edward capable of that. He was too prone to resent those who hurt him. How could she trust that, when the glow of their romance wore off, he would be able to find the deeper love it would take to make a marriage last?

And now that she was out of danger why should she even think he would repeat his proposal? She had rejected him with scathing reflections upon his character. He might well feel the same disgust for her he had felt toward Estella, even though he had done what his pride demanded and rescued her from the predicament their shared heedlessness had put her into. Now that she was safe, he might be glad to see the last of her. He was still Lord Lightning, eccentric and unpredictable. He was the last person on earth she should be turning to for comfort now.

As if he had read her thoughts, he said, "Regrettably, you will be forced to spend a little more time in my company, but I see no alternative. You have no one here to depend on save myself, so I must still take full responsibility for your safety until we return to London, which we will do as soon as I make a brief stop at my mother's house to pack. While we are there, I will go to the magistrate's to retrieve your things, though the swine himself will be unable to assist me. He suffered a crippling accident in the course of his flight from the town hall—one I'm happy to say I had some small part in facilitating. His friend, too, is now severely indisposed. You can rest assured they will never again harm another woman. Once I've recovered your books we can be on our way."

"But surely, if you leave Brighton now, you will lose your inheritance."

"I have claimed as much of my inheritance as I care to."

"But won't your mother lose her home if you leave Brighton now?"

"My mother never ran the slightest risk of losing her home. The clergyman who attended my brother on his deathbed offered to testify that my brother was not in his right mind when he made his will. She knew that all along. That's why she felt safe in attacking me through you."

"But if that was the case, and you had nothing to hold over her, how did you get her to release me?"

"I did what I had to do." His face took on a shuttered look. "There is no point in discussing it further."

He took a deep breath. "When we reach London, I shall offer you any assistance you might accept from me so that you may return to living out your life in whatever manner you see fit. You need not tolerate my presence any longer. And until then, you may rest assured that I will not burden you with any further expression of those sentiments you can have no pleasure in hearing."

She nodded, wordlessly. He was right. She could not wish to hear him repeat his proposal, not when she had not the courage to commit herself to spending her life with him. Were he to ask again, she must offer him only a second humiliating rejection. So she bit her lip to keep herself from making any reply and looked down into her lap, though she still felt his warm brown eyes fixed on her. Indeed, such was the intensity of his gaze, she would have almost thought he was waiting for her answer to the proposal he had just promised not to renew.

She sank more deeply into the rich fur, hiding herself in the shadow of the carriage as they rode on. Edward again was the first to break the silence. "I shall not raise this subject again, Eliza, but my honor requires that, as difficult as it might be, I must remind you one last time that if there should, indeed, be some consequence of the night we shared together—"

"You will open your purse generously."

A look of what might have been pain flitted across his face. "No, I will not."

Shock echoed through Eliza. Had her rejection angered him that much? Did he hate her now as he had once hated Estella? She fought to let none of her perturbation show and said coldly, "I took full responsibility for what I did that night. I was no longer the innocent I was when I first met you. I knew what might result from our encounter and chose to engage in it anyway. I have no intention of becoming a burden to you."

"You misunderstand me," he said quietly. "You could never become a burden to me. I mean only to say, that should you be carrying our child, I shall insist you marry me. No child of mine will grow up with the shame of bastardy. And though I know how much you wish to avoid a fate like your mother's, I trust I have proved to you that I am not like your father. Should our marriage become necessary I would do what I could to ensure you would have no cause for regret. But otherwise, I will make no claim on you. You may live the life you choose. And it is possible you are right in thinking that the quicker you resume your life without me, the better off we will both be."

She felt a swift stab of loss at his words, for she knew, as he could not, that there would be no child. This very morning her courses had begun. So they would go to London and there they would separate forever. She would be left with her memories of the few glittering days that had transformed her life and with the haunting vision of his face as it appeared to her now in the faltering twilight, his pale lashes lowered as he struggled to reassume the ironic mask that was Lord Lightning's, the mask that protected Edward Neville from feeling any pain.

She wished she, too, had some way of damping down the pain she felt right now, but she didn't. How unfair it was to feel so much love for him, when it was so wrong and dangerous to feel it. When to give in to it would be to bind her to him for life. The price was too high. So she only murmured, "Thank you, Your Lordship," and nestled more deeply into the reassuring warmth of the fur.

Her aunt had said, "There are some things in life we are not meant to know," but her aunt had not spoken of the suffering caused by that uncertainty.

At length they arrived at his mother's house. It reared up in the night, the black-and-white of its façade rippling in the shadows. "Are you warm enough?" he asked. "I shall leave you here briefly while I collect my things. You can have no wish to come inside."

"Of course. I am fine."

She thought for a moment he was going to kiss her, but it was just her imagination, for he only let himself out of the carriage and left her alone to her thoughts. She snuggled deeper into the wrap, feeling how rattled she was, still, by the events of the day, and grateful to have a chance to be alone.

But she was to have no chance to nap. No sooner had she settled back into the corner of the carriage, than the door opened again. It was one of Lady Hartwood's footmen.

"Lady Hartwood requests a few moments of your time, within, miss."

Eliza shivered. She had no desire to see the woman whose malice had put her into prison.

"Her Ladyship will brook no refusal," the footman added. "She demands to speak with you."

She thought of refusing whatever Her Ladyship might command, but she had not the energy for it. There was nothing to fear in giving Lady Hartwood what she asked for. It was most likely that having had her revenge, she now wished only to gloat. Well, let her. It did not matter. In another day Eliza would be back in London, on her own, and there was little possibility she would ever see Lord Lightning—or his mother—again. And even if his mother intended to do her more mischief, Edward would be there to protect her. So steeling herself for a final, unpleasant interview, Eliza slowly extricated herself from the carriage and let the footman lead her into the house.

Lady Hartwood awaited her in the parlor, seated in her customary position in her chair. At Eliza's entrance, she dropped the embroidery she had been working on and sat up straight. Her heavy corset creaked. She favored Eliza with the sort of look she would have given a chambermaid found stealing and said, "Well, you have come out of this tawdry affair in far better shape than you deserve to. You should know you have *me* to thank for saving you. I have called you in to allow you to express your gratitude. Where is your curtsey, woman? Do you know nothing of how you should behave before your betters?"

Eliza stood up straighter. She would not be cowed. "I have already bestowed my gratitude where it belongs, Your Ladyship, on your son. It was he who saved me, not you."

"Little fool. I imagine you think he did so because he loves you."

"I think no such thing. He is a man of honor and he acted honorably."

"The word *honor* comes strangely from the mouth of a creature like you." Lady Hartwood sniffed. "If my son told you he rescued you out of love, you would be a simpleton to believe him. He has merely become enraptured with the idea of himself as a selfless lover. It is a novel sensation. It will pass."

Despite herself, Eliza shivered. Lady Hartwood still had the knack of putting words around her own, darkest fears.

Then Lady Hartwood leaned forward and let her voice drop. "Did my son tell you how much I extracted from him in return for your freedom?"

"He said nothing about it." But even as Eliza spoke she wondered what Lady Hartwood could be alluding to.

"How very nobly he is acting," Her Ladyship

sneered. "It must be yet another new sensation for him. But I should have thought he would have told you how much he paid, if for no other reason than to ensure you remained with him until he was ready to send you away. He hinted you were losing your enthusiasm for his attentions and there is nothing he would hate more than to be rejected before he had the opportunity to reject."

The import of what Lady Hartwood had just told her only now struck home. "Lord Hartwood paid you to have me freed?"

"A great deal. It was very careless of him to brag about his wealth to me."

Lady Hartwood picked up her embroidery and took a stitch before continuing, "There was no other inducement he could have given to make me relent. As much as I would have liked to see you hang, I prefer to live out the rest of my life in comfort. The arrangement I forced him to make will make that possible. That was the price of your freedom, missy. When he abandons you, you may console yourself that no doxy of his has ever before cost him what you have."

Eliza turned away from her tormentor. To think that Edward had made a sacrifice like that for her and had said not a word about it, even after the way she had reproached him with his selfishness in the gaol. She felt her heart open. That was not the act of a resentful soul.

She paused for a moment to collect her thoughts. Then she wheeled around to confront Lady Hartwood. "You have placed me forever in your son's debt, for there is no way I can ever repay him. But I shall cherish the memory of his selfless act for the rest of my life—for it was selfless indeed. You are wrong in thinking he would use his generosity to force me to stay with him against my will. He said nothing of it, nor did he attempt to use it to compel me to do anything I knew would not be prudent. We shall separate as planned on our return to London."

A look of satisfaction swept over Lady Hartwood's features. "Then have you learned, at last, what it means to love a man like Edward?" she asked. "He told me he offered for you and you refused him. Is this true?"

"It is."

"Did you finally come to understand, before it was too late, that my son is a man who cannot love?"

Eliza said nothing.

"Come, girl. I wish to know your answer. You defied me once and mouthed a bunch of twaddle about him. But clearly you thought better of it, if you turned down his offer of marriage. Admit it. You learned at last that he is a cold, cruel man who cannot love."

"No. I did not. Your son is passionate and warm, and he would love me if I would let him. It is my own character I've learned to understand better, not his. Though I love him with all my heart, I am a coward. I urged him to believe he could love, but when he tried to live up to my urgings, I had not the courage to trust he would succeed."

Lady Hartwood sneered. "Why should you trust him when all he has done is seduce you with his charm as he has so many others? His father was just like him, you know. So handsome. So deft with words. He recited poetry to me and it came alive, and I wished nothing but to be in his arms. Nothing else mattered to me then. But it did matter later, oh how it mattered!"

Anger surged within Eliza. "He's not like his father at all, though you did everything you could to make him believe he must grow up to be just such a libertine. It's a wonder there's any goodness left in him. But there is. He *is* a kind and loving man, despite what he believes he must be because of his father."

A look of scorn twisted Lady Hartwood's face. "He knows nothing about his father," she said with contempt.

A tall spare form loomed in the doorway. "You're wrong, Mother." Edward pressed forward. "I know all about my father. My real father."

"Mrs. Atwater told you?" She looked horrified.

"She didn't mean to, but she let something slip and from there it was not hard to winkle out the rest."

"What are you talking about?" Eliza demanded.

Edward took off his hat and let his pale curls spill out to frame his face. "You were so right, Eliza, when you insisted that Lady Hartwood was indeed my mother. Your charts told you the truth. And you were right, too, when you told me there was some mystery surrounding my birth which could explain my mother's implacable hatred for me."

Lady Hartwood sprang up from her seat. "Edward. Not in front of a stranger!"

"Eliza is hardly a stranger. She suffered greatly because I didn't know the truth about my birth. I owe her an explanation, and so do you. And besides, without her prodding I should never have discovered that truth."

He turned back to Eliza. His deep brown eyes met hers and she saw within their depths a joy she had never seen in them before. Had he overheard her protest her love for him? The thought terrified her even as she felt her heart swell with the hope that he had learned, at last, the truth of those feelings she had not had the courage to reveal to him.

Trying to keep her voice from trembling, she asked, "What did you learn, Edward, that fills you with such joy?"

He took a step toward her and took her hand. At his touch she felt a burst of warmth flow into her heart. He squeezed her palm gently, just once, then again met her eyes. "I hardly know how to tell you, Eliza," he said. "But I think you of all people will understand what it means to me. You see, you were right about what you told me you read in my nativity. I am indeed my mother's son, but to my great amazement and relief, I find, after all, I'm not the son of the man I thought to be my father. I'm not Black Neville's son."

It took a moment for the full meaning of his

words to sink in. Then her mouth dropped open. But she had no time to reply, for Lady Hartwood had risen out of her chair and was leaning heavily on her cane, her eyes wild. "Edward, consider what you do! Would you put us both in her power? You may delight in destroying *my* reputation, but consider what such a revelation means for your own." She sank back into her chair, her breast heaving. Edward made no reply but merely waited patiently as his mother regained control of herself.

When she could speak again, Lady Hartwood clenched her teeth. "How you must enjoy having me at your mercy," she said. But even as she spoke these last words her voice faltered, and a look of confusion filled her hardened features. "And yet," she said, "you *must* have known the truth when you came to beg for Eliza's freedom. You had already been to see that Atwater creature when you came to see me—after she wrote me that disturbing note."

"I did."

"But if you'd discovered my shame, why didn't you use it against me? When you came to beg me to secure Eliza's freedom, you gave me no hint of what you'd learned from that terrible woman. I thought you had nothing left to bargain with. Yet if you knew, you could have threatened me with exposure. You could have set your own terms instead of letting me impose mine. How could you have known about my shame and not used it against me?"

Edward dropped Eliza's hand and took a step toward his mother. "I didn't wish to, Mother. You've suffered enough for the one mistake you made in your youth. And as I am *not* Black Neville's son, I have not inherited his heartlessness. So I can forgive you as he could not. You sacrificed so much to keep your place in society, and as it is all he left you with, I would not take it from you."

"Truly? You won't expose me?" Lady Hartwood's eyes were blinking rapidly.

"I won't. There's no way of changing the past, and I have no more desire than you do to see the Hartwood name shamed."

"Well, I must be grateful for that." His mother fought to recover her composure. "I suppose you are delighted now to think that your real father was a better man than Black Neville."

"No, that would be foolish, Mother. I am, as you have often pointed out, a cynical man of the world. Though I cannot know what kind of man my real father was, I can well understand what led him to seduce you. You were a young and passionate woman who had been slighted by her husband. That's an opportunity few men could ignore."

Lady Hartwood remained motionless except for her left hand which she was clenching convulsively. "He didn't seduce me," she said quietly. "I went to him willingly. He had such a beautiful voice. Your voice is so like his, just as you look like him. You always have, ever since you stared up at me from your cradle with those deep brown eyes of his and that pale, pale hair. I couldn't bear it."

And to the amazement of them both, a single glistening tear coursed down Lady Hartwood's granite cheek.

"Was he a man who could not love?" Eliza demanded. "Did you learn that too late? Is that why you have been so vehement in your warnings to me?"

"I don't know what he was," Lady Hartwood replied. Her voice held a wistful tone. "Our connection was so brief. He was all sweet words, such sweet, sweet words. He spoke of love, but I didn't know if I could believe him. He begged me to leave Hartwood and come along with him and join the troupe. He said he could teach me to be an actress, that I had a gift for it. But how could I do a thing like that? I was Lady Hartwood. I couldn't give that up to become an actor's mistress, not when he might abandon me at the next town."

"So it was you who left him, not the other way around?" Eliza asked.

"Of course. What choice had I? For months after the troupe moved on he sent me letters. But I burned them unopened, every one—except the one that the stupid servant girl handed to your father. Black Neville gave it to his solicitor to hold hostage, knowing it was all he needed to divorce me. I never read that one, either, but I fear it must have been quite indiscreet."

"So my real father might have loved you, Mother," Edward said softly. "And he might have been a good and loving man."

"Or he might have been an arrant rogue worse even than my husband. I shall never know. But I have to believe I made the correct choice and that I would not have been happy had I been foolish enough to forget myself and follow him who knows where."

"Which is why you couldn't bear any sign you saw in me, who was so like him, that suggested I, too, might be a good man," her son said softly.

She shook her head. "Sin begets sin. How *could* you be a good man? Your birth had ruined my life." Another tear dripped from her bleary eye.

He crossed the room and embraced her heaving form. "Mother," he said, "I'm glad I was born, whatever it might have cost you. I am glad, too, that I am not the son of the cold, implacable man who punished you so cruelly for doing once what he had done with impunity all his life. How much fear you must have lived with, knowing that if you displeased him you could be dismissed like a servant."

She nodded fervently. "It was worse than that. Had I shown any partiality to you, I think he might have harmed you. So I schooled myself to show none, and after a while, it became second nature to me."

As his mother dabbed ineffectually at her eyes, Edward walked over to the mantelpiece. "Perhaps James wasn't wandering in his wits when he was on his deathbed as Mr. Hoskins thought," he said quietly. "By forcing me to come back to Brighton, James removed a great burden from my heart, and

I must be grateful to him for that. I must thank you, too, Mother, for your candor. I do not expect you to love me, not after so long. But I no longer need to hate you, and that is gift enough. I hope James found some comfort at the end in knowing that he might reach out from beyond the grave to undo some of the damage his father did."

"James knew the truth, you know," his mother said as if to herself. "He overheard your father reproaching me. It wasn't something a young child should have heard. But he did, and I fear that learning what he did about his mother, so young, did not help him grow into the man I would have wished him to be."

Lady Hartwood sat sunk in her thoughts for a moment longer. Then her expression hardened and she turned back to Eliza. "Young woman, what will I have to pay to buy your silence? Edward trusts you far too much if he believes you will hide my secret from the world. You can have no reason to forgive me, even if he has found one."

Eliza could barely reply, her heart was so full. Though she shared Edward's relief that he need no longer believe himself condemned by a toxic heritage, it was nothing compared to the happiness that had welled up within her at seeing him forgive his mother. That he could show such selfless love to the person who had hurt him so badly meant far more to her than the generous sacrifice he had made to free her. That could have been explained by his partiality for her. But his mother had done nothing to earn the loving sacrifice he had made for her and likely never would. What a transformation he'd undergone!

But she forced herself away from her selfish rejoicing and addressed the concern she saw in his mother's teary eyes. "You need have no fear, Lady Hartwood. I care too much for your son to spread a story that could only cause him pain."

"You care too much for my son, period," Lady Hartwood said tartly. "But he is a charming devil, and you may have no choice about it. I would have liked him to marry a girl of good birth, but perhaps it takes a woman of your kind to sort out a rake like him. The lord knows I could not sort out his father."

Edward laughed. "Mother, Eliza is of gentle birth. Better birth than you or I."

"What?"

"She is Pythagoras Farrell's daughter."

Lady Hartwood's eyes widened. "Evesbury's boy? Well, that explains the Greek! But the man is as mad as a hatter. Not a speck of common sense. No wonder she fell into such disreputable society as you run in. Still, it is a relief to know that my grandchildren will have noble blood running in their veins after all."

"But that can only happen if Eliza will have me," Edward corrected her. "She has already refused me once and I haven't the courage to ask her again. Whoever her father might be, I'm not sure she is mad enough to accept my offer."

"She'd be a fool not to," Lady Hartwood snapped. "But I shall hold my tongue. Whatever

I say, she is sure to do the opposite. The girl has spirit. I will give her that. And there is no denying she has made a change in you."

When they had made their adieux and resumed their places in the carriage, Edward said, "Now that my mother has given us our blessing, I expect there is no hope you will ever have me."

Eliza felt herself smile. "It does add a new twist to a subject already twisted beyond untangling. But after observing you over this past hour, I must tell you I am truly proud of you, Edward. I know what it must have cost you to forgive your mother, and yet you did it."

"I take no credit for it."

"Oh yes. I know you wish to take no credit for any good deed and I've promised never to see good in you where you assure me there is none, but your grant of forgiveness to your mother was an act of love, disinterested love, which must be the highest kind, since you could expect to receive nothing in return for extending that forgiveness to her but the knowledge that you did the right thing."

"How could I have done otherwise? Her husband's treatment of her was truly monstrous."

"How indeed?" Eliza said. "With the good heart that hides beneath your breast, you had no choice."

"I will not argue. You are making me resigned to owning a loving heart." He grinned, for only a moment, then a troubled look swept over his handsome features. "Still, I must be honest with you, Eliza. I have given much thought to your reproaches, for they were well deserved. And as much as I would wish to change myself to better deserve your love, I cannot woo you under false pretenses."

For a moment Eliza's heart stood still. What would he confess to her now? Terrible possibilities flooded into her mind, replacing the joy that had filled it only a moment before. She sat bolt upright, trying to be brave. As she awaited his explanation, it struck her with renewed force how much she loved him and how hard it would be to give him up.

He sensed her dismay and his voice softened. "I have nothing *that* terrible to confess," he reassured her. "No wife tucked away in the country or anything like that. It is only that I don't think I shall ever be able to give up playing, even if it would win your heart for me. My true father was an actor, after all."

He had reassumed that nonchalant look and now lounged against the rich upholstery of the carriage, but she was not deceived about the depth of the emotion with which he awaited her answer. She met his eyes and let her smile convey the love she felt in her heart. "I'd much rather learn that your father was an actor—not a rake and a reprobate. But you're probably right. Your life remains dramatic even when you attempt to give up playing. Consider, in just this single day I've been made captive and you have rescued me quite cleverly, to say nothing of making a stunning discovery about your birth and engaging in a scene of reconciliation that must bring a tear to every eye. All that remains, I should think, is for some god to ride down from the heavens on a piece of stage machinery and give us our happy ending."

"Would that I could bring that about, too," Edward said with a faint smile. "Then a chorus of maidens would accompany us to our marriage bower as the curtain slowly dropped to great applause. But it is a serious thing to join our lives together. I'm not the easiest man to live with, no matter who my father might have been."

"Of course. Uranus rules your life, so it will always be filled with unpredictability. But if I'm to be honest, I must admit your playfulness and unpredictability are a large part of your appeal to me. I delighted in Lord Lightning long before I learned to know and trust Edward Neville. Indeed, I should be hard-pressed to say which of the two I love better."

The smile of relief that filled his face was so genuine, she had to pause for a moment before continuing, "I also have a confession to make. I know myself now to be too firmly under the sway of the planet Uranus to love a man who did not embody its energies as you do. I should not love you half as much if you behaved as you ought to. That's why my aunt was so afraid I would grow up to repeat my mother's imprudence—and why I let her fears become my own."

She gave up speaking, to better enjoy the way his deep brown eyes glowed with unconcealed delight that seemed to grow greater with each passing moment.

"And do you still fear to repeat her pattern?" His question was dead serious.

"How could I not?" she replied, in a tone as sober as his own. She saw his face fall and, seeing that, had not the heart to torment him any longer. "When your mother shared her painful story with us, Edward, it made me consider something quite unexpected. For *she* did the prudent thing in staying with her husband, and look at what a mistake that turned out to be. Her prudence ruined her life."

"Then you must take warning from her example, and avoid prudence lest it ruin yours," Edward said, dropping to his knee awkwardly and looking up at her from under his long pale lashes with eyes empty of every emotion but love. "You know, Eliza, you really would make me the happiest of men if you would have me. I'll lead you a merry dance, no question about it, but I've come to think you rather like dancing. And I cannot bear to give you up."

Eliza sighed. "I can't bear to give you up, either. And as terrifying as I find the idea of marriage, I don't think you'd let me stay on as your mistress anymore."

"No, I certainly wouldn't," he said with a grin. "It would be far too exhausting. Indeed, if you'll have me, I vow I'll never have a mistress again."

His face had suddenly grown serious. "I mean it, Eliza. I love you."

She reached out for his hand and lifted it to her lips. "I love you, too, Edward. As I probably have from the moment you first abducted me. So I suppose there's no help for it. I shall have to marry you and take the consequences."

"You will? You'll really have me?"

When she nodded, he enfolded her in his embrace and pressed her to his heart. Then he released her and with his mahogany eyes full of mischief added, "There is nothing to keep us from driving all the way to Gretna. I'm capable of doing it, you know."

"You're capable of anything, Edward. Don't think I don't know it! But London will do just as well for marrying, and it's a great deal closer."

"To London then, to get a special license, for it's long past time you became my Lady Lightning."

"Lady Lightning, indeed! Though with my imprudence so well rewarded, I am afraid that together we shall set a terrible example to the world."

"I warned you from the start that I love to set a bad example."

"I cannot deny it." She laughed, remembering the first time he had said that, the first night they had spent together at his town house. But the time for banter was over and now she wished only to give herself up to the happiness of his embrace. As she leaned toward him, he met her lips with his, and together they luxuriated in the contentment that engulfed them as they kissed. It was only after a very long time had passed that Edward relaxed his hold on her and Eliza recovered the ability to speak.

"Such a *very* bad example we will set," she said, breathing a sigh of pure happiness. "It will be a puzzle to know what to tell our children when they ask how we first met."

"Not at all, my dearest." He grinned, fixing her with Lord Lightning's most impudent smile. "Only this: That you read my horoscope and saw the love that lay hidden in my heart, while I discerned *your* wisdom in the glorious constellations of your freckles."

A Few Last Words
from the Author

I hope you've enjoyed sharing the adventure as Eliza's astrological charts came alive—at times a bit more than she bargained for. You can be sure that even though she's found the lord of her House of Love, she'll still be peering at her charts, especially the one that answers the question, "Is it a boy or a girl?"

If you've read this far you might be interested to know a bit about the actual way astrology was used in Eliza's time. Most history books report that astrology fell out of favor in the West during the Age of Reason because it was unable to recover from the blow to medieval cosmology delivered by the discovery of Mr. Herschel's new planet. But this is not true. Though astrology did almost vanish on the continent, it continued to be practiced in England throughout the eighteenth and nineteenth century.

Moore's popular astrological almanac, *Vox Stellarum*, had a print run of 393,750 copies in 1803, and the number published almost doubled in the succeeding decade. Several astrological magazines were also published during this period, as well as textbooks by astrological authors like Ebenezer Sibley and John Worsdale.

The first known English woman astrologer was a Mrs. Williams, who in the 1780s advertised her practice in London and at the fashionable watering places of Bath and Bristol Hot Wells.

Many astrologers in this period practiced the kind of astrology described in William Lilly's book, *Christian Astrology*, published in 1647 and still in print today. Because accurate birth data was hard to come by, these astrologers often relied on horary charts which were cast for the moment when a question was asked, though the kind of character delineation that Eliza uses here was also popular.

For readers who are curious, Eliza's birth information is 11/29/1788 01:42 P.M., London. Edward Neville's is 7/29/1785 10:30 A.M., Brighton. Astrologers who review these charts will see that I have played fair with my interpretations, though I have also taken hints from the placements of Neptune and Pluto to get deeper insight into Eliza and Edward's personalities.

Neptune was only discovered in 1846. One

hopes Eliza would have lived long enough to have learned how helpful it is in understanding why both she and Edward had such a penchant for self-delusion, as well as why the circumstances of Edward's birth were shrouded in such secrecy and caused him so much pain. But Neptune also gives the capacity for selfless love which both Eliza and Edward would need to build the kind of life together that would truly satisfy them. Pluto of course was not discovered until 1930.

Those familiar with midpoint composite charts may notice that the midpoint composite chart describing their relationship bears a Sun-Mercury conjunction near the midheaven that could be read as describing a relationship filled with banter, or, alternatively, one that occurs in a book. The North Node on the Ascendant on the Capricorn/Cancer axis of the midpoint composite chart also suggests that their relationship would be one that would help Eliza and Edward come to terms with issues of parenting, security, and emotional control.

Readers who would like to learn more about how to use astrology to analyze character should read Donna Cunningham's *How to Read Your Astrological Chart* or Stephen Forrest's *The Sky Within*. For a fascinating look at historical methods of reading charts, read psychiatrist Anthony Louis's classic, *Horary Astrology Plain and Simple*.

*Unforgettable, enthralling love stories,
sparkling with passion and adventure
from Romance's bestselling authors*

At Avon Books, we know your passion for romance—once you finish one of our novels, you find yourself wanting more.

May we tempt you with . . .

- **Excerpts** from our upcoming releases.

- Entertaining **extras**, including authors' personal photo albums and book lists.

- Behind-the-scenes **scoop** on your favorite characters and series.

- **Sweepstakes** for the chance to win free books, romantic getaways, and other fun prizes.

- Writing **tips** from our authors and editors.

- **Blog** with our authors and find out why they love to write romance.

- **Exclusive content** that's not contained within the pages of our novels.

Join us at
www.avonbooks.com